A DEATH IN GLASGOW

EVA MACRAE

CENTURY

CENTURY

UK | USA | Canada | Ireland | Australia
India | New Zealand | South Africa

Century is part of the Penguin Random House group of companies
whose addresses can be found at global.penguinrandomhouse.com

Penguin Random House UK,
One Embassy Gardens, 8 Viaduct Gardens, London SW11 7BW

penguin.co.uk

First published 2026
001

Set in 14.2/17pt Fournier MT Pro
Typeset by Six Red Marbles UK, Thetford, Norfolk

Printed and bound in Great Britain by Clays Ltd, Elcograf S.p.A.

The authorised representative in the EEA is Penguin Random House Ireland,
Morrison Chambers, 32 Nassau Street, Dublin D02 YH68

A CIP catalogue record for this book is available from the British Library

ISBN: 978-1-529-94691-8

A DEATH IN
GLASGOW

For my grandmother,
Janet Davidson Macrae

A DEATH IN
GLASGOW

PROLOGUE

Holly knows she's being followed. The baseball cap pulled down, hood up, face shadowed, but she knows. She keeps craning back over her shoulder, pretending to be on the phone. Maybe that'll make them back off. But there's no one she can call. Nobody will believe her; else they'll say it's her own fault.

Along Union Street, the pubs are emptying into the cold neon night. Shapes come barrelling into her, forcing her off the icy pavement into the path of buses and Deliveroo bikes. *Haw, hen, watch where you're going.*

The temperature's plummeted. With her big coat on and her legs pumping like pistons, her hair's sticking to the back of her neck while the beads of sweat freeze on her face. That last vodka, or three, is climbing up her throat. She can't stop to chuck up. She'll be caught and then what? *I only want to talk. I only want to give you a wee cuddle. I only want to . . .* When she gets to Central station, there'll be plenty folk around. A public place. Safe.

Suddenly, the station entrance looms on her right like an escape hatch and Holly bolts towards it, elbowing through the drinkers, tripping on some homeless guy huddled on the floor. The steps up are mountainous but she's taking them

I

two at a time in her platform boots. At the top, she risks a wee keek back. Nobody. Her guts unclench a fraction. Was she wrong? Was it just someone who'd been behind her for ages, going the same way? Dark clothes and a hoodie. Could've been anyone. What happened in the pub was a shock, made her think she was being followed again. She just panicked. Deep breaths, her therapist said. She tries now, but the cold and the vodka are getting in the way.

On the concourse, Holly is hoping for calm and bright, but the station shops are all shut. No families or commuters, only gangs of drunk lads. The high glazed roof that floods the station with light in the daytime now feels like it's coming down to trap her like she's a bug under a glass.

There's a big bunch of lassies out on a hen night, and maybe she can stand with them for a bit till her heart isn't thumping and the floor stops tilting. She staggers forward, her arm brushing a handbag. One of them turns and snarls at her – *she's after robbing me, get the fuck away you* – and Holly body-swerves the group in case the mad cow and her pals decide to jump her.

The heels on her boots looked great when she was getting ready to go out to the pub, but now they're a liability. The floor's shiny white, slippy-wet. Like a cloud. Holly can't see where to land her feet. She slides, arms cartwheeling like a one-woman flash mob starting a performance. The lads all start laughing – *fancy a wee dance, darling* – and shout how they could give her the horizontal boogie of her life.

Holly spins back, looking for the way she came in, getting her bearings.

This time, she's sure. Their eyes lock. The choking sensation is back, she can hardly breathe.

Instead of coming straight for her, they're moving round the edge of the concourse, cutting off her escape to the taxi rank at the other exit. She searches desperately for any station staff in their hi-vis – not the police, the bastards'd have her in the cells. But what'll happen when they finally catch up with her? They'll tell the staff she's drunk (not a lie) and that they're looking after her (aye, right) and they'll get her home safe. The polis will always believe them over her.

Then it hits her through the fog in her head. None of her mates from college live on the southside. She was never planning on sharing a cab. The illuminated sign for platform 9 swings across her vision like a beacon. It's on the other side of the concourse, further than she remembers. Always platform 9 to get home. Holly fumbles in her bag for her ticket, pulling it out in triumph. Can't follow her through the barriers.

Holly sets off with her Bambi-on-ice totter and sees the gate coming towards her, and oh my God, it's even open. Go. Quick. Get away. Too late she realises her mistake. If she didn't need to swipe through the barrier, then neither will anyone else. She stuffs the ticket like a betrayal into her coat pocket and runs.

The surface is gritty and there's a better grip, but the flares of her trousers are flapping against her legs like broken wings. Her bag slips off her shoulder, a weight pulling her backwards.

On one side of the platform is a forest of big green pillars studded with rivets like the stumps of broken-off branches. If she can't run, she can hide. In the distance, out across the river, she can see the train snaking towards the station.

The end of the platform is in darkness. Holly dodges behind a pillar, telltale breath pumping out of her like a steam engine. She puts a gloved hand over her mouth, tastes the wool, breath hot in her palm.

The train is coming; big blocks of light speeding towards her.

She peeks out. There's no sign of anyone. She's done it.

The train will take her home. Relief floods through her and an intense bubble of laughter expands the tightness in her lungs as she steps out from her hiding place.

Suddenly, she feels someone behind her, like a panting beast.

Holly sprints for the train, hand out like it's a bus and it'll stop. If she can just make it stop, she can get on.

Holly! Holly! She turns before she can prevent herself and sees a face, twisted and angry. Over the screeching of the train, she hears her own screaming. A bright palm is coming through the dark to grab her. She's caught and there's nowhere left to run. Any second, the fingers will curl like claws, and it'll be all over. She was daft to think she could escape. The train is close, but it's too late. She's shaking her head. Knowing what she says, what she is, doesn't matter.

The hand keeps coming. But when it reaches the front of her coat, it's not a grab. It's a push.

CHAPTER I

Sergeant Mackay's boot had just hit the third step on the flight of stairs up to her office when she heard a shout behind her.

'May!'

It was Jimmy Wallace, a fellow sergeant who'd been stationed at Cathcart Police Office in the south of the city for as long as anyone could remember.

'Can you be a pal and do us a wee favour?'

May stepped down to his level and rested the bundle of case files she was carrying on her hip like a box-shaped bairn. 'I've calls waiting, Jimmy. You know what it's like first thing in the morning. Kit on, straight out.'

He was her equal in height, rank and years of service so she didn't immediately bat him away as she did the younger officers – *you're perfectly capable of sorting that for yourself* – although never hard enough to stop them asking if they really needed her help. She narrowed her eyes at him just the same. 'What's the problem? If it's sheep again, it's a no-go.'

'Sheep?'

'Two sheep up a close. Calder Street. Fella keeps calling. I've given CID the nod about a potential illegal butchery operation, but I can't send Toni again, she's scared of them, and PC Kennedy says he's allergic, and it's too early to look at a rash. Call the council dog warden. See if he's got a stray Border collie that fancies the exercise.'

'It isn't sheep.' He stood, shoulders bowed, hands on hips, as if the burden he was attempting to shift her way was a heavy one. 'There's a woman at the front desk. She's not happy. Picking up personal effects for her deceased daughter. Suicide.'

In typical Glaswegian understatement, *not happy* could mean anything.

'Are we talking lightly vexed or breaking the furniture?' If Jimmy wanted assistance, it was likely the higher end of the scale. May ran through a mental checklist of her current cases and came up empty. No suicides.

'Lassie jumped in front of a train at Central station last night,' Jimmy said. 'The mother's kicking off about it not being a suicide. It's the lad on the front desk's first day. Bit out of his depth.'

'That's a British Transport Police job. How come the deceased's effects are here?'

Jimmy spread his hands and gave a shrug, the universal symbol for *there's been a cock-up somewhere*. 'Family are local to us.'

This wasn't May's responsibility, but in this brief exchange something unspoken passed between them. May knew if she was in this woman's position she'd want to speak to someone with training, experience, and a hefty dose of empathy. She knew because she had been there. Jimmy in his clumsy kindness knew it too. Work of this nature used to be viewed as a job for the WPCs – *one for the lassies* – and it still was by some, but Jimmy wasn't one of them.

'Speak to her for me?' Jimmy said. Less a question than a plea.

'Got a room you can put her in?'

'Aye.'

'Give us a moment. I'll come down.'

Ten minutes later May opened the door to the interview room, her body language doing its best to convey amicable and unthreatening. She wore the regulation black top and trousers but had left off her personal protective kit of stab vest, cuffs, extendable metal baton and PAVA incapacitating spray. May knew she could be physically intimidating, not a bad thing in a polis, but not always useful in a delicate situation. She had the height and heft of her Highland ancestors, many of whom had been recruited by the Glasgow police to keep in line a population whose own stature had been stunted by industrialisation, a process which seemed only to have concentrated their belligerence. With her green eyes and red-blonde hair, faded from its original brilliance but still carefully highlighted and trimmed every six weeks, she was the picture of mature professionalism.

By contrast, Jackie McNally was a mess. She seemed to have absorbed the cramped room's colour scheme – grey walls, grey furniture, grey face. Her thin frame had crumpled over the bulky personal effects bag on the table, head down, a wounded animal protecting the remains of her young. The supermarket trouser suit and block-dyed dark bob hinted at effort and employment, but the chipped and bitten nails along with the scuffed shoes said it wasn't all plain sailing, which fitted with what May had been able to find out.

She'd got the bare bones from the control-room log. It was as Jimmy had said. Jackie's 22-year-old daughter, Holly Campbell, had thrown herself in front of the incoming Neilston train at Glasgow Central station. Life pronounced extinct by attending paramedics at 11.20 p.m. A quick records search showed an address in the lattice of sandstone tenements in Govanhill, a district in the city's southside which had miraculously avoided the 1960s council wrecking ball and was one of the most ethnically diverse places in Scotland. Last time anyone had checked there'd been fifty-two nationalities and thirty-two languages within thirteen tenement blocks. Govanhill was on a journey to gentrification, but a substantial number of residents had missed that particular wagon. The area was characterised by an equal balance of trendy cafes, gourmet delis, drug deaths, squalor and crime.

Jackie McNally, her ex-husband and her daughter had been spoken to multiple times by response officers after neighbours' complaints about loud arguments and the sound of breaking glass. Holly had previously taken an intentional overdose and received a psychiatric assessment and treatment. In addition, there were other branches of the McNally family tree known to the police.

Jackie raised her head and her bloodshot eyes met May's. 'She was everything to me. It wasn't suicide.'

May nodded and sat down opposite. She'd have liked to

offer tea, but hot liquids became offensive weapons in some hands.

'I'm May.' She indicated the bulky brown paper bag into which items of clothing had been roughly stuffed. 'These your Holly's things? Can I have a wee look?'

Jackie hesitated then cautiously relinquished the bag.

May slid it across the table. 'D'you want to tell me what happened?'

'The polis came to my door at five this morning. Said Holly had killed herself. But she'd never do that.' Jackie stopped and eyed her. 'Aren't you the polis?'

'I'm a sergeant with the response team here.' Then, seeing Jackie's bewilderment, she added, 'The officers who came to see you were detectives from the British Transport Police. They deal with incidents on the railways and at stations.'

May pulled a pair of blue nitrile gloves from her pocket and slipped them on, more to reassure Jackie that she was taking her concerns seriously than from forensic awareness. She picked up the blood-stained T-shirt and folded it carefully. If nothing else, Jackie would go home with her daughter's possessions in respectful order.

'Five o'clock, you said?'

Jackie nodded.

May checked her watch. It was just after 9 a.m.

Outside it was barely light, the time of year when Glasgow seemed to be sinking and would never come up for air. On May's half-hour traffic-clogged drive to work from the city's West End, the sodium glow of the streetlights had turned the fog a sickly yellow, accelerating the sense of terminal decline.

Still, less than twelve hours since the lassie's death. The transport police hadn't wasted a minute in coming to their conclusions. Must have been a grim job, working through the night to get the trains running again. The body would have gone to the mortuary at the Queen Elizabeth hospital. Technically, this was a *fatality* until the post-mortem and Procurator Fiscal declared the cause of death, but then the BTP dealt with hundreds of these incidents every year and knew the score.

'Tell me about Holly,' May said quietly as she took the black puffer jacket, white stuffing blotched with blood and oil spilling from a ripped seam, and searched the pockets. Jackie watched the reverent care with which May completed her task and it seemed to calm her. They could have been two women folding laundry.

'She was clever. A clever lassie.'

'Did she work?'

'At college. Coding. On computers. I don't really know what that is, but you have to be dead clever to do it.'

'When did you last see her?'

'Last night. Afore she went to meet her college pal.'

'And how did she seem to you?'

'That's it, that's it,' Jackie declared, triumphant. 'She was fine. And we were going clothes shopping tomorrow. It was her birthday just by. She had money to spend.'

'What d'you think happened?'

'Somebody killed her.'

'She didn't leave a note?' May said gently. 'Or call you?'

Jackie shook her head vigorously.

May rested her arms on the table and leaned forward, studying Jackie intently. 'Who do you think killed Holly?'

'I don't think. I know. Her ex. That bastard ned Scott Galbraith.' Jackie must have seen something flicker in May's carefully neutral expression. 'Aye, you know him too, don't you? I had to stop him battering her in the street. And I tell you another thing, she was clean. No drugs for a year. Not since she dumped him. She was clean and going places, and . . .'

At the reminder of what she'd lost, Jackie grabbed Holly's newly folded T-shirt, buried her face in it, and sobbed.

May wanted to tell her that the passing of time would, one day, soften the pain of losing her only child, but it was a lie. It only got harder. At least May had her son, Rory, although he was in Australia with his wife and three kids, her grandchildren, who seemed to have grown by large increments in every new photo and video call. And she had her husband Tam – lovely, wonderful Tam – to share the pain.

Two years ago, after a long struggle, May's daughter Isla, had lost her battle with life. There was no doubt she'd meant to do it. Isla had climbed over the railing of the Squinty Bridge that crossed the Clyde, cut her wrists, and jumped. Tam, a folk musician, had agonised that his love of Scots and Irish myths had somehow given Isla the idea that a blood sacrifice to the river deity would send her straight to Tìr nan Óg, the Land of the Ever Young, a kind of Celtic heaven. May had merely thought that their daughter had never done anything by halves. If they'd known what she'd been thinking, could they have stopped her? Everyone who experienced the suicide of a loved one asked that. She'd heard it repeated all through her police career as both a detective and a beat cop, but she'd never come close to an answer.

Jackie needed answers too. Answers the BTP, however correct in their procedures, had failed to give her. May carefully folded and bagged Holly's remaining clothing and possessions – torn trousers, ripped jumper, one glove, empty shoulder bag and smashed phone. Christ, this was brutal. What were the transport cops thinking sending this to the mother?

'Aye, you're alright there, hen.' May patted her hand then gave her a moment to compose herself before taking the T-shirt from her unresisting grip and placing it in the bag. 'Come on, I'll take you back home.'

Jackie smeared her eyes with a dirty tissue. She looked unsure but lacked the energy to come up with a different solution.

'Okay. Thanks. But can you just drop me at the corner.'

May understood. In that area, you kept your distance from the cops, no matter what the circumstances. She stood, then put her hand under Jackie's elbow, encouraging her to her feet. There was a mountain of cases, welfare checks and follow-up interviews to assign to her constables.

'He did it. He killed her,' Jackie said, her calm certainty unnerving after the storm of her sobs. 'I'm asking you, as Holly's mother, will you find out what happened to my wee girl?'

'Listen, Jackie . . .' May began, but found she couldn't continue.

Holly Campbell was a young woman with a socially

deprived and domestically violent background, a history of drug use, and a previous suicide attempt. May could see why the transport police thought this was an open-and-shut case. The lassie had travelled to Central station, like many before her, with the express intention of ending her life. Her mother was just a broken and confused woman who couldn't process what had happened and was throwing wild accusations in the air like birds, hoping they might fly towards a different truth.

The hypothesis that this was a tragic suicide fitted except for one thing, the item May had found in the young woman's coat pocket: a return ticket to Glasgow Central.

Why would you buy a return if you were never coming home?

'Leave it with me,' May said eventually. 'I'll see what I can do.'

CHAPTER 2

There were straightforward ways for a police officer to gain information. Pick up the phone. Ask a direct question. But May had the feeling neither of those would produce results in this instance. Central station wasn't on her patch, or even on her route back from dropping off Jackie in Govanhill, but she made the detour anyway.

The station was laid out on two levels. She slotted her patrol car into an emergency services parking space, then walked straight to the high level, bypassing the British Transport Police office, to find platform 9. On the way she found a bin to dump a carrier bag of empty Irn-Bru cans and greasy food papers she'd cleared from the cup holders and door pockets of the squad car and cursed the likely culprit. P C Rab 'the Kebab' Kennedy would be getting a rocket later.

For May, the place always had a poignancy. It was Scotland's busiest rail station, and in a city and nation marked by the generations of emigration, it was hard not to think of all the people who had left. Gone south. Gone over the water. Gone for good. The span of girders and glass, the wood-panelled buildings that curved like the sterns of sailing ships around the wide-open space echoing with travel announcements, the famous four-faced hanging clock, would have been their last glimpse of home. True, the station was no longer the soot-, steam- or diesel-fumed cavern of yesteryear, but still the ghosts of the departed lingered. Some old, some recent, thought May as she turned towards platform 9.

A stiff breeze blew up from the River Clyde. A muffled member of the station staff let her through onto the platform, not even checking her ID.

'That on?' She indicated the CCTV camera pointing directly down on the ticket barrier. He shrugged behind his scarf.

The trains were running normally; the only evidence of last night's tragedy was a stray ribbon of crime-scene tape flapping in the breeze at the far end of the platform. As May walked towards it she took in the lack of further CCTV.

It would've been all hands to the pump to get the scene cleared before rush hour. Suicide by train was a depressingly regular occurrence but few commuters had much sympathy for the victims, especially if it meant there'd be a bollocking from the boss and no time for the cappuccino run.

She glanced back towards the main concourse. Two station patrol cops were approaching her at an unhurried pace.

'What happened with this sudden death last night?' she asked when they arrived, not waiting for introductions. 'Were you on shift?'

They were young, prodded into obedient reply by the directness of both her questions and her gaze as much as the sergeant's tabs on her shoulders. The taller of the two had a neatly trimmed dark beard. The other was stockier, a tribal tattoo poking out of the cuff of his long-sleeved top. Both shook their heads.

'Must be hard for your mates though, seeing a lassie jump in front of a train.'

The blank looks confirmed what she already suspected; none of the station police had witnessed the suicide. The grisly details would've been all round the crew room by now if they had.

'So she wasn't walking around the station distressed? She didn't ask for help?'

Again, the headshakes.

Given Holly's history, she could understand why she might not have considered approaching a police officer.

'What about witnesses? Other passengers waiting for the train?'

'Weren't any. The train was terminating,' the stocky officer said. 'Not due out again until the morning. Empty platform. Guess that's why the lassie chose it.'

'What about the driver?'

They both shrugged.

'Are you . . . ?' the taller one began.

'A real cop? Aye, I am. But next time you meet a superior officer, introduce yourselves and find out who you're talking to. I could be bloody anybody.'

She strode past them, back towards the barrier.

For the first time since Isla's death, she wondered if Tam was right. As their daughter's depression had progressed, May had switched from detective sergeant in Glasgow Central Division to a plain sergeant in uniform. The pay was the same, but with set shifts and no last-minute late nights and weekends chasing cases, it meant she and Tam had been able to tag-team Isla's care, so she'd never be left alone. It had been an act of love on May's part, but it still hadn't been enough to save her daughter.

Tam thought May was delaying a move back to detective due to lost confidence because she couldn't unravel the reasons why Isla had done what she'd done. But it was more complicated than that. At Cathcart, in response policing, she went home at the end of the day having helped people and accomplished something, positive actions that saved lives. And, though wild horses wouldn't drag it out of her, there was reward in supporting and moulding the young officers in her charge, a role she could no longer deploy to Isla's benefit. But now she felt the familiar investigative itch.

On the surface, the sparse details of Holly's death did point to suicide, but she couldn't shake the thought of the return ticket. She needed to know all of Holly's story – the how and why of its end – but also the beginning. She wanted to understand every twist on the path that had brought this young woman to Central station – a place from which she'd failed to return – and had ripped out Jackie McNally's heart.

Looking around at the unforgiving steel rails, the mundane squalor of fast-food wrappers blowing across the platform, hearing the shrill squeal of brakes, May felt inescapably sad. There might come a time when Jackie and the family would want to lay flowers at the spot. They'd think it a good idea right up until the moment they arrived, and the reality of Holly's death struck them, at which point it would be anything but cathartic. If Jackie asked her, she'd advise against it. There was no comfort in this place.

Back at Cathcart Police Office, May had just passed Inspector Mark Ward's door when he stuck his head out.

'May. A word.'

The constables were calling him Markie the Meerkat due to him continually popping up and admonishing them for minor misdemeanours. To May, he was too young, too inexperienced and too promotion-focused. Response policing needed officers prepared to get elbow-deep in the dirt, sometimes literally. With his neatly pressed uniform and fresh complexion she always had the urge to shout at him to get back in his room and finish his homework.

She came just far enough into Ward's office to lean on the door frame in her habitual pose. He preferred it when people sat down, but if he wanted to play bank manager, he should have chosen that profession, and she didn't have the time.

'Why were you at Central station this morning?' he said.

'How d'you know I was at Central station?'

'Transport police called to say you were at Central station. So, if you can enlighten me as to why you were at Central station we'll all be up to speed.'

May wondered how many times she could say *Central station* back before he lost his rag. He'd love to chew her out over it and, to be fair, he was making a game go of frowning his disapproval, but he was on a hiding to nothing. He had just enough sense to realise getting on the wrong side of her would be very bad indeed.

'Jackie McNally came in,' May said. 'Her daughter, Holly Campbell, went under a train last night.'

'Yes, a suicide. The transport police said they'd had one. I mean, it's not uncommon with troubled girls. The family is a mess, so it's understandable.'

May felt a contraction in her chest so powerful she had to fight to suppress a gasp. From a colleague it would be thoughtless. But from her inspector – and line manager – it was unforgivable. Her own daughter's suicide was the reason she was even standing in his office right now, and none of it was understandable. As an officer he had a third of her experience, a quarter of her intelligence, and about one-sixteenth of her balls. She waited, giving him the chance to consider what he'd just said, but he merely blinked at her. Fighting the urge to take a bite out of him, she took a deep breath instead and pressed on.

'Jackie McNally is adamant the ex-boyfriend pushed her daughter.'

'Did the BTP interview him?'

'Don't see how they could have. Holly was declared dead at half-eleven last night and the mother was told at five a.m. it was suicide. If they've dotted all the i's and crossed all the t's in that time, well, all I can say is I admire their work rate.'

'Who's the ex-boyfriend?'

'Scott Galbraith. Had him before the sheriff a few times. Started off as a dealer of the baggies-for-blowjobs variety, now fancies himself up-and-coming. God knows what his empire-building will do to our crime figures – housebreaking, street crime, the works.'

Markie sat up in true meerkat fashion. It was pitiful watching the struggle on his face. Potential shit for interfering in a BTP investigation balanced against the glory of arresting a player under the noses of CID and cutting his monthly returns in one fell swoop. It was exactly what May had calculated.

But a moment later he shook his head. 'Can't see anything there for us. Let the transport police deal with it.'

A sour mix of frustration and disbelief bubbled up inside May. If he couldn't join the dots, she'd have to do it for him. She walked forward, placed both hands on his desk, and was rewarded by the flash of uncertainty in his expression at her looming presence.

'Scott Galbraith's the thread we pull on and maybe we'll land a bigger fish. Jackie is Michael McNally's sister. She's made a serious allegation against one of her brother's dealers.'

'Michael McNally is a high-profile legitimate businessman,' Ward countered. 'I know you believe otherwise, but there's no evidence of his involvement in any criminal activity.'

'Only cos nothing has stuck.'

Rumour of common or garden criminality circulated freely – backhanders to councillors, deals done with planning committees, but May had always suspected there was more to Michael McNally than that.

'If he's head of an organised crime group, then he's the root source of most of our business,' she shot out, suddenly aware how loud her voice sounded in the quiet of the office. Her face felt hot and she knew her colour must have risen with her temper. She made a conscious effort to step away from the desk and put her case calmly. 'It's worth chapping Galbraith's door on this. Check his whereabouts.'

As if freed from the pressure of her proximity, Mark Ward sprang up from his seat.

'No, May. This isn't our case. It isn't any case. And even if it was a case, it's the BTP's case. Is that clear?'

May held his gaze. Just what was his problem? Did he think she was after his job? Inspectors' pips and a role in middle management had never appealed to May, and she made no secret of it. It was more likely Ward just didn't want to rock the boat with his bosses and a prominent public figure like McNally and maybe dent his promotion chances.

When she didn't answer he repeated himself. 'Is that clear, Sergeant Mackay?'

'Yes, sir,' May said eventually.

Let him have his petty victory. This wasn't the end. She was just getting started.

CHAPTER 3

That afternoon May was kept busy by a string of treble-nine calls – domestic disturbances, road traffic collisions, two out-of-control dogs, and a shoplifter attempting to make off with a cut-price frozen turkey inside his jacket which resulted in him tripping and sustaining broken ribs.

Tam was home and had already started cooking when she arrived. He looked smart. His dark beard and hair were neatly combed, and he had on black jeans and a favourite cream Aran sweater beneath the denim blue apron. For a moment, May felt a flutter of panic that she'd forgotten some social arrangement, but then she saw his fiddle case on a chair, a folder of music on top, and remembered he'd been rehearsing for an upcoming show which was due to be filmed by BBC Scotland.

'How's my braw man?' She put her arms around him from behind, resting her cheek against the thick wool of his jumper.

'Missing his bonnie lassie.' He took one of her cold hands and, without turning, pressed it to his warm lips. 'How'd it go today?'

'The usual, with the additional highlights of two males fighting with fire extinguishers at a petrol station, and a woman giving birth in a pub. We're running bets on what the wean will be named. I said Special Brew, which is obviously gender-neutral, but Ross Reid reckons Stella for a girl and Heine-Ken for a boy.'

She expected him to laugh, or maybe groan; instead she felt him tense.

'No close calls today?' he asked with a serious tone.

May gently shook her head. 'You needn't worry. All fine.'

Tam had made no secret of the fact that her daily exposure to violence bothered him. When Isla had died, he'd wanted May to quit the force so they could make a fresh start with their son and his family in Australia. And why wouldn't she? What future was there here? For him it was a straight choice between basking in the Australian sunshine surrounded by grandkids or never knowing them beyond dwindling Zoom calls and Christmas cards. In time, he and May would mean nothing but a meagre inheritance when they went.

Conscious that the conversation might easily take a turn in the direction of Australia, she peered over his shoulder at the stir-fry he was making. 'See I got home just in time. Smells great.' She released him with a final squeeze and plucked cutlery from the container next to the sink. 'So how was your day? Rehearsals go okay?'

'Aye, grand. But I heard from the centre that our funding is being cut again,' he said, and May realised she wasn't the sole cause of his worry.

Tam worked for a small charity, the Aspen Trust, helping young people tackle addiction and mental health issues. His previous experience in the public-housing sector made him a valuable asset, and he'd taken a lead on homelessness and how best to navigate the system.

'Again? Seems to me you're fighting a war on all fronts with the current funding, never mind less. I don't know how you do it.'

Scotland had one of the highest imprisonment rates in Western Europe. At some point, the cases May dealt with progressed through the justice system and became someone else's problem – the fiscal's, prison officers', probation officers', social workers' – although a significant proportion of offenders were caught in the revolving door. Reconviction rates were scarily high. If you waited long enough the same folk would come around again.

'Aye, well, no' just a pretty face, eh?' He winked, and stroked her arm.

'And if you were, you'd still be enough for me.' She smiled in return.

Before she could ask him what the funding cut meant in real terms, he clapped his hands together. 'Right! Plates.'

They sat at the old pine table in the warm kitchen to eat, a habit they'd fallen into since the table in the bay window of their front room had become too large for their reduced family. They still used it when guests came round, but the spectacular view over the trees with the lights of Glasgow behind didn't bring them the satisfaction it previously had.

When they'd finished eating, May propped her chin in one hand and reached out the other to take Tam's.

'Sorry everything is so shit.'

'It's not. No' really.' He gave her a tired smile. 'Just one of those days.'

'Tell me.'

'I don't need to tell you. You know.' He smiled again.

'I had a woman come in, Jackie McNally. Her daughter went under a train. She doesn't accept it's suicide.'

Tam's face seemed to age before her eyes, the lines of grief deepen. 'Aye, well, we've all been there.'

'From what I've found, neither can I.'

'Oh, May.' He came round the table and wrapped his arms around her. 'Isla wouldnae have wanted you to suffer like this. It's not like we'd ever forget her, even on the other side of the world.'

How could she tell Tam that she couldn't leave behind a city where she saw her daughter in every street? She heard her voice in the snatch of conversation on the subway, a burst of laughter in a bar, or among the young lassies sharing a joke on their way home from work. She saw her a hundred times a day, in the corner of her eye. But whenever she turned, she was always just a fraction too slow to catch the tilt of Isla's head, the mocking brown eyes rimmed with barricades of liner, the fingers obsessively tugging at the long golden hair.

And then there was the job, simultaneously horrifying and irresistible. Perhaps she and some of her fellow officers – the ones who secretly craved their next shift, and who believed they hid their compulsion from their partners and families – weren't so different from the vomit-crusted, piss-soaked addicts they hauled in. Better uniforms, marginally better hygiene, fewer communicable diseases, but that was all.

May patted his arm, then nodded towards the front room. 'Go and put your feet up.' She began clearing the table, conscious his eyes were trying to meet hers in hope. 'I'll wash up, since you cooked. Find us something good to watch; ideally no cop shows or gritty drama. We've both had enough of that already today.'

CHAPTER 4

May was in the office at 6.30 a.m. the next day. She liked to get her kit out of the locker room before her constables arrived. It gave them the opportunity to bond as a team through shared grievances, otherwise known as bitching behind her back. It saved time. The more experienced officers generally dissuaded those who thought complaining to her in person was a hazard-free occupation.

The brief window between shift changes also helped gauge the mood on the streets. The outgoing night crew provided not just the official handover of cases and arrests, but scraps of intel to be tucked away. Last night there'd been a number of domestic assault calls dialled in by neighbours but dismissed by the victims themselves as mistakes. The departing sergeant had reeled off names. *You know any of them,* he'd asked. *I know them all,* May had replied. Next time the calls came in she'd try to make it the last time by urging them to accept support and doing all she could to get the perpetrators locked up.

She grabbed a coffee and headed for the briefing room. PC Rab 'the Kebab' Kennedy was labouring along the corridor from the direction of the back stairs, dragging a bin bag in one blue-gloved hand. Their eyes met and his expression quickly slid from pissed off to suitably contrite. 'Morning, Sarge.'

Last night, she'd assigned him the task of clearing out squad cars before he went out this morning, the total number he was required to do rising with every protestation that it hadn't been him who'd left the cans and food papers in the car May had used yesterday. She'd chewed him out: *I had to take a bereaved mother home in a skip.*

'Good morning, PC Kennedy. Keep up the good work,' May said, indicating he was on his way to forgiveness, but wasn't quite there yet.

With experienced cops retiring and recruitment falling she was lucky her team of four female and seven male constables had only a single vacancy. Response officers in Police Scotland were never single-crewed, mainly due to the requirement of corroboration central to Scots law. The evidence of one witness, however credible, wasn't enough to proceed with a charge. Two officers working together was also safer. Being one cop down meant May sometimes had to take a spot in a squad car while fielding calls from her other constables and dealing with the additional responsibilities of rotas, budgets and keeping the bosses happy that came with sergeants' stripes.

The briefing room was small and the oval table in the centre meant that when kitted up even the slimmest cop had to navigate sideways, and two attempting to pass each other caused gridlock. She set her coffee down and nodded to a couple of officers. The rest filed in carrying hot drinks and paper bags of rolls filled with square sausage or bacon, dragging with them aromas of hot fat and the cold morning air as they greeted each other and found seats.

'Right, boys and girls. Hope you've had your Weetabix cos it's going to be a busy one,' May said, to a chorus of groans.

Even on a Thursday morning they'd a backlog of work to get through, and she tapped the table impatiently, a signal to settle down. At least the recent move away from paper notebooks to the digital Pronto device was saving everyone at least an hour's admin each shift – time they could remain on the street. As well as direct access to person and vehicle checks, everything from initial job taskings to golden hour actions – audio interviews with witnesses and victims, evidential photos – were now logged via the pimped-up smartphone and automatically stored in the command-centre vault. May had heard even old-timers agree it was the best piece of kit to come along in twenty years.

Most of the overnight drink- and violence-related taskings had been processed, but there were still some jobs to chase. Moped in a pedestrian area had clipped a pensioner. Twenty-five-year-old male glassed in pub after heckling the karaoke singer. Youths damaging shopfronts.

'Right, follow-ups for today. Lauren, I want you and Toni to check the CCTV at the shops. See if you can identify our would-be Banksys with the spray-cans and penchant for kicking folks' doors in. Visit their parents and have a word.'

The two female officers, already sitting next to each other, fist-bumped.

'We can mibbaes get the youngsters into a Violence Reduction scheme if the parents are no-hopers,' PC Lauren

Paterson said. She was steady and efficient, an expert juggler of responsibilities, which included a toddler and a pre-schooler of her own.

Her beat partner nodded in agreement. PC Toni McAleer was Parkhead-born, in the city's east end, and had been adopted out of domestic violence aged six. Police officers had been her first positive role models, and she'd joined up to help others the way she'd been helped.

'Yes. Good,' May replied. 'Let's not have these lads up before the sheriff until we've exhausted all the other options.'

She scanned the room till she found Ross 'Keep the Heid' Reed, sitting with PC Mohan Pannu, a third-generation Punjabi Sikh who'd grown up in the family furniture shop in Paisley.

'I need an update on our karaoke heckler, and his likely prognosis.' She levelled her pen at them. 'Mo, Ross, I'm putting you two down for that.'

Both in their late twenties, with active social lives, they'd likely find common ground with the victim. Ross shrugged his agreement. He was short, with heavily muscled shoulders, and had started out as a nightclub bouncer. He'd earned his nickname by exhorting those who objected to being arrested, sometimes violently, to calm themselves or *keep the heid*, a phrase probably picked up in his previous profession. Earlier in his police career, it was advice he'd occasionally failed to take himself. These days, he seemed to be perpetually studying for his sergeants' exam but never taking it.

'Is he at the Royal?' Ross asked. Glasgow Royal Infirmary

was north of the river but was the closest accident and emergency.

May checked her notes. 'Queen Elizabeth.'

Ross shifted in his chair, and exchanged a look with Mo, acknowledgement that a transfer to the newer university teaching hospital probably meant the victim needed sewing back together by an expert.

'So, was this guy getting glassed for a clash of musical tastes, or what?' Mo leaned back and folded his arms. May saw his mind was working along the same lines she'd just travelled. Their enquiries might mean the difference between an assault charge or wounding with intent, which carried a maximum sentence of life imprisonment. Three years into the job, May reckoned he'd likely be a high-flyer and would join his girlfriend in CID soon.

'Arresting officers say it was a difference of opinion, but I want the full story,' she replied. 'We've got the perpetrator in custody, but his pals might decide they're honour-bound to dissuade the victim from co-operating with us. Eyeball any known faces hanging around at the hospital. If this is gang-related best we know now before anything else kicks off.'

'Aye, okay, Sarge,' Mo said, pulling out his Pronto and making a note.

Two teams down, four left. She did a quick headcount. One officer was in court this morning, another had picked up a tasking as he was driving in and was already at the scene. There'd been a call from the ambulance. Suicidal man. Had had to force entry. Police Scotland attended around 20,000 mental-health-related incidents each month.

Nine out of ten didn't involve a crime. Now May was a constable down while they waited for the joiner to turn up and secure the door.

She was glancing at her notes and doing a quick reshuffle of priorities when there was a knock, and Inspector Mark Ward came in. As one, the team pushed back their chairs to stand, but he motioned them to remain seated and stepped aside to reveal a petite young woman.

'This is DC Dimple Sharma from British Transport Police,' Ward said, shooting May a look that said, *I haven't worked out how, but this is your doing.* 'Purely a courtesy visit. I'm sure she won't take much of your time.' He gave May a further meaningful glance before making a rapid exit as if he'd be tainted by association, or May might ask him for resources to pursue the case.

DC Sharma smiled tentatively at the sea of expectant faces that greeted her from around the table. May thought she looked so slight that a gust of wind would topple her. To reach detective constable she must be at least mid-twenties, though she appeared younger. She wore a dark grey trouser suit and her glossy dark hair was tied back in a simple knot. DC Sharma began to extend her right hand, as if to come forward and formally introduce herself to May, but the press of bodies around the table made that impossible, so she tucked a stray lock behind her ear to disguise the action and gave the room another nervous smile.

May caught the look of relish on some of the officers' faces. They expected her to make the BTP cop pay for the unexpected interruption to her briefing. But to May this was less of an interruption than an opportunity. She pointed to a chair in a corner by the door and gave the young woman a warm smile.

'Take a seat, we're nearly done.' May turned back to her team. 'Now I know some of you think our pals in the BTP aren't proper cops, but we can't all be the chosen ones.' A ripple of laughter ran around the room. May's expression became grave. 'DC Sharma is here to make enquiries regarding the sudden death of a young Govanhill woman named Holly Campbell. I do not anticipate that you'll be called to assist at this stage, but if you are, I expect you to give her all the help she requires.'

Her message was clear, and under May's watchful eye the same officers who'd smirked a moment ago now nodded respectfully to the newcomer before turning their attention back to the briefing.

May allocated the remaining tasks to the team, then sought out PC Kennedy.

'Rab, does your encyclopaedic knowledge of cars extend to bikes?'

'Bikes aren't Formula One.'

'There you are. Knew you were the expert. That moped in the pedestrian area that hit the elderly gentleman. CCTV. Get a make and model, and index number. Check if it's stolen.' Other officers might have seen this as further punishment, but Rab Kennedy, though a capable officer, was happy with mundane tasks.

May lifted the remote and activated the screen on the briefing-room wall.

'Familiarise yourself with our most wanted, pals old and new.'

A mosaic of headshots appeared – current top five muggers, court no-shows, those in breach of bail conditions, and anyone sought for questioning or reported missing to look out for, including a male who'd absconded from a psychiatric unit.

Some were more memorable than others.

Suspect known to keep a machete beneath the driver's seat of his vehicle.

Suspect last seen naked doing press-ups on the roof of a bus.

Suspect claimed direct descent from William Wallace and attempted to headbutt police.

'Any questions?' She gave each officer the once-over, a sweep around the table inviting replies, but also speed-checking their demeanours. Some hid stress levels better than others. Shift briefings aside, only on rare 3 a.m.s when calls miraculously stopped coming in was there anything like a full crew in the office. It was a common mis-conception that CID did all the investigating, but each member of her team had their own caseload to manage – housebreakings, assaults, thefts. Nights were when they'd attempt to progress outstanding cases in a vain attempt to catch up with the backlog. On those eerily quiet shifts, May had the urge to lift the blinds and check if Armageddon had wiped the city of inhabitants yet somehow bypassed Cathcart Police Office. It was the only possible explanation for silent phones, since every other day was just the usual apocalypse-in-progress – fire-, sword-, drug-driven pestilence, and death.

She stood up, signalling the end of the briefing. 'Right. Look after yourselves, and each other.'

When the room began to empty, May made her way to where the BTP cop was standing in the corner by the door.

'DC Sharma, you're coming with me to knock on a drug dealer's door.'

The BTP detective quickly suppressed a look of surprise tinged with apprehension.

Toni McAleer gave Sharma a playful nudge. 'No luck, eh, hen?' She grinned.

'You commenting on the job or the company, PC McAleer?' May raised her eyebrows at the young officer who was zipping up her utility vest.

Toni held up her hands in surrender and gave the BTP cop a sly wink. 'Neither, Sarge. Honest. Good luck, DC Sharma.'

'Please, call me Dimple,' she said, smiling at the two response officers.

The drug dealer May had in mind was Scott Galbraith, who'd previously assaulted his girlfriend, Holly Campbell, in full view of her mother. She was hoping he'd open the door spliff in hand and resist; she hadn't used her baton in a while.

CHAPTER 5

The sullen red of the traffic lights was the only colour that morning. The blast of the car's heater chased the damp chill around but failed to banish it as May and the young detective threaded their way through the warren of tenements that made up Govanhill.

Dimple, it turned out, was a local lass, happy to be on familiar ground and share anecdotes from her childhood. Her father's corner shop. Her auntie's laundrette. The school she'd attended where her sisters' kids now went. Sensing her nervousness, May let her talk. The squad car was nearing its destination when Dimple revealed Holly Campbell's death was her first case.

'Well, not really a case, as far as my boss is concerned,' she admitted. 'He wants it wrapped up and off our hands.'

Snap, thought May.

'So, why are you here?' Inspector Mark Ward might have bought the whole *courtesy visit* idea but May didn't. Who had the time these days? 'An email, a phone call would've done.'

As they turned the corner into Allison Street, May glimpsed Dimple's sheepish smile, admission that she'd hit the mark.

'Three or four women a week kill themselves on the railways,' Dimple began, her voice low and serious. 'I want to know why. Transport cops and rail staff make thousands of interventions every year. When I was patrolling in uniform, we were always told a moment of kindness might save a life.'

'So that's why you're here? As a kindness?' May said, aware her tone gave the question a more cynical edge than she'd intended.

'I want to know what happened to Holly. But aye, I suppose you could call it a kindness.'

Whatever May had expected it wasn't this. She'd thought simple ambition had brought DC Sharma to Cathcart Police Office. A keen youngster anxious to shine, to catch her boss's attention. But now she wondered if there was more to this young woman than met the eye.

They pulled up at an address near Victoria Road. It wasn't the worst street in the area – no cars on bricks – but it still had the overflowing bins, a leaf-litter of takeaway boxes, and the vibe that no Uber driver in his right mind would pick you up from here.

'So, Holly's death?' May unclipped her belt. 'How far have you got? Any useful CCTV?'

Dimple shook her head. 'We have Holly on the concourse. But power was off to the barrier and the platform nine lights.'

It chimed with what May had seen on her visit to Glasgow Central, and she knew from her encounter with the station cops that there'd been no witnesses – no staff or folk on the train.

'What about the driver?'

'He's called Billy Mackenzie and lives over Giffnock way. He's in bits. Signed off work. He said Holly came out of nowhere. Train cameras don't give us any more than that.'

Dimple sighed. 'He asked me about her. This is his third fatality. I told him she was twenty-two and from Govanhill, and he said he'd grown up here too. Seemed to make it worse, like they had this connection.' She stopped, looking at May from the tail of her eye. 'Shouldn't have done that, should I?'

'You only said what'll be on the TV and in the papers,' May replied. If it even makes the news, she thought, but didn't add. 'And it's best to answer a straight question with a straight answer, when you can. It helps gain the witness's trust.'

Dimple pushed out her bottom lip, considering, then nodded. 'So, who's this guy you think we should talk to?'

May recounted Jackie McNally's visit and her accusations of previous assaults by Galbraith on her daughter.

Dimple's mouth formed a small O. 'And do you think he's involved in her death?'

'I think folk who sell drugs to schoolkids are capable of anything.' May knew all too well how criminality in one area could spill into abuse in relationships. 'You haven't spoken to Jackie?'

'My boss did. He didn't mention this.' Dimple left May to draw her own conclusions about the weight he'd given to the accusation against Scott Galbraith.

'After what you've told me,' May began, 'Galbraith being involved in the lassie's death is a leap, I'll admit.' She had nothing but Jackie's words and her own gut feeling that the present career trajectory of Scott Galbraith would, sooner or later, see a murder charge added to his CV.

'What's he like?' Dimple said, her sharp, dark eyes fixed on May.

'He's twenty-four and officially an apprentice electrician, but he didn't buy *that* on a trainee's wages.' May nodded towards a new bright blue BMW, incongruous in a line of elderly Hondas, Toyotas and a Kia with a mismatched door panel. 'Up-and-coming dealer. Father died in prison when he was ten and he got hooked up with the G Block young team.'

'That still a thing?' Dimple wrinkled her nose.

Though Scotland's culture of *young teams* – youths wanting a buzz and having nowhere else to get it except tracksuits, drinking, drugs and battering the fuck out of rival gangs – wasn't the issue it had been ten years ago, the raw material was still around.

'I mean,' Dimple continued, 'I remember as a kid lads jacking Ferraris from Shawlands, blocking off streets, then tormenting the thing doing doughnuts until it died. But the Violence Reduction programmes, treating crime as a social problem, stopped most of that.'

'I don't think we can claim all the credit,' May replied. 'Social media's just made it easier to act the big man without risking getting your head kicked in. Nice cars, breeding and selling expensive dogs, five-hundred-pound polo shirts. Stick it all on Instagram. It's still a big dick-measuring contest, and some lads are always going to make the leap to gangster.'

Dimple suppressed a grin. 'The research doesn't quite put it like that, Sarge, but I think you're right.'

The spectral presence of Michael McNally slipped once more into May's mind. She felt certain he was cultivating just such proto-gangsters, whatever his *businessman* tax return claimed.

Dimple was leaning forward, craning up at the tenement through the squad car's windscreen, processing what May had told her and making her assessment.

May wasn't the only one who suspected McNally. A month before she'd transferred from CID to care for her daughter, her partner, Detective Inspector Andy Wilson, had been found floating in the Clyde with two bullet holes in his skull. There were rumours of corruption, that he'd failed to deliver confiscated drugs back to their owner, or had taken a backhander to make a charge go away only to renege on the deal. May knew none of it was true, and the subsequent investigation had uncovered nothing. But shortly before his murder, Andy had revealed to her his suspicions about Michael McNally, sketching out a web of connections that led from legitimate businesses to criminal enterprises and back again, but nothing could be proved. Not yet. Shortly afterwards, he'd been murdered.

Just old unfounded rumours, May had been told by the murder team, when she'd relayed what Andy had said. None of her own CID colleagues had backed her up. And that was that. After two years, the case remained open but stalled.

Sometimes she wondered if those two tragedies – losing both Isla and Andy Wilson – had fused themselves in her mind, making her see ghosts and shadows where there were none. Maybe that's what had happened to Jackie McNally. Either way, she needed to find the truth.

Dimple sat back in the passenger seat, her expression resolute. 'You're right. We need to talk to this guy.'

'Aye, we do,' said May. 'Let's go.'

CHAPTER 6

The security door to the close was wedged open with a half-brick, giving them the advantage of surprise when they reached the third-floor flat. Shadows moved behind the spyhole when they knocked, then the door was wrenched open.

The guy was big, bearded, tattooed. There were enough chunky gold rings on his fingers to double as knuckledusters.

A second figure appeared behind him and lightly tapped his shoulder.

'S'alright, Malky.'

Galbraith matched May for height but he'd bulked up in the year since she'd last seen him in court. His dark hair was shaven close, a spider tattoo curling from his sweatshirt collar. For the briefest moment he rested his pitch-black eyes on her, flicking to DC Dimple Sharma and back. Remembering the petite clothes she'd folded with Jackie McNally, May was struck once more by Holly's fragility and felt a curl of anger at how utterly powerless she'd have been in the face of such an individual.

But May wasn't powerless.

'Mr Galbraith. Can we come in?' She took a step forward, but Malky the man-mountain needed a second tap on the shoulder from his boss to stand aside. The dynamic of the relationship was clear. Malky was there for protection, not for his sparkling conversation.

'Officers. What can I do for you?' Galbraith's voice was light, like a wee boy trapped inside all the pumped-up meat.

The dim, square hallway had five doors – kitchen, bathroom, two bedrooms all closed; the only open one leading to a front room.

'I'm Sergeant Mackay, this is DC Sharma from British Transport Police.'

'Lost yer train, hen?' Galbraith growled. 'You'll no' find it here.'

To her credit, Dimple didn't react, and May thought she'd probably had plenty of practice with football crowds, drunk revellers, and the persistent threat of terrorism to be bothered by a ned like Galbraith.

'Shall we go through?' May took another step and this time both men stood aside. She instinctively put out a hand for them to lead the way. Best if they weren't between her and the door. Dimple was quiet and tense beside her, but she was taking in every detail of the flat.

Light streamed from half-open curtains on the street-facing bay window. Two games controllers lay on a low glass table, littered with plates and mugs, in front of a black leather sofa. An enormous wall-mounted screen showed a fight in progress. The men resumed their seats and stared at May.

The lack of curiosity, questions or even concern displayed spoke volumes about their past encounters with the police.

They were waiting for her to make the first move. Or they already knew why she was here.

'I'm sorry to tell you, Mr Galbraith, that your former girl-friend, Holly Campbell, is dead.'

Nothing. Not a flicker in those shark eyes.

'I've got that right, haven't I? She was your girlfriend.'

'As you said, ex.'

'Did you have anything to do with her death, Mr Galbraith?'

Dimple slid her Pronto from her pocket and opened a note file.

'Aw, come on. You're no' serious.'

'When was the last time you saw Holly?' May said.

'Can't remember. Weeks. Months.'

'Did you see her on Tuesday night?'

'No.'

'So where were you on Tuesday night?'

'Nelly Dean's. It's a pub.'

'Aye. I know. All evening?'

Galbraith nodded.

'What about Glasgow Central station? Were you there on Tuesday evening?'

A shake of the head.

'What time d'you leave the pub?'

'Late. Half-elevenish.'

'On your own? Anyone with you?'

'Malky was there, weren't you? Playing pool.'

The big man grunted in response.

'Anyone else see you at the Nelly Dean?'

He reeled off a couple of names familiar to May as dealers. They'd back him up if he said he'd been on a trip to the moon.

'So you didn't see or contact Holly Campbell on Tuesday night?'

He made a show of considering. 'I mean, I can't say I didn't pass the lassie in the street and no' notice her.'

The vagueness was a tease. A challenge. *Prove I did.*

'When did you last contact her?'

A shrug.

'Did you ever hit Holly Campbell?'

'Never.'

'We've a witness who said you did.'

She saw him calculating who that might be and how much weight their testimony carried. His face didn't register concern. Either he wasn't worried about Jackie, or the occasions of violence had been too numerous to pick out an individual witness, who might in any case be intimidated into silence. Galbraith gave her a blank stare.

'Did you ever supply Holly Campbell with drugs?'

He snorted. 'I'm no' gonna dignify that with a reply.'

'Mr Galbraith, you and Holly were together for a couple of years. Did you love her?'

There was a flash of emotion before the mask fell back into place. He had felt something for Holly, May was sure, but whether that was love, possession or hate, and whether Scott Galbraith even knew the difference, was another matter.

'She was just some lassie. Now she's dead. Not my problem.'

44

Oh, it is, pal, May thought, because I'm about to make it very much your problem.

Galbraith's brow lowered as he detected the threat in May's silence.

'So, Mr Galbraith, you wouldn't mind showing me your phone? The last time you contacted Holly Campbell.'

'You've no warrant. That's it – you two, out.' He plunged his hand down the front of his tracksuit bottoms and jiggled it about. 'That's 'less you're gonna arrest me for scratching ma balls.'

Malky sniggered as he got to his feet.

May didn't react to either man and looked calmly around the room. No sign of drugs. No weapons, other than Malky. She'd need a warrant to do a thorough search. Unless he'd watched them draw up there'd have been no time to move stuff. If he had drugs on the premises, they'd be well hidden.

May exchanged a glance with Dimple confirming she had no other questions.

'Well, I can see you're busy, Mr Galbraith. Another time.'

As they reached the front door, Galbraith stepped in front of May and her hand went automatically to her PAVA spray. Galbraith's face was inches from hers. She could smell the bacon on his breath. She stared back and held her ground, impassive. Dimple had tensed beside her, eyes fixed on Big Malky.

'Just so we're clear, Sergeant Mackay,' Galbraith began, 'I know nothing about Holly Campbell's death.' He emphasised each word with such menacing clarity it left May with only one conclusion. He was lying through his teeth.

CHAPTER 7

Chapping neighbours' doors proved equally fruitless. May was sure there were folk inside but if you had predators nesting above you then you'd think twice about breaking cover and talking to the polis. She wanted to know if anyone had seen Holly recently. Jackie thought the relationship between her daughter and Scott Galbraith had been over, but skilled as he was at maintaining the hard man exterior, there'd been a reaction when May had asked him whether he'd loved Holly. If they could place Holly at the flat in the days before her death, they'd be a step closer to placing Scott Galbraith in Glasgow Central, or at least breaking down his statement that they were no longer in touch.

'What d'you think, Sarge?' Dimple said when they returned to the squad car and were retracing their way through the maze of tenements, each street a bleaker sibling of the last, until they hit the main drag of Victoria Road and its cultural kaleidoscope of small businesses and shops.

'I want to hear your thoughts,' May replied, braking to avoid a woman in a hijab wrangling a pram and two toddlers across the street.

'Quite the charmer, isn't he,' Dimple replied. 'And in a

coercive or violent relationship it's often when the woman tries to leave that she's in the most danger.'

'Aye, that's true.' May thought of her constable Toni McAleer, whose mother had been battered to death when she'd tried to get herself and her kids to safety.

Dimple crossed her arms. 'But why do it so publicly? He's a big guy. Could've just lifted her off the street, bundled her into the boot of his car.'

'Perhaps he didn't set out to do it. He was stalking her, or it was just chance they were getting the same train home from town. A confrontation that escalated.'

'Aye, mibbaes,' Dimple said, but she didn't sound convinced.

'Now you've had a good look at him, you'll be able to find him on the concourse CCTV. We'll get a sheriff's warrant and go through his place.'

There'd been no gear visible. No smell of weed. Apart from the expensive gaming equipment, she'd spotted two laptops. Be interesting to see what was on them. The days of dealers scribbling lists of customers' accounts on the backs of envelopes were long gone. They all fancied themselves as *techno-dealers*, running spreadsheets and photographing anyone who owed them money so bad debtors could be dealt with by third parties. Electronic devices were now among the top five items on the forensic shopping list – flat, phone, car, laptop, bank accounts. With luck they'd nail Galbraith for Holly's death and sweep up an entire network with it.

When Dimple didn't reply, May said, 'You've still got access to the CCTV?'

'Aye, of course,' she replied. 'If he was there.'

'Oh, he was there alright.' Galbraith had been rattled. It was what he hadn't said that told May she was on the right track. 'Me he knows of old, but he didn't ask why a transport cop was chapping his door.'

'Already heard how Holly died?'

'An offender with his record should have been shouting *lawyer* the minute we arrived. He's got something to hide, he just hasn't worked out the best way to do it yet. Your lot told Jackie McNally it was a suicide. It'll be all round this place by now. He's been thinking if he kept his head down maybe no one would come looking for him. We've just blown that idea out of the water.'

They drew up outside the Nelly Dean. Inside, the decor was old man's pub, wood-panelled booths, the whole place in shades of brown. *Nobody gets out sober*, said the jokey sign behind the bar. *Nobody comes in sober* would have been a more accurate assessment of the place. Every punter through the door would be looking for the same thing. Something to take the edge off.

It didn't seem like a trendy fit for Galbraith, but the barman confirmed he'd been in on Tuesday night playing pool. CCTV? No, broken, as May somehow knew it would be.

'If his alibi checks out . . .' Dimple began when they'd returned to the squad car.

'If the BTP are willing to take the word of a scrote like the landlord of the Nelly Dean as gospel, it's a wonder you solve any cases.'

Dimple flushed and looked down at her clasped hands.

'Look,' said May more evenly, 'I truly believe you want to understand why Holly Campbell died, and if there are any lessons to be learned that stop further tragedies, I'm right behind you. But don't think it's gonna be simple. You'll no' find answers in a couple of hours. It's never simple.'

The young detective studied May's determined and not unkind expression, then nodded.

'We need to talk to Jackie, but first, what's the train driver's address?'

'He's on sick leave.'

'Aye, so he'll be at home.'

'He's already given his statement.' Dimple shifted uneasily. 'He was really upset. I don't want to put him through it again.'

'We'll be gentle,' May said, and pulled out into the traffic before Dimple could argue.

CHAPTER 8

The train driver's house in Merryburn Avenue, Giffnock, was a semi-detached bungalow set back from the road. May surveyed it while she took a call from one of her constables about a rota clash for an upcoming football match. Behind the living-room curtain a figure was watching them.

In the passenger seat, Dimple looked uneasy.

'It'll be okay,' May reassured her when she'd ended her call. 'It's just a quick chat.'

The woman who came to the front door wore a green Scottish Ambulance uniform. May felt a jolt of shock, a certainty that she was too late and the driver had harmed himself. *His third fatality,* Dimple had said.

Beside her, the young detective had gone white, her mind working along the same lines. 'Oh no,' she breathed, and May put a steadying hand on her arm.

But if paramedics were here, where was their vehicle?

'I'm Sergeant May Mackay from Cathcart Police Office. I'm looking for Billy Mackenzie. Is everything alright?'

'Aye, everything's fine.' The woman had sharp features and cropped blonde hair. The name badge on her breast pocket said *Emma*. 'I'm his wife. What's this about?'

May felt a wave of relief, but also the strong impression that Emma Mackenzie didn't welcome the sight of two cops on her doorstep.

'Is it possible to have a quick word?' May said. 'I'll not keep your husband long.'

'This about the other night? He's already given a statement to the station cops.' Her gaze travelled to Dimple and the BTP ID lanyard around her neck before hardening into a scowl. 'He wasn't responsible. I don't want him upset.' Emma crossed her arms and leaned against the doorpost, a signal she'd no intention of letting them anywhere near her husband. 'D'you know what these drivers have to put up with? Two hundred and forty deaths there were in the last year, not counting the Tube in London. For you and I, it's the job, but not them.' She stopped and gave May a shrewd look. 'Did the lassie try to kill herself before?'

May knew that Emma Mackenzie wanted to tell her husband something that would make him feel better, to emphasise the inevitable trajectory of Holly Campbell's life towards self-destruction. It was just a random piece of bad luck that, this time, the lassie had chosen his train. But he was strong. He'd get through it. Perhaps it was even better him than another driver less equipped to deal with the hand fate had dealt them. May didn't blame Emma. She'd protect her own officers in the same way.

When May didn't answer Emma's question about Holly's previous attempts, the woman nodded, drawing her own conclusions. 'I feel for the lassie's family, I really do, but why are you here?'

'We just wanted to clarify a few points,' Dimple said. 'And check Mr Mackenzie has support.'

'Aye, well, he's got me for that, and his union rep. We appreciate your visit, but if you want to talk to him, it'll need to be with his lawyer present. Now, if you'll excuse me.'

As she went to close the door, Billy Mackenzie emerged from behind her.

'It's alright, Emma,' he said, reaching past her to pull the door open. He was clean-shaven and mid-thirties, dressed smart casual in jeans and a plaid shirt. He stood gripping a half-finished mug of coffee to his chest. 'You'd better come in.'

In a neat living room furnished with two leather sofas, Mackenzie laid out the events of the evening of Holly's death methodically and precisely, exactly as he'd told the British Transport Police officer who'd taken his statement an hour after the fatal incident. His train had been terminating, ready for the morning. There were no passengers on board. The signals were all clear. He'd approached the unlit platform at a safe speed. Isolated power circuit problems were not uncommon, likely a tripped switch or fuse that would be fixed overnight. With no passengers, it wasn't an issue and did not affect the safe running of the train.

'I heard Emma ask you if the lassie had tried to kill herself before.'

His wife took his hand into her lap. She didn't interrupt but stared at the two officers sitting opposite like they were predatory animals who at any moment might leap on her husband and devour him.

May nodded. There was no point in withholding this. Whether it made him feel better or worse was up to him and his therapist to deal with at a later date. 'And you saw no one else with Holly?'

He hesitated. May felt a pulse of adrenaline at his reaction.

'Emma, love,' he said, handing his wife the empty mug he'd been clutching like a life raft. 'Can you make us all some coffee?'

'That'd be great, thank you. Just black, please,' May said, sensing there was something he didn't want to discuss in front of her.

Dimple had also taken the hint and rose to her feet. 'I'll give you a hand.'

Emma required repeated reassurances before she was willing to leave her husband alone with May.

'What did you see on the platform?' May said, her voice lowered.

'I'm not sure,' he said slowly. 'And what's the point saying there was someone? The electrics were out, no CCTV. Maybe I imagined it.'

'You saw someone? What did they look like?'

He shook his head, working his bottom lip between his teeth.

'Male or female? Tall or short?' May persisted. 'Don't think too hard, just tell me what your impressions were at the time.' She held up her empty hands. 'I'm not writing anything down. Not recording it. Tell me what your first thoughts were.'

'A shape, really. Dark clothing. About my height. I saw

the lassie turn. It looked to me like she'd heard someone calling her name. There weren't any staff on the platform that tried to stop her, were there?'

'Not that I've heard. The BTP told me there were no witnesses.'

'Aye, they said that to me too.'

'Did you tell them you thought you saw someone?'

He shook his head. 'Didn't think they'd believe me.' He took a deep breath, as if steeling himself for what was coming next. 'I've had jumpers before. Some folk go onto the line backwards, like she did. Maybe easier for them that way. Can't see the tracks or the train coming. But you need to stand right on the edge of the platform for that. It was more how she fell, or didn't fall. It's no' that easy to jump backwards and know you're going to land on the tracks. It was like she was . . . propelled.'

'Pushed? You thought she was pushed?'

Billy Mackenzie rolled his shoulders in a movement that was half shrug, half confirmation. Then he sat back, letting his shoulders sag, as if telling the story had been a physical release.

'You could put the person in front of me and I'd be no use,' he said. 'But I tell you what, they must have been fit.'

'How's that?'

'Station staff were there quick. I was out of my cab in five or six seconds and they were long gone. My wife thinks it's the shock. My subconscious trying to find ways to deal with the guilt, to make myself think I wasn't responsible, that someone else caused her death. And she's worried I'll lose my job if the train company think I'm mentally unfit and seeing things that arenae there.'

'That's reasonable. We cops feel it too sometimes. Guilt that we didn't get there quick enough. Guilt that we didn't lock someone away first time around before they went on to kill someone.' Guilt that I still don't understand how and why my daughter killed herself, when I was keeping watch over her so closely, May thought but didn't say.

Mackenzie nodded, reassured that his difficult admission hadn't been minimised or swept aside.

'But you do think you saw someone? That Holly Campbell was pushed?'

This time, the nod was clear. 'Aye. But I've no idea who it was.'

CHAPTER 9

As they headed towards Jackie McNally's flat twenty minutes away, Dimple listened patiently as May recounted what the driver had told her, then shook her head.

'Why didn't he say this in his statement?'

'He'd already been told there was no one else on the platform,' May said severely. It was a breach of protocol, allowing witnesses to confer before they'd been interviewed and Dimple's silence told May she'd understood this. 'And he's scared of losing his job.'

'Mibbaes he's mixing Holly's death up with the other fatalities?'

'It's possible,' May conceded. 'But his experience also means he knows better than most what suicide by train looks like.' The certainty that Galbraith had pushed Holly had been solidifying in her chest until it was an ache that could only be allayed by action. 'Review the station CCTV. If there's anything, anything at all, that might back up the scenario of a second person on the platform, then ask Billy Mackenzie if he'd like to amend his statement.'

After a hesitation, May was gratified to see Dimple pull out her Pronto and type herself a note.

*

It was still early when they arrived at Jackie McNally's, not even lunchtime, but an open bottle of wine sat on the kitchen worktop, most of it gone. May told Dimple to take the woman through to the living room, then she poured the last dregs down the sink and switched the kettle on.

The two-bed flat was the same layout as Galbraith's but without the hi-tech gadgetry and hot-and-cold running intimidation. From the front, the bare treetops of Queen's Park could just be glimpsed over the opposite tenement. The rear-facing kitchen had new units and looked out over the back court where washing lines criss-crossed over family gatherings of wheelie bins. The ceilings weren't as high as in May's own flat in the West End, and the original cornicing, skirting boards and window shutters were long gone, but the place was cleaner, and less chaotic, than she'd expected.

May placed the milky coffee in front of Jackie, who was pale but composed in jeans and a black sweater. A photo album lay open on the table and Jackie was pointing out the pictures to Dimple. Holly in high-school uniform. Holly with braces on her teeth. Holly posing with a guide-dog puppy at an outdoor fundraising event.

'That Queen's Park?' Dimple said, and Jackie nodded. 'My mum used to drag me and ma sisters there all the time, even when it was pelting down. For the fresh air, she said. I just wanted to be home on my laptop.'

'My Holly was the same.' Jackie smiled at the memories, but then her expression flattened and faded, her eyes empty. 'But then she got awful bad with the drugs, and it was Scott Galbraith that was giving them to her.'

May had seen the file. Cannabis, diazepam, cocaine and MDMA, the intentional overdose with sleeping pills. It seemed both mother and daughter had found life difficult. Thin white scars and rounded indentations of burn marks from self-harm were dotted across Jackie's forearms. She saw May looking and self-consciously pulled down her sleeves.

'She was the world to me. Just the two of us since . . .'

Since Holly's father, Darren Campbell, had left the family. May had read that in the file too, noted the call-outs for loud domestic arguments and how Holly's problems with addiction could be traced back to that time.

Although she was convinced the driver had seen Galbraith, May recognised it would be a further cruelty to raise Jackie's hopes at this stage, even if her own were already soaring.

'Jackie,' she began, 'you know we might not be able to find out what happened.'

'I know that.'

'And also . . .'

'You might find something about Holly that I don't want to hear.'

May nodded and Dimple squeezed Jackie's hand.

'I don't care.' She gave the young detective a watery smile. 'I need to know, cos it wasn't suicide.'

May nodded to Dimple who pulled the Pronto from her pocket and clicked the record function.

'Tell me from the start when you last saw Holly, Mrs McNally.'

'Call me Jackie, hen. Holly went out just before seven p.m., to meet her friend Mhairi under the clock in Central station.'

'What's Mhairi's second name?'

Jackie shook her head. 'Don't have her number but she's on the same course.'

'And you were here on your own all night?' May said.

'Neighbour from downstairs brought back a couple of folding chairs she'd borrowed at Christmas. Stayed for a cuppa. Went afore ten.'

May wasn't seeking to eliminate Jackie. She had no suspicion that she'd been the shadowy figure the driver believed he'd seen, but it was vital to know who was where, and when, and what they might have seen or heard, even if they didn't yet recognise its significance.

'Did Holly call or message you?' Dimple said. 'Was she upset or worried?'

'No, that's the thing. She didn't. And she would've. I'm sure of it.'

'And you told Sergeant Mackay that Scott Galbraith had been threatening her. When did he last contact her?'

'I'm no' sure. But she was scared of him.'

'Okay, you're doing really well, Jackie,' Dimple reassured her. 'This won't take much longer. Who are Holly's friends around here? Might she have talked to any of them recently, about Scott?'

'There's Gemma Thorne, they were at school the gether — though I havenae seen her around lately.'

May scrutinised Jackie, but there was nothing. Gemma

was a dealer of spectacular proportions, but Jackie betrayed no indication that she saw the significance of what she'd just said. If Holly was visiting Gemma, she was likely back on the junk, and that alone might account for her taking her own life.

'Anybody else?' May said.

They went through other college friends that Holly had mentioned, and any professionals she might have maintained contact with. Social workers, case workers, psychiatrist, addiction councillors. Dimple thanked her and ended the recording.

'Have youse two interviewed Scott Galbraith yet?' Jackie said.

'We saw him this morning. Says he has an alibi.'

'Well, he's lying.'

'We've spoken to the landlord of the pub. He confirmed he was there.'

Jackie leaned forward, her elbows on her knees as she scrutinised the two officers. 'Don't believe it though, do you? Loads would tell lies for him cos they're mates or scared.'

It was on the tip of May's tongue to say *we're just trying to build a picture*, but she knew that stock phrase wouldn't wash with Jackie, so she gave a tight smile which she hoped conveyed her agreement. No, she didn't believe Galbraith's alibi. Proving it was another matter.

Apart from the calls over domestic disturbance – which hadn't resulted in prosecutions – and Holly's drug issues, Jackie was clean. Not even a misspent youth. No shoplifting, no breach of the peace, no sheriff's warnings. Yet she was a McNally. May framed the question as casually as she could.

'What's Scott Galbraith's connection to your brother, Michael?'

Jackie blinked once, then it was like someone had pressed her off switch. A complete shutdown.

May waited while Dimple looked anxiously between the two women.

If they were ever lucky enough to get Michael McNally to court, his defence counsel might claim she'd used his sister's grief to put words into her mouth about his wrongdoing. And perhaps there was some truth in that. But sooner or later the nest of vermin that Michael McNally presided over would have to be opened if it was to be dealt with, and Jackie could be the key. Jackie thought Scott had turned her only daughter into a junkie and then killed her. She had every reason to destroy his character by linking him to a suspected gangster. But she sat as still as the photos in the album, and didn't utter a word. Frozen in fear. It was as May had suspected. Jackie's abuse hadn't started in her marriage, but much, much earlier, when she was growing up.

'Can we see Holly's room?' May said, ending the silence. There was no point in pressing her on the topic of her estranged brother.

'You'll no' find anything,' Jackie replied, her eyes still on the photographs. 'I've looked.'

CHAPTER 10

Holly's room was the smaller bedroom of the two. Beside the window which overlooked the street, a shiny white desk, with old-fashioned filing-cabinet drawers, was pushed against the wall. There was a laptop connected to a large iMac screen, and above it a pinboard surrounded by fairy-lights. Wooden letters, *HJC*, sat on a shelf (her initials: Holly Jacqueline Campbell) next to an old My Little Pony mug with pens in it, and a cactus.

'Jackie's in quite a state,' Dimple hissed to May. 'Is it fair to ask her about her brother? Is he relevant?'

'I don't know if it's relevant, that's why I had to ask her,' May replied quietly, her eyes searching the photographs on the pinboard. 'Like I said. Won't be simple. Won't be easy either.'

A well-loved cuddly toy dog, not unlike the one in the photograph album, sat by the pillow, a substitute, perhaps, in a domestic set-up that wouldn't support the real thing.

Isla had wanted a dog, but May and Tam had been united in their opposition to their daughter's request. No garden. Everyone out all day. Not possible. If they'd agreed, and the animal had offered even a small degree of emotional support, would Isla have still been here? The question had slipped unbidden into May's consciousness. She knew by now that it was no more than a reflex. She'd told Jackie she might not be able to give her answers, the how and why of her daughter's death, but it wouldn't stop May searching. It was a hard truth she hadn't heeded herself.

In contrast, the walls were covered in dark-themed posters from horror movies and a collage of black-and-white prints – crows, a woman in a graveyard, skulls, decaying flowers. The effect combined to show someone with one foot in adulthood, the other still in a childhood that was perhaps an imaginary one.

'Gothic,' Dimple said, indicating the pictures. 'The style.'

'I know,' May replied. 'My daughter went through a phase.'

'What's she into now?' Dimple said, surveying the walls.

Nothing, May wanted to say. She's dead.

Instead, she pointed to the pinboard. 'That's Holly there.' She studied the young woman's clothing. 'Looks the same as what she had on the night she died.'

The wee lassie from the photo album now hidden beneath heavy eyeliner. May raised her phone and took a snap of the picture, and nudged Dimple to do the same. Holly was in a bar somewhere, wearing the black top with the white skull design, the black jeans and the platform boots that May remembered from the personal effects bag. Small and slim, with grey-blue eyes like her mother's, and long, dark hair hennaed to a deep red. A goth girl – her skin pale, her stare intense – she seemed to be challenging the camera and the world. *Do your worst.* She couldn't have imagined the answer would come so quickly and be so devastating.

May wasn't sure what she was looking for beyond a sense of the victim, which came in only faint echoes. The wardrobe held just a few clothes, mostly black. She pulled open a bedside drawer, noted down the medication names on the back of the empty pill strips. There were a few battered paperbacks and manga comics. It all seemed oddly impersonal. Her own daughter Isla's room had been a riot of dried-up make-up containers, dropped clothes and shoes, books, half-completed art projects, fluffy cushions, guitars, and a music keyboard thick with dust.

May's gaze came to rest on the desk and the laptop.

Dimple followed her look. 'Holly was studying computers. Perhaps there's something online that could tell us more.'

'If we want to follow her there, we'll need the sheriff to authorise it. Without evidence of foul play that's not gonna happen.' She looked pointedly at Dimple who accepted that this would be down to what she could recover from the CCTV with a resigned nod.

They photographed the remaining pictures on the pinboard, including a group May thought were Holly's college pals. At the door, she took a last look around. May's eyes lingered on the laptop. On impulse, she picked it up and closed the door behind them.

'You can't just remove it from Holly's room . . .' Dimple said, her face a mixture of horror and awe.

'Course I can.' May brushed past her and went back into the living room.

Jackie was wiping her eyes. She stopped when she saw what May was carrying.

'Jackie, can I take this with me? I promise you'll get it back.' When the woman hesitated, May said, 'I'll write you a receipt. It'll not leave my possession. Holly might have been talking to someone online.'

After a moment, Jackie nodded. 'You hear about these folk on websites, egging kids on to kill themselves, don't you? Holly wouldn't have done that.'

'I don't think that's the situation here,' May reassured her. 'But it'd be good to know if someone was hassling her.'

They all knew she meant Scott Galbraith.

Jackie gave her a canvas shopping bag. May slipped the laptop inside and held it out to Dimple who looked like she'd just been asked to courier a ton of cocaine. Eventually, she accepted the consignment. May gave her a *told you so* wink.

'You gonna be okay?' May said to Jackie.

'Aye, I'll be fine. Ian'll be here soon.'

'Who's Ian?'

'My partner.' Jackie dipped her head, both proud and coy. 'We've been the gether for a couple of years. He doesn't live here. Don't know what I'd do without him.'

There was a noise in the hall and a voice called out, 'Hiya.'

Jackie's expression turned momentarily anxious, then she fixed on a smile.

The man who walked into the living room looked in his early fifties, broad-shouldered with thinning sandy hair. His face rang a bell with May. Someone she'd arrested? Jackie hadn't mentioned anyone before, and May mentally kicked herself for just assuming there was no partner on the scene. If he had filled the role of Holly's stepfather, he needed checking out. It also put a new light on why Jackie had wanted to be dropped at the corner the previous day, and the anxious look that had just crossed her face. Perhaps it wasn't just the neighbours who'd take a dim view of her consorting with the polis.

He stopped in the doorway, looking from Jackie to the two women, inviting an explanation.

'I'm Sergeant Mackay from Cathcart Police Office.' May held out her hand, keen to head off any confrontation. He took it, which in May's experience was a favourable sign. 'And this is D C Sharma from the British Transport Police.'

'Ian McDonald. Good to meet you.' He shook both their hands, his grip firm and accompanied by a cautious but welcoming smile. He was smartly dressed in a dark suit and held himself like a professional.

'Did you see Holly on Tuesday evening?' May said. 'Just a formality,' she added, though he didn't show any surprise at the question.

'No, I was working late.'

Jackie sat down, then shuffled along the sofa, inviting him to join her. May and Dimple remained standing, signalling the interview wouldn't take long.

'You had that office thing, in town, didn't you?' Jackie prompted.

He nodded. 'And I don't live here. I've a place over in Shawlands. It was a works night out at the Hilton. I'm a risk manager with Cobalt Maritime Services. My colleagues can corroborate I was there.'

'What time did you leave?' May asked as Dimple took notes. The hotel was about half a mile from the station. A fast ten-minute walk, and a man offering up *corroboration* was familiar with legal terms.

'I got a taxi just after eleven.'

'How much did they take off you for that?'

He slipped his wallet from his inside pocket and rummaged through it until he produced an A B C Cabs receipt for £30.

May held up her phone and, when he didn't object, snapped a photo. 'Ouch! The price of living in the leafy suburbs.'

He gave her a good-natured shrug.

Ian McDonald retook Jackie's hand, shooting his partner a quick consoling glance. He seemed in no hurry to eject May and Dimple from the flat, but she still felt a jangling undercurrent of recognition that she was anxious to place. Dimple took down his home address. A quick check through her Pronto would reveal if he had a record.

'Well, I'll leave you to it,' May said, and pressed a hand lightly to the woman's shoulder. 'Jackie, hen, try and get some rest. We'll be in touch when we have something.'

CHAPTER 11

The neighbour in the flat below confirmed she'd gone up to visit Jackie on the night in question, then gave May a five-minute tirade about Scott Galbraith.

'That wee shite needs putting away for good. See that cracked window on the stair? That's his doing. Had Holly by the throat and bashed her against it.'

'You could report Scott Galbraith attacking Holly to me now?' May ripped the Velcro strap of her pocket open and took out her Pronto. Here was an independent witness to Scott Galbraith's violence who could establish an escalating pattern of behaviour. This woman, with her sleeves rolled up over meaty forearms, looked as if she could take on an army of neds.

The neighbour's face clouded with apprehension. 'Didn't see it. Just heard the glass go. Anyways, Holly's gone. Killed herself.' Before either May or Dimple could say anything else, the door swung shut.

'This is what we're up against,' May said to Dimple as they went down the remaining flights of stairs. 'For most folk around here, the chance of getting justice, of locking up the bad guys, is always outweighed by what'll happen if they get to you first.'

'Oh, aye.' Dimple gave a resigned nod and May realised that, having grown up in a local family shop, a constant target for pilfering, vandalism and violence, this must be old news to her.

'Listen, do me a favour,' May said as they came out of the close and into the drizzle. 'Look up Ian McDonald. I know that guy's face.'

'Already did,' Dimple said, fishing her Pronto from her pocket. 'No criminal record. I googled him. There's a profile on the Cobalt Maritime Services website. Senior risk manager, with a career background in security.'

She turned the screen towards May. It was heavy on the corporate language, but light on fact, or previous employers.

' "Experienced at identifying potential project risks and developing mitigation strategies",' May read aloud. 'I thought preventing things from going tits-up was part of everyone's job, or is that just us cops?'

Dimple giggled. May scrutinised the accompanying photo, trying to place how she knew him, but drew a blank.

They put the laptop in the boot. May was about to discuss their next move when Dimple's phone rang.

She checked the screen and grimaced. 'My boss. He'll want me back. Can you drop me at Queens Park station?'

'You came by train?' May said.

'Perk of the job. Plus no parking tickets.' Dimple grinned.

'You need to check the station CCTV for Galbraith. Tell your boss—' May began, but a tap on the driver's window made them both jump.

Ian McDonald stood outside, nervously shifting from

foot to foot, although the bitter wind that blew through the canyons between the tenements might have been part of it.

As Dimple answered her call, May got out of the car and eyed him. 'How can I help you, Mr McDonald?'

'Glad I caught you. Thought maybe we'd met before.'

'Oh, aye, why was that?' If he was going to fess up to some brush with the law it'd save May digging any further.

'I used to be a cop.'

She blinked at him, pictured a uniform but came back with nothing.

'Ex-CID. West Division.' He gave her a self-conscious smile. 'It's why me and Jackie keep our relationship low-key – because of the area, you know? Jackie won't leave, though I keep asking her to move in with me. And then, well, there's her family's connections.'

The McNallys.

'That why you resigned from the job?'

He nodded, bashful that he'd been caught out. 'And it was time to move on. I had some issues with alcohol. Didn't see them getting any better. And I met Jackie in rehab.' He shrugged, smiling.

May didn't believe for one minute that he'd given it all up for love. He'd probably done enough years to qualify for a pension and saw the opportunity to jump straight into a well-paid job with none of the hassle of his previous career. The old days of cops numbing their traumas in the pub after work were gone, but it was still brave to admit his alcohol problem to a relative stranger.

He told her about his new job. Casual, self-deprecating, but with a touch of pride, like he wanted to impress a fellow cop, and show he wasn't on a downward slide.

'So how do I know you?' he said, giving her a quizzical look.

'Central CID, most likely.'

He pointed a finger at her uniform, waggling it up and down, inviting her to explain.

'Straight shifts work better for me at the moment.'

He nodded, and didn't question her further.

'Listen . . .' he began.

May sensed this was the meat of the matter, the real reason he'd caught up with her.

'Jackie wants to go on social media about what happened to Holly,' he said. 'Put up pictures, make an appeal.'

The open photo album on the table took on an additional significance.

His forehead creased into worry. 'I mean, she'll get all sorts of weirdos contacting her. I don't think it's a good idea.'

'I agree, that might be a problem,' May replied carefully. 'What d'you think happened with Holly?'

'You know, when I left the police, I considered social work, but I wasn't sure I could handle it.' He gave her a wry smile. 'It's like I ended up doing it anyway.' He paused, hands on hips as he shook his head. 'The last six months, I think she found college harder than she was letting on.' He stopped again, biting his lip, the struggle evident on his face. 'I'm not her real dad. Darren Campbell has made it clear he doesn't want to know. I tried to support her, we both did, but it was like . . .' He lifted one hand, glided it out, then let it fall. 'She was just moving further and further away from us. I think she took her own life, and part of me isn't surprised. But if I'd known she was this bad, this low . . . I wish there was something more I could have done.'

'It's a natural reaction,' May assured him, understanding the need to dislodge the inevitable sense of helplessness. After Isla's death, her husband Tam's way of dealing with it had been to give up his job at the Glasgow Housing Association and retrain as a youth councillor.

'I'm worried that Jackie not processing Holly's suicide will lead to another breakdown and her hitting the bottle again.'

May considered telling him about the train driver or about the wine she'd poured down the sink that morning, but decided against both. It felt like a betrayal to Jackie. As an ex-cop, he'd work out if she was already drinking. As someone who'd experienced alcohol dependence, he'd know what to do.

'You don't think there's anything in this murder idea, d'you?' he said.

May kept her face neutral but in the empty air between them she saw him draw his own conclusions.

'Oh.' His shoulders slumped, then he braced himself upright again.

'Do you think Scott could've harmed Holly?' May asked.

'Wouldn't put it past him,' he said wearily. 'I thought he was well out of the picture. If I missed something, and me a former detective, I'll never forgive myself.'

'If opportunities were missed, it wasn't down to you,' she

told him, her voice firm as she remembered the neighbour's reluctance to report the stairwell incident. And even if the police had known, it still might not have been enough to save Holly. 'And don't go round to Scott Galbraith's thinking you can sort this out,' she warned. 'You just leave him to me.'

CHAPTER 12

May left work just after 4 p.m., in time to see the sun slip below the Clyde as she joined the conga line across the Kingston Bridge. The temperature had plummeted and telltale flashing blue lights in the distance indicated a possible shunt. Dimple had promised to update her as soon as she'd reviewed the station CCTV. May's texts had gone unanswered, but, as she inched through traffic, the BTP detective's name flashed up on her phone.

'Have you got him?' May said as the taillights ahead came on again.

There was a pause.

'No, Sarge. I'm sorry.' Dimple sounded quiet and far away.

'What, nothing? No sign of Galbraith on the concourse at all?' She was so sure he'd been there that a cold wave of disappointment broke over her.

'It's not that,' Dimple said.

There was another pause and May thought the signal had dropped. She was about to grab the phone to redial when Dimple spoke again.

'My inspector has closed the case. He says we've got nothing to contradict the original finding and the driver isn't a reliable witness.'

'Does he think evidence gets dropped down chimneys by storks,' May snapped. 'We'll no' find anything unless we go looking. I'll call him.'

'I've been trying to change his mind. But he's got a point.'

'How's that?'

'Is Scott Galbraith pushing Holly credible? He's a nasty piece of work, but what've we got? We've already reviewed the CCTV from the train. There's nothing. Sarge, are you sure you don't want this to be him for other reasons?'

Despite herself, May felt a sting of betrayal. There was no logic to it. DC Dimple Sharma wasn't one of her constables, but in the short time they'd spent together it seemed like a partnership of sorts might be possible. And she was wrong about May's motives.

'No, I don't,' May began, her voice as icy as the tarmac outside. 'I want justice for Holly. As far as I'm concerned, getting Galbraith, and any of his associates, off the streets would be a welcome bonus. Billy Mackenzie, the only witness, believes there was someone else on the platform. Holly's mother outlined an escalating pattern of violence, and we have a potential motive in that Holly broke off the relationship. The lassie left no suicide note, nor was there any indication of declining mental health. And she had a return ticket in her pocket. I thought you wanted to understand what had happened to Holly?'

'I do,' Dimple replied, sounding chastened but determined. 'I just don't think pursuing Scott Galbraith is the way to accomplish it.'

'Well, it seems we'll have to agree to differ on that,' May said, and ended the call.

By the time May reached home her anger, driven by frustration at the BTP's action but topped up by the atrocious traffic, hadn't dissipated. She ranted about the injustice of the situation to Tam until he gave her a look that said, *Enough*.

When he put a plate in front of her she couldn't eat, so he suggested she take herself off and have a glass of wine and a hot bath. In her heart, she knew he meant it kindly, but she had the sense she was being sent to her room to have a good think about her attitude and behaviour, and perhaps she deserved it.

Later, as May and Tam lay in bed, her mind circled back once more to Holly Campbell. The image of Jackie clutching her daughter's T-shirt to her breast, gutted and uncomprehending, wouldn't leave her. She reran Scott Galbraith's reaction to her question – *did you love Holly?* – and Jackie's assertion that he was lying about where he'd been when Holly had died.

'I can't let this go,' May said, her voice calm. 'I don't believe Holly killed herself. I think her ex-boyfriend murdered her because she knew something, or as revenge for leaving him, or just because he thought he could. She didn't do this to herself. She was intelligent, resourceful, determined. What?'

Tam had put down his book and given her a look that was all softness, that strove to convey his understanding.

'You could be describing Isla.'

May stared at him. 'No. That's not what's happening here. I just don't think she did it.'

'Why?' Tam said. 'Because of the return ticket? Could have been spur-of-the-moment. Not everyone—' He stopped.

'You were going to say not everyone plans it as well as Isla did.'

'Aye. But you know what I mean. Not always planned. Some just see the opportunity and take it. She'd been out drinking. Maybe she'd taken something else. Wasn't thinking straight. In pain and wanting the pain to stop and thought that was the cure.'

'But you'd think if she was going to do it, it would be at the times when things were bad, not when they were getting better. She had everything to live for. She'd been through therapy. She'd got clean. And if you're gonna do it, why not just do it at the station you got on at. A through train, a fast train, not one pulling to a halt thirty metres up the track.

'Like I say. Spur-of-the-moment.'

She thought of Dimple's comment when she'd challenged her about understanding why Holly had died. That this wasn't the way to accomplish it. Perhaps the lassie was right. She had to consider the broader picture in order to find evidence on Galbraith.

'I need to talk to her friends. Know her state of mind recently. Build a case that points away from suicide. The Procurator Fiscal will need to review it.'

'Oh, May. Don't take this on.'

'I have to.'

'Why? It's not gonna bring Isla back.'

'I know that.' She waved away the accusation. 'But what if her mother is right? What if a vulnerable person has been targeted by an unscrupulous individual, for whatever reason? You're asking me to let a murder go. It's not only about getting closure for her mum, but also about getting justice for a young woman who's died, and God knows there's not enough of that around.'

Tam rolled over and reached for the bedside lamp. 'Aye, well, it sounds like you've made up your mind,' he said, and plunged them into darkness.

After a moment's silence, when she felt him lying still and not going through his customary routine of duvet straightening and getting comfortable, she said, 'D'you think I'm wrong?'

The question seemed to hang in the dark room like the ghost of previous conversations, whose meaning and purposes were long forgotten, but whose disharmony had lingered, a rare visitor during their twenty-six years of solidarity against the world.

'No. Yes. Maybe. Och, I don't know, but I know you, May. You'll not be happy until you've found out, one way or another. I'm just worried that maybe there isn't an answer. Maybe it's like most suicides. We never really know why. And we don't need any more reasons to be unhappy.' He turned and reached for her in the dark. 'I love you, May.'

'I know you do,' she said, and curled into the space he'd made, resting her cheek against his chest. 'I love you too.'

CHAPTER 13

May rose in the small hours, walking through the flat's hallway and cavernous front room, inviting sleep as she'd done with Isla when she had been a baby. But as the clock crept towards 4 a.m., she gave up the battle. Outside, the sky was starless, but the city was a twinkling carpet of lights slowly coming to life. Heading to the office in Cathcart was a possibility, the chance to catch up on some paperwork, but she knew before she'd even reached her car where she was going.

Glasgow Central station closed its doors briefly overnight but it hadn't slept either. Until a few years ago, the night mail trains would've been arriving, their cargo coursing through the tunnels in the heart of the old station and out through arteries to the furthest fingertips of the city. During the First World War, the perpetual cold of these long caverns had served as a mortuary for soldiers' bodies transported back from the Front. Now, delivery vans for the shops on the concourse and laundry and catering suppliers for the hotel came and went like busy insects, and a small army of cleaning and maintenance staff laboured through the dark hours.

May wasn't sure what she'd achieve with this early-morning visit, but she'd been driven from her bed by unabated anger and the fear that chances to provide Jackie with answers were slipping away. And in this unsleeping beast of a station, she was sure such a shocking incident hadn't gone unnoticed, or unremarked upon, no matter what the BTP chose to think.

On the main concourse, a cleaner had just finished pushing a polishing machine across the brilliant white floor. Above, the glass roof still retained the ink-black of the sky beyond and the four-faced clock hung like a glowing pearl, showing the time as 4.30 a.m.

A thin trickle of early commuters were boarding the first train to London Euston. May looked around the concourse for any staff in the local uniform but saw only the cleaner, who was still watching her.

'That sudden death you had the other night . . .' May began when she'd strolled over and greeted her with a nod.

'You're no' one of the station cops. You a reporter?'

May wanted to spread her hands in an ironic gesture of incomprehension. She was Police Scotland branded from her cap, through her black fleece down to her boots. Instead, she treated the question with due seriousness.

'I'm from Cathcart Police Office.' She showed her ID and the woman nodded, apparently satisfied. She was in her fifties, in jeans and a logoed green fleece with a high-vis waistcoat over the top.

May brought Holly's picture up on her phone screen. 'Ever see her about?' Holly had a distinctive look and would've used the station almost every day on her way to college.

'Bonnie wee thing, isn't she,' the cleaner said, then shook her head.

'Her mother would like to know if anyone came across her that evening,' May said. 'She's very distressed. I'd like to support her in coming to terms with what happened. I think if she knew the full story it would help.'

'Aye, I know what you're saying. Poor soul.' She reached out and patted May's hand. 'If we understood more, mibbaes we could stop people from doing it. And good on you for helping out the poor lassie's mother. Tell her everyone at the station is thinking of her.'

'Thank you, I will,' May replied, genuinely touched.

'Remind me what time this happened?'

'Just after eleven p.m.,' May replied.

'Now, see the folk in blue and orange?' The cleaner pointed out a group of train stewards making their way towards platform 1. 'They're West Coast mainline staff. No' be much use, the last train by that operator departs afore seven p.m. It's the Caledonian Sleeper staff you want. All done in tweed and tartan, you'll no' miss them. That service leaves at a quarter to midnight, so you'll need to come back later to catch them.'

'Good tip. Thank you.'

'But what I'd do is ask the station cops to put an appeal on the announcements.' She indicated the space next to the train destinations on the electronic board, currently showing a warning about unattended luggage. 'We get a hundred thousand passengers a day through here. Might be worth a try.'

It was so obvious May could've kicked herself. Jackie had wanted to use Facebook. They might still get bogus calls, but it was a much more targeted approach. All she had to do was persuade the BTP to play ball.

'I need to put you on the payroll,' she told the woman with an appreciative smile. 'Thanks again for all your help.'

'That's alright, hen. It's the wee folk you don't see that know what's going on.'

She gave May's arm a last squeeze and began wheeling her polisher across the concourse.

The smell of coffee made May's stomach grumble. Commuters were now flowing steadily through the station entrances like bees into a hive. There was a cafe open that also sold tourist gifts. She showed the barista Holly's picture but the young man just shook his head. As May waited for her Americano, she browsed the display spinner, picking out a card sporting the Glasgow landmark of the Duke of Wellington statue, complete with the customary traffic cone on his head. The practice had started in the 1980s thanks to late-night revellers. Occasionally, in keeping with Glaswegian egalitarianism, his horse got one of his own too.

While her anger at the BTP hadn't lessened overnight, guilt at the way she'd treated Dimple had seeped in. Tam had given her a severe look when she'd told him about abruptly ending the call and he'd asked how she'd have felt if someone older and more experienced had treated Isla like that. *You'd have knocked their head off their shoulders,* he'd said. He was right, of course. Holly Campbell's death was like an itch she couldn't scratch, causing her to behave in ways she couldn't comprehend, but it was no excuse. She accepted the coffee, paid for the card, and pulled up a stool to begin her apology.

You're a good officer with potential to be a great one, because you listen. She added, *And I'd have you in my squad – if you ever decide to join the proper cops.* She signed it: *Sarge.*

CHAPTER 14

May took the steps down through the low-level platforms, pushing through a thick stream of travellers, and dropped the card addressed to DC Sharma into the BTP office.

South of the station, below the glass-walled railway bridge that carried the main high-level tracks into the concourse, ran a section of Argyle Street, a perpetual twilight of neon-lit fast-food places, cheap jewellers and twenty-four-hour convenience stores. It probably had another name, but to every Glaswegian since the nineteenth century it was the Hielanman's Umbrella, a meeting place for displaced Highlanders like May's own Gaelic-speaking ancestors to get the news from home and any potential jobs going.

She plunged her hands into the pockets of her fleece. Here you were at least out of the rain that had started, the black pavements at either end now a kaleidoscope of taillight reds and streetlight yellows. But below the bridge, this deeper darkness conspired with the prevailing westerly to make it a raw and bitter place.

If the BTP weren't interested in constructing a timeline for Holly's death, she'd need to do that herself. Working backwards she considered the ways Holly might have entered the station just before she'd died. Earlier in the evening,

she'd arrived on the 18.50 train from Queens Park to rendez-
vous with her college pal, Mhairi, under the clock. What had
happened between that train journey and just after 11 p.m.
when she'd met her death on the tracks? May ran a variety
of hypotheses. Where could Holly have gone in those four
hours? Who might have seen her, and understood her state
of mind? Had any of them spotted Scott Galbraith?

The station had three entry points. If Holly had indeed
left the concourse with Mhairi at some point, and not spent
the intervening four hours wandering in an increasingly distressed state, which even the BTP cops would have picked
up on, then where had she re-entered the building? To May's
left, at the junction known to the locals as the Four Corners
and to the cops as a magnet for trouble, was a McDonald's that
operated till the small hours. Had she gone in there? They'd
have CCTV but were unlikely to hand it over to May without
the proper authorisation. What about the countless bars in the
area? The late-opening shops? The jewellers probably ran
their cameras round the clock.

The possibilities criss-crossed until she was left with a rat-
run of overlapping routes and itineraries that tangled in her
mind. It wasn't so much that there was a lack of possibilities,
but an excess, and to whittle them down into something useful
she needed people to talk to her. Top of her list was Holly's
friend Mhairi, but even if she could get Holly's college to
hand over contact details, it was too early in the morning to
call them.

On the greasy pavement, a man wrapped in an old sleeping
bag thrust a paper takeaway cup at the few muffled figures as

they hurried past. He had a cardboard sign propped up in front of him. *I served my country. Hungry and homeless.* As he saw May approaching, he jumped to his feet and scrabbled up his belongings.

'You can take me in, if you want,' he said, a note of hope in his voice.

She was a Glasgow cop on a Glasgow street. She had jurisdiction but no back-up, utility vest, cuffs or other enforcers of authority. What she didn't have, either, was any notion of a crime having been committed. Breach of the peace would be a stretch.

'What, like a stray cat? I'm no' taking you anywhere.'

He grinned at her. He was tall, but thin and hunched, a thatch of thick grey hair pushed to one side of his lined face. She estimated he must be in his early sixties, but he could've been anything from forties to eighty – although homeless folk rarely made it that far. Strong, though, the way he'd jumped up at her approach. She wondered how often the local beat colleagues gave him a meal and a bed for the night.

'How long you been at this lark? On the streets?'

'A few years.'

She looked into the paper cup he was still clutching, emphasising the gesture so he saw her take notice of the meagre contents. 'Not very good at it, are you?'

'It's early. Tough crowd. This is a cracking spot.' There was mock indignation and a twinkle.

'Oh, aye.' May said, heavy on the scepticism. He was obviously the type that enjoyed some verbal sparring. Might be the only friendly interaction he got. 'What's your name?'

'James Alexander MacDonald Fraser. But everyone calls me KitKat. Kit for short.'

'Like a biscuit, do you?'

He pushed his right fist from inside his sleeve and uncurled it. 'Only four fingers.'

May steeled herself not to flinch. His remaining digits curled straight from his wrist. More a flipper than a hand, the skin was torn and stretched where it'd been roughly sewn back together, and the dirt that now encrusted the appendage gave it the appearance of old wood.

'Where'd you leave your thumb?'

'Royal Navy. Falklands.'

'I could call you James, if you'd prefer?'

'Kit's fine. Only my mother called me James and she wasnae a nice person.'

'Okay.' May nodded, judging it best not to enquire further. She made a show of surveying the street once more. 'Maybe not such a bad spot.'

'Aye, I've got my regulars,' he said, a note of pride.

'You ever go into the station?'

He gave her a look of disgust. 'Station cops kick me out. Bastards.'

He, at least, wasn't mistaking her for a BTP cop. Enough experience to know the difference.

'But you must know everything that goes on around here.'

'Aye. A fair bit,' Kit said, cautiously eyeing her.

'You know anything about the lassie that died the other night? Went in front of a train.' May pulled up a picture of Holly on her phone and turned the screen towards him.

But he shook his head. 'I sleep well. Never see a thing.'

'What about any of your mates?'

'Don't have any. See me, I'm a lone wolf.'

'Righto. So, do lone wolves prefer coffee or tea with their Maccies breakfast?'

'Don't mind. Omnivore.'

'Right, c'mon then. You can tell me some more about all the things you haven't seen.'

CHAPTER 15

Kit proved an affable breakfast companion. The station cops did regular sweeps to eject the homeless and anyone they thought was loitering, but otherwise their patrols were sporadic, reserved for big football matches or other high-profile events. The regular cops were better and mostly tried to help, but the hostels were full of addicts and you were safer on the street. When she left him, he promised to ask around about Holly, but May wasn't hopeful anything would come of it, or that he'd even remember their conversation once he'd taken the drink he was so obviously hankering after.

May had just pulled into Cathcart Police Office car park when Dimple called.

'I had a think about what you said,' the young detective began, 'about going out and looking for evidence. You're right. Oh, and thanks for the card, by the way. Can't tell you what it means to have your approval, Sarge.'

'Aye, well, keep it to yourself or everyone'll be wanting it,' May replied, more relieved than she was willing to admit at having mended this particular bridge. 'Has Holly's file gone to the fiscal?'

'The boss is sending it this morning when he gets the post-mortem paperwork. Don't know how I can stop him.'

To May, this was further confirmation that Dimple's inspector had pre-judged Holly's death, though unless the post-mortem provided some unexpected revelation – a stab wound or other cause of death, and that seemed unlikely – she wasn't sure herself what it would add to the investigation.

'Tell him,' May began, 'that you've heard from me, and Holly's mother intends to contact her MSP and raise a complaint about the BTP's handling of the case.'

The involvement of a Member of the Scottish Parliament would bring the kind of media spotlight Dimple's inspector wouldn't want.

'Oh my God, is she? Don't scare me, Sarge.'

'Put it this way, she will when she learns that Holly's case has been closed. I'll help her write the email myself.'

'Ah. Right,' Dimple said, as the penny dropped.

'We just need time to talk to those who knew Holly, pursue every avenue we can. You were right to question whether the focus should be entirely on Scott Galbraith,' May said evenly. Tam would approve of this sudden burst of self-reflection and May acknowledged that her former CID colleagues' tendency to develop a laser-like focus on a single individual, inevitably moulding the evidence around them, had always made her uneasy and had contributed to her leaving.

'What about Holly's laptop?' Dimple said in a low voice, as if retribution for her part in acquiring it was already on its way. 'Can't see my boss authorising that from his budget.'

The device was safely locked up in May's desk. Despite what she'd said to Jackie about evidence of possible threats, on reflection Holly's knowledge of computers, programming and software would have probably enabled her to block anyone sending threatening messages.

'I don't think the laptop is a priority,' May replied. She remembered her conversation with the cleaner. 'But can you persuade him to put up an appeal for information on the station's electronic information board? That shouldn't break the bank. And point out it'll look good under press scrutiny.'

'Okay.'

The other officers for May's shift had begun streaming into the car park.

'And can you find me contact details for Holly's friend, Mhairi? Give the college a call. Or better yet, go over and flash your badge – it'll be quicker.'

'Okay. What are you going to do?'

'I'll chase down some of the folk Jackie mentioned yesterday, local friends and Holly's case workers. Then I'll check in on her and see if she's remembered anything else. And Dimple, the CCTV?' she said, and heard the responding sigh. There'd be hours of it, too much for one person. 'Get some help. I've got to go. We'll catch up later.'

After the morning briefing, May took out a squad car. She was providing back-up for five teams of response officers, giving procedural advice and visiting crime scenes in person when required. May parked up and got a coffee and a pastry from a Turkish bakery on Govanhill Street. She was about to start phoning the names on the contacts list Dimple had sent her when the first call came in.

PCs Toni McAleer and Mo Pannu had been called to an

assault on a dog walker in Queen's Park. When they'd turned up, both victim and assailant had been sitting on neighbouring benches.

'Is the gentleman with the dog injured?' May asked over the phone, taking a bite of her *künefe*.

'He said the lad grabbed him by the throat, but he's okay,' Mo said.

'Why'd he grab him?'

'Toni's talking to him now. Seems he saw the wee spaniel being yanked on its lead. Didn't like it. When he asked the dog walker to stop, the old fella told him to fuck off. So he just grabbed the victim's collar from behind to see how he'd like it.'

'And he didn't run off?'

'Naw. Says he can't believe he did it.'

'Intoxicated?'

'Nope.'

'Previously been in trouble with us?'

'Clean as a whistle.'

'Police warning then. If he comes to our attention again, it'll be the cells.'

'Thing is . . .' Mo began, 'he's a bit teary, really upset about this dog, which, by the way, is totally fine. Keeps saying how sorry he is and how he's been struggling lately.'

'You think he needs to talk to someone?'

'Aye, I do.'

May checked the time. Not yet 10 a.m. She scrolled through her Pronto. A couple of other active jobs, nothing they couldn't handle.

'Talk to the dog walker. If he's happy not to press charges get this fella up to the hospital. See if there's a psychiatric nurse available. But Mo, I can't have you guys waiting with him, right?'

It could easily take hours for him to be seen. There was a chance he'd just walk out on his own. May thought of the train driver, Billy Mackenzie, of Holly, of her daughter, Isla. Police Scotland wasn't designed to deal with the thousands of mental health incidents that came in every week, but until there was something better, they were it. May knew a small moment of kindness could save lives.

'Listen, Mo, it's fine. Get him a cup of tea, settle him in at the hospital. I'll call you if we need you.'

May drained her coffee and finished the last mouthful of pastry. She flicked through her list of names. A call to Holly's psychiatrist went to voicemail. Gemma Thorne, drug dealer and school friend of Holly was next.

May checked her Pronto. A steady flow of jobs was being allocated by the control room and picked up by her team. She got on the radio and told them she was doing a welfare check on Gemma Thorne due to information received. Jackie McNally had said she hadn't seen Gemma around lately, so it was mostly true.

CHAPTER 16

Gemma Thorne's registered address was in a pebble-dashed low-rise block near to where the M74 and the railway line carved a deep groove through the city, separating Govanhill from the neighbouring Hutchesontown. A hand car wash was operating on the empty lot next door to the flat. Three skinny and under-dressed young men (two Asian, one white) hunched their shoulders against the cold and gave May's squad car a wary look as she pulled up. Was this another McNally enterprise? Every spare postage stamp of land seemed to be theirs. If it was, there'd be a dozen shell companies between them and the dirty sponges, but May noted the location just in case.

On one side of the front steps to the flats, two abandoned supermarket trolleys clung together for protection. The other side was piled with a mattress, cardboard boxes slowly decomposing in the rain, and an expired plastic Christmas tree. In the window of one ground-floor flat hung a Scottish saltire flag, doubling as a curtain. Gemma resided in the other flat on this level. May rang the bell.

Gemma Thorne didn't seem surprised to see her, and May wondered if Jackie had already put in a call. In the front room, a wee girl no more than a toddler played with a toy kitchen while a property show ran on the TV.

'You want a cup o' tea?' Gemma said. She wore an over-sized yellow sweatshirt and black leggings and looked at least a decade older than her twenty-two years. There was another child registered as living here, a boy, Dylan, who May thought must be at school. She took a quick glance at the kitchen. It looked clean enough.

'Aye, go on then.'

May pulled apart the Velcro straps on her utility vest and sat down. The room was icy but neither mother nor child seemed to notice. After giving May the once-over, the child ignored her and went back to feeding her dolls.

The place was sparsely furnished: old sofa, a small table with two dining chairs. The TV didn't look particularly new.

'I'm not in business any more,' Gemma said, handing May a mug. 'It's got milk but no sugar in it. Hope that's okay.'

'Aye, fine. Thanks.' May cupped her hands around the hot drink, grateful for the warmth. The fact Gemma had any food or drink in the house, that the electricity was still on, *and* that she still had possession of both her children said more about an upward trajectory than any declaration that she'd given up dealing.

'I heard about Holly. Poor lassie. Jackie called me,' she said, confirming May's suspicion. 'She wanted to know if I'd seen her lately.'

'And have you?'

Gemma shook her head. 'Not for six months or so. She

came to tell me she was getting clean and was deleting my number. I appreciated her letting me know. No' all my regulars were that considerate.'

'I thought she'd been off drugs for a year?'

'Oh, aye. She had been. This was just a bit of weed. But she was right to elbow that. Gateway drug to the hard stuff.'

So Holly hadn't been quite honest with her mother. The advice for all reformed addicts was the same. No drugs of any sort. Don't think you can just have one joint, one pill and go no further.

'Could Holly have gone to anyone else?'

Gemma shrugged. 'Free country.'

'Might she have got it from Scott Galbraith?'

Gemma stiffened. 'Don't know. Mibbaes.'

'Was he your supplier?'

'I don't like to talk about a' that. Drags me back. An' it's for my own protection, you know?'

May nodded. Hardcore addicts needed about £70 a day to fund their habit and Gemma's thriving enterprise would have been bringing in thousands every week for her supplier. They wouldn't have taken kindly to her shutting up shop. Her silence was their price for letting her live. And there was always the chance she'd come back into the business, when her kids were older and she'd got tired of giving them second-hand stuff.

'Holly was smart – I mean, really switched on,' Gemma said. 'Could've gone anywhere, done anything. The one stupid thing she ever did was getting hooked up wi' that evil bampot. All calm on the outside, but a major screw loose. I telt her but she wouldnae listen.'

'When was this?' May edged forward in her seat.

Gemma waved her hand, 'Och, way back. He used to hang around the school gates. She thought he was the cat's pyjamas cos he had a nice car. Said she felt sorry for him cos he lost his parents. Tell ye, she was easy meat, but weren't we all. He . . .'

She stopped. It was likely Scott, or someone in his circle, had recruited Gemma to start with, destroyed any possible chance she'd had for a different life.

'And how are you doing?' May said. She'd come to learn more about Holly, and she had, but she also felt a sting of regret for encouraging Gemma to look back at an existence that, like Holly, she'd worked so hard to escape from. 'You know, you can always contact me if you need help.'

'I'm okay. I've got an access course three days a week. There's a creche. Shyanne loves it. It's the boredom you've got to watch for. Drugs are shit, but being clean is a different kind of boring shit. Did Holly really kill herself?'

'We're keeping an open mind,' May replied. 'Is there anything you can tell me that might relate to her death?'

Gemma thought for a moment then shook her head. 'Wouldnae surprise me if she did. I'm lucky I've got ma weans. They keep me busy. If it wasn't for them, I'd go the same way Holly did. Jump in front of a train. Life? I wouldnae fuckin' bother.'

CHAPTER 17

In the afternoon, May could've returned to Queen's Park and enjoyed the view across the city to the Campsie Fells beyond. Instead, she chose a spot outside Scott Galbraith's flat off the Victoria Road. It was central, a convenient place from which to provide back-up and advice to her constables. She'd already supported officers with the arrest of a couple of shoplifting sisters. She'd had words with folk over illegal parking, lack of car insurance, and an out-of-control dog. She'd advised Rab the Kebab and Lauren Paterson about an elderly woman, known to be vulnerable, who'd dialled 999 to report an intruder in her flat, which had turned out to be a pigeon. Once the bird had been encouraged to leave, May had told them to call the woman's niece, whose number was on file.

Parking behind the rear bumper of Scott Galbraith's bright blue BMW was absolutely not intimidation or unauthorised surveillance on a known drug dealer and all-round bawbag. The fact that it might discourage his junkie customers and put a dent in his business model, if he was selling from the flat, was just a bonus. There'd been no visible evidence when she and Dimple had called, but that wasn't surprising. If Galbraith was as smart as she thought he was, there'd be nothing in his home to incriminate him. Maybe they'd cuckooed a downstairs neighbour. Drop the cash in one flat, collect from another. Been done before. May made a mental note to check out who else had recently moved into the block.

The winter light had already dropped. It was quiet, the street enjoying a brief afternoon lull before the schools came out. May had been going for nearly twelve hours and, after her disturbed night, an ache of tiredness had settled behind her eyes. Napping here wasn't an option. They'd have the wheels off the patrol car.

Caffeine poisoning was a serious risk if she drank any more coffee, so she got out of the car and stretched. Above, in Galbraith's flat, she thought she saw a curtain twitch. Good. Let the bastard sweat.

As she got back into the patrol car, she thought about Gemma's parting words. There was no doubt the lassie was sincere in her desire to stay clean, but May knew the young mum would face an uphill task and she thought that Gemma knew this too.

May put in a call to the control room asking for another welfare check on Gemma in a fortnight's time. PC Lauren Paterson who had two young kids of her own would be the best option. She'd hoped for more from Gemma, ideally the report of a conversation within the last few weeks where Holly had specified Galbraith's threats after the breakup of their relationship. She should have sent Dimple. Perhaps they'd have bonded. They came from two completely different cultures, but in the melting pot of Govanhill ethnicity counted for less than the shared challenges of growing up in

Glasgow's southside. May admired Gemma's determination to provide a better future for her children, but she also knew that the lucrative offers of an established drug network might one day prevail. If she was allowed to remain living in the area unmolested, that meant the drug gang hadn't let her go. They were merely biding their time.

A scruffy young man in a hoodie and dirty jeans was eyeing her from across the street. He'd walked past the entrance to Galbraith's close twice already. After a third pass, he took off back towards Victoria Road. May smiled, satisfied her presence was already acting as a deterrent.

She took out her phone again and after answering a text from Tam to reassure him she was fine and wouldn't be late, made a series of calls to the professionals Holly had encountered. The social worker was cautious but not unfriendly. The psychiatrist was regretful but not surprised by May's call. A therapist seemed to take the news of Holly's death as a personal failure. None would release case files without a sheriff's warrant, but May was familiar with the merry dance she and other professionals engaged in when they wanted to help. They spoke in what they called *general terms* that were anything but. By the end of her calls May had added disordered eating and anorexia to Holly's drug addiction, anxiety and depression and suicide attempt. All confirmed Holly had experienced a violent and abusive relationship, but, mindful of their legal position, none would name Scott Galbraith as the culprit.

May replayed the conversations, sifting them for any missed clues but they all amounted to the same thing. Both the scenarios – suicide and murder – were equally supported by what she'd heard. It was Jackie's freedom from any doubt that tipped the balance for May, but that alone wouldn't be enough for a jury. She checked the taskings. All quiet. She texted Jackie. A reply came back immediately. *Come round, now.*

As she drove away, May gave a last glance up at the flat. A dark shape moved behind the window. Scott Galbraith had definitely seen her. What he hadn't seen was the last of Sergeant May Mackay.

CHAPTER 18

When Jackie opened the door, May thought the woman seemed smaller, shrunken inside her black jeans and pink sweatshirt as if grief was consuming her.

A glimmer of hope ignited in Jackie's eyes. May's arrival signalled news.

She owed it to Jackie to be honest, but what did she have to tell her? The train driver thought he'd seen someone but without corroboration it meant zero. It would confirm in Jackie's mind that Holly hadn't committed suicide, but it would also open up a whole new world of pain. Until she had solid confirmation from Dimple that a review of the CCTV might yield something, May could say nothing. It felt simultaneously kind and cruel.

'Jackie, love. I just came to see how you were.' May saw the hope diminish, the flat reality of Jackie's life stretch out before her. Her only child was dead. In the absence of anyone else to hold responsible, she could go back to blaming herself. May couldn't bear it. On impulse she said, 'There's something I need to tell you.'

'Good.' Jackie seemed to shake herself and her mouth settled into a determined line. 'I was going to call you cos I've got something to tell you too.'

*

Brittle winter sunshine poured through the bay window of the front room. There was no sign of an opened wine bottle, or Jackie's partner, Ian. May had made some discreet phone calls about the ex-detective sergeant. His former team in West Division had a reputation for getting results, but also for bending the rules. The same could be said about most CID units, including her own colleagues. There were always officers with an eye on promotion and a hefty dose of what her detective inspector had liked to call *over-enthusiasm*. Nothing that May had heard suggested Ian was one of them. He'd taken the opportunity to change his life. She didn't blame him. Perhaps she even envied him a little. It was the kind of future Tam wanted for her, but for reasons she couldn't explain, even to herself, she wasn't quite ready to take that final step into civvy street.

Jackie made May a coffee and set it before her on the low table. The photo album of the previous day was gone, in its place neatly stacked magazines and a notebook.

'Milk, no sugar. I remembered,' Jackie said proudly, setting down the mug with a flourish and sitting opposite. 'And look what I've got.' With barely suppressed glee she produced a mobile phone from her jeans pocket. The screen was cracked but May recognised the distinctive black case with a white spider's web design. With a jolt she also remembered the tattoo on Scott Galbraith's neck.

'That Holly's?' The design was almost identical. Why had Holly chosen to be reminded every day of her ex-boyfriend? Did she keep it because there was still a romantic attachment, or as a reminder to stay out of his business? May preferred to think it was the second possibility. 'The phone's broken though.'

Jackie gave her a mischievous smile and, like a magician revelling in their sleight of hand, pressed the home button.

'Battery was flat. Just the cover thing that's smashed.'

The screen illuminated, the image of a raven beating its wings against the splintered glass appeared. Jackie shuffled through images like a pack of cards, then handed the phone to May.

There was a stream of abusive messages from a contact listed as *Scotty*.

Call me.

Why haven't you called me?

Call me now. You know whats gonna happen.

You want ma fist in your tits?

Didnae like it last time, did ye?

Call me.

Call me.

Call me.

Why haven't you called me.

Want to see yer mother with acid all over her face?

Call me.

Call me.

RIGHT NOW, BITCH.

'It's Scott Galbraith,' Jackie confirmed, though May had already made the leap. Holly would've been very unlucky indeed if she'd had two psycho bastards called Scott in her life. She checked the date of the last message. It was a month ago.

Jackie took the phone back and clicked on another message stream. 'Look at this'.

It was a message from an unattributed number – *Meet me, Holls. I only want to talk.*

The date and timestamp said Tuesday night. It was unsigned but the use of such a familiar diminutive – *Holls* – indicated they knew each other. Holly hadn't responded, but she'd received the text around an hour before her death.

'It's him,' Jackie said, an expression of righteous victory on her face. 'Scott Galbraith on a different number. Holly said he has all these burner phones for his drugs business. It'll be one of them.'

May called the number on her own phone. Straight to voicemail.

'I tried that too. Same thing.' Jackie clasped her hands together. 'Right, so that's the phone.' She looked about as if searching the room until her eyes lighted on the notebook. She picked it up and handed it to May. 'Aye, so, this is Holly's diary, had the same one for ages. Goes back about three years.'

The light blue cover was decorated on the front with silver stars and doodled loops, obviously from before Holly had hit her goth phase. *PRIVATE. KEEP OUT* had been inked in multicoloured dots. May turned the pages. The early ones were full of angry scrawls, then the handwriting became neater, the entries more measured.

'I keep hearing Holly moving around the flat,' Jackie said. 'Like she's looking for something. That's what made me think about mibbaes trying the phone. It was like she was telling me to. I knew where she hid the diary, in a box under her bed.'

The most recent entries were dated in the last few weeks, the pages once more filled with desperate scrawls. The last one stopped May in her tracks – *I THINK HE'S FOL-LOWING ME. I CAN'T TRUST HIM.* She scanned back through the pages but couldn't find a name. She turned the notebook around to face Jackie.

'Who's she talking about here?'

'Galbraith, of course. Look.' Jackie sat forward and began counting off on her fingers. 'We've got the abusive messages on the phone. We've got the diary saying she was scared o' the bastard. I'm a witness to him attacking her in the street. His alibi is rubbish, you said. That's got to be enough to make them railway cops listen, right?'

When May had arrived, Jackie had seemed like she was shrinking in on herself, but here was a woman transformed by action. Bright mother to a bright and talented daughter. How far Jackie might have climbed in her own education and career if the deep mental and emotional scars (and the physical ones Jackie had carved into her own arms) hadn't stopped her.

But although the diary, the phone and Jackie as a witness all confirmed that Holly had been in a violent and coercive relationship, it didn't say that Galbraith had killed her. The fiscal would argue that, with her treatment for depression and her previous attempt to end her life, all the phone and diary did was reinforce the case for suicide.

When May didn't answer, Jackie frowned. 'You don't think it's enough. You said you had something to tell me? Is it about the funeral?'

'No, it's not that. The BTP will probably call you soon about returning Holly to you.'

'Then why'd you come?'

May knew she couldn't delay her decision any longer. Jackie was calm and sober. Best just get on with it.

'I spoke to the train driver.'

Jackie's hands flew to her mouth. May pressed on.

'He thinks there might have been someone on the platform with Holly, but this isn't corroborated by any of the other staff. He's off work. Pretty traumatised.'

Jackie was nodding, the tears pooling in her eyes. 'I knew it. I knew it. Could he tell it was Galbraith?'

'The description is vague, but it doesn't rule him out. The driver didn't report it to the BTP. Didn't think he'd be believed.'

'I believe him.' Jackie rubbed her sleeves across her eyes. 'Can you tell him that from me? I believe him.'

May reached out and took Jackie's shaking hands in her own. They were small and cold, their fragile scaffolding of bones prominent beneath the pale skin. She wanted desperately to give this woman some hope.

'My colleague DC Dimple Sharma who you met yesterday is looking again at the CCTV. We just have to be patient until she has something. It won't be long.' May bristled at the thought of Inspector Mark Ward's likely observation that *all we have is a grieving alcoholic mother with a history of mental illness and a traumatised train driver who doesn't know what he saw.*

'We're going to make Galbraith pay, aren't we?' It was

half statement, half plea. Jackie picked up the diary and the phone and shoved them into May's hands. 'You can go back to the train driver. Get him hypnotised or something, help him to remember. What about all the awful messages? Malicious communication, that's a crime, isn't it?'

May didn't have the heart to say to Jackie that with the victim dead, the fiscal was unlikely to pursue a case on the strength of some texts, threatening though they were.

'Yes, of course we're going to get him. Leave it with me. But I want you to call Ian.'

Jackie looked defiant, but after a moment her shoulders drooped and she nodded.

CHAPTER 19

As May drove past the front of the police office, she spotted a familiar figure. Janine McCulloch had been one of May's regular call-outs until they'd finally locked her husband up for half killing her. She was short and wore a yellow-and-white beanie hat and a long black coat, at least two sizes too big for her, and stood beneath the falling sleet staring up at the sky. If May hadn't known the woman it would've been like encountering a particularly off-course penguin.

May pulled the squad car to a halt and got out. As she came closer she saw Janine was clutching a bag to her chest. She had three young children. None of them were with her.

'Janine, hen, how are you doing?' May touched her gently on the arm and the woman turned to look at her.

'I was just praying,' she said.

May felt an uneasy chill creep across her back. 'What you praying for?'

Janine held out the bulging carrier bag and May looked gingerly inside. Wads of twenty-pound notes were secured by elastic bands.

'I'm praying I don't weaken. I had a big win on the bingo. The debt collector won't accept it.'

'You won this on the bingo?' There must have been five grand.

'They gave me a cheque but I made the bank cash it.'

'Janine, it's not safe for you to be carrying this much money around.'

'Aye, I know. I want them to take it off me. Clear ma debt. Can yous lot help?'

'I can't do anything about that, Janine, love. It's a civil thing. Have they threatened you?'

'No' out loud.'

'What's been said then?'

'Nothing. But everybody worries about petrol through their letter box, don't they?'

'Why would they put petrol through your letter box if you're offering to give them money?'

'Well, you know.' Janine shrugged. 'They're daft bams. If they'll no' take my money, who knows what they'll do?'

May shook her head in exasperation. 'Who is it?'

'Stephenson's. Got an office over the laundrette in Cathcart Road.'

'As in Danny Stephenson?' She knew him. Bookie's runner, or had been. One rung up from pond life.

'Maybe if you come with me, he'll take the money.'

'I can't do that. Just turn up in uniform?'

'I took the loan out when I had three kids to feed and no man about. I've got a new man now, and he's saying I should do this.'

Not many would have said that. They'd have had it off her and be straight down the pub or the bookie's.

'That's good advice. Will he no' come with you?'

'Said I need to do this alone for ma self-respect.' The phrase unfolded like she'd had it tucked in her pocket. A note of his confidence in her. A wee gold star.

May thought of her lovely Tam, and about how Ian had supported Jackie in her battle with alcohol. There were good men around if you looked hard enough. Though maybe Janine's fella was sending her by herself because he was scared of the debt collectors. Perhaps not such a catch after all.

'And he's minding the weans,' Janine added.

So more a work in progress, May thought.

'Make Stephenson take the money, Janine. You're no' scared of him, are you?' The guy was eight stone soaking wet. Rumour was he got his clothes from Asda's kids department.

'It's no' him. It's the McNallys.'

'Danny works for the McNallys now?' May felt her pulse quicken. That was an interesting wee bit of intel. Danny Stephenson had slithered up in the world and the McNallys were inviting folks to sell their souls for a payday loan right on her patch.

'Please,' Janine begged. 'If you don't come wi' me, I'll just weaken. This is a lot of money.'

She didn't need to say it out loud. May knew what she meant. Drink, drugs, slot machines. That money could have gone any number of ways.

May checked her watch. 'Right. Okay. I'll come with you as far as the door.'

May put Janine in the squad car and they drove the short distance to Danny's Stephenson's office, one room in a tenement block, above the SpinTime Laundry and VIP Ironing Service.

A minute later, Janine was back. Shaking her head, bottom lip stuck out.

'Fucksake.' May took the stairs two at a time.

'You here in an official capacity, like?' Danny Stephenson's voice was a nasal whine. He eyed May from the swivel chair behind his desk. She bet his feet didn't touch the floor.

'Officially I'm on my break, but that might change, Danny. I'm here in the interest of community relations. And what I can't understand is if this woman wants to pay off her debt, why you'll no' let her?'

'Can't discuss individual accounts with third parties. Data protection.'

'It's almost like you want to keep her on the hook. And you can put down your phone and stop texting till I'm finished talking to you.'

Danny placed his phone obligingly on his desk. 'Her debt's too big for her to pay off.' He looked at May nervously. 'You can't make me take it,' he said, as if she were holding a venomous reptile or a grenade with the pin popped. 'It's all perfectly legal.'

'Legal, yes. Moral? Well, that's debatable.'

'Look, I need to keep ma customers. She's no' the one with a gun to her head.'

'Who's holding a gun to your head, Danny?' She wanted him to say it. If he was wrapped up with the McNallys he'd be on a work schedule. Generate cash or lose fingers.

He batted her words away. 'Forget it. Figure of speech. There's nothing you can do to make me take that money. Can't arrest me.'

May studied her watch again. 'Alright, Danny, break time over. What's it to be? A wee phone call to the Financial Conduct Authority? I'm sure they'd be interested in your business practices. And I've heard HMRC make a hell of a mess. All your nice neat files. And any business associated with yours might come under scrutiny as a result. Your mates are gonna love you for that. Want me to give them a call?'

The look on his face said no. He was rattled now.

Before he could grow a spine and change his mind, May went to the door and bellowed down the stairs.

'Janine! Get up here.'

She stood back from Danny Stephenson's desk as Janine counted out the money and he handed over a receipt.

'Alright, Janine. Just give me a minute with Mr Stephenson here. I'll see you downstairs, pet.'

May took a card from her pocket and placed it on the corner of his desk.

'You know, I've more sympathy for your predicament than you might expect. Can't be much fun having someone else telling you how to run your own business. If you ever want to talk about the McNallys, give me a call.'

She waited for him to deny he had any connection to them, but he just sat there staring at the cash on his desk like it was radioactive. He'd been counting on racking up the interest, May thought. Putting a few extra grand on an initial loan that probably hadn't even amounted to four figures. She'd said she had sympathy, but not much. For his clients, yes, but not for the likes of him.

'Did it start with protection, Danny? Did you get behind

and now they own your business? Own you. Liam McNally and his pals pay you a wee visit, did they?'

He shot her a glance that told her she'd hit the mark.

'It doesn't have to be like this.'

'Aye, it could be a whole lot worse. You see your pal D I Andy Wilson around lately?'

May felt the blood drain from her face. It was like he'd punched her. 'What d'you know about that?' She pointed a pistol finger at him. 'You saying the McNallys were behind his murder?' His eyes went to the door, desperate for an exit. She advanced on him. Another step closer and she'd be dragging him across his desk while he coughed up everything he knew. There was a noise behind her.

'Janine, pet, go back downstairs.'

'Sorry, darlin'. No can do,' replied a deep male voice.

When May turned, she saw a short, well-groomed middle-aged man in a cashmere coat. He had perfectly cut dark hair above a high, lined forehead and sympathetic brown eyes. On one side of him stood Scott Galbraith, on the other, the lean blonde figure of Liam McNally. For a moment May wondered if just using his name had, like the devil, conjured him up.

'Sergeant Mackay,' Michael McNally said smoothly. 'An unexpected pleasure.'

They'd never met.

That he knew her name was both a threat and a confirm-ation of everything May believed about this evil, duplicitous, parasitic bastard.

CHAPTER 20

May stood with one hand on her baton, the other on her PAVA spray, the threat implicit. She doubted she could incapacitate them all before calling for assistance so she kept her eyes on the main threats: Liam and, above all, Galbraith, who was staring at her with undisguised hatred.

Michael McNally stretched out his arms and smiled, as much an acknowledgement of the tension in the room as a signal for his attack dogs to stand down.

'Something we can help you with here, Sergeant Mackay?'

'Just passing, were you, Mr McNally?' May said, shooting Danny Stephenson a look sharp enough to make him flinch. He was regretting his jibe about her former CID partner's death, but caught between the law and a hard place, May had no doubt whom he feared most. He must have texted Liam McNally when she'd arrived and had indulged in a moment of foolishness knowing the cavalry were on their way. Now he realised both sides had the potential to make him pay for it.

'We like to take an interest in the small businesses of our community,' Michael McNally replied. 'Help where we can.'

Help yourself, more like. May fought to keep her expression neutral and not roll her eyes.

Galbraith gave McNally an approving nod, and May realised with sick recognition that he was in awe of this man.

'I was very sorry to hear about your niece, Holly Campbell,' she said to Michael McNally.

Galbraith started like an electric current had run through him. His face was white with anger as he tried to take a step towards May, but again the older man put out his hand.

'It's a shock, right enough. Only a young lassie. But we weren't close. Thank you anyway for your kind words.'

After a tense silence, he clapped his hands together, a signal their exchange was over. He nodded to Danny Stephenson who sank further behind his desk.

She was still watching Liam and Galbraith. Holly's cousin affected a bored air, phone half out of his pocket, surreptitiously scrolling. But her ex-boyfriend's attention was still clamped on May, his fists curled, the veins on his neck visible. Compared to their meeting at his flat, the confident, restrained malice had slipped and was mixed with something else. Less certainty, more apprehension, and maybe just a touch of fear.

'How's business, Scott?' she said, holding his gaze. 'You must be doing very well judging by that car of yours.'

He blinked at her. 'What?'

Michael McNally frowned.

'Not everyone would have Mr McNally's forgiving nature.'

It was clear from the growing terror in his eyes that he expected May to repeat her earlier accusations that he was somehow responsible for Holly's death. Liam, alerted to the reignited tension in the room, stopped scrolling and looked up from his phone.

Michael McNally tipped his head to one side. 'Your point, Sergeant?'

'Oh, I was just thinking that employing someone with a criminal record shows a great deal of community spirit. I suppose as an apprentice electrician, Scott here can do you a good deal on rewiring.' She looked around the shabby office. 'This place certainly needs some TLC.'

McNally gave her his businessman smile, all teeth and cold eyes. 'So many youngsters have a tricky start, and the police do a good job, but I know' – he held up his hands like he was dispensing forgiveness – 'they can't be every-where. Scott's paid his debt to society and I'm proud to support him and many others through opportunities in my companies.'

'Aye, it's never easy to break the chain of criminality. But no matter how bad you think things are, there's always options. Our doors are always open.' She was looking at McNally, but she felt Galbraith tense further. In a flash she saw him as he must have been: parents dead, a frightened lad with few options. Michael McNally, a new father, strong, suc-cessful, a ready-made brother in Liam, both would keep him safe. Suddenly, the spiderweb tattoo on Galbraith's neck took on a new significance. A maker's mark, a stamp of ownership from the spider himself.

She'd laid out her terms. Come to me and I will help you out of this trap you're caught in. Whether Galbraith accepted her offer was another matter.

Michael McNally's affable manner had evaporated. 'We won't take up any more of your valuable time.'

Galbraith took his cue and jabbed a finger in her chest, his eyes wide enough to show a band of white around their jet-black irises. 'You've no business being here. Be on your way, Sergeant.'

Their eyes locked and she saw it. Scott Galbraith was shit-scared. He had every reason to be.

May stormed down to the kit room and threw her utility vest into her locker and slammed the door. If she'd been back in CID she'd have had Galbraith under surveillance and turned Danny Stephenson inside out till he gave up what he knew about Andy's death. Her hands shook and she forced herself to take a deep breath. She thought of calling Dimple for an update, but didn't want to risk venting her frustration on the lassie again. Don't get sidetracked, she told herself. Holly Campbell's death is the priority.

A few of her constables were also there, hanging up wet kit and checking their radios and Prontos. She caught the look that passed among them. Nobody said a word. The rest of the squad were already done, shuffling about in the corridor outside, itching to get away before the traffic, or their sergeant, got any worse.

She was happy to oblige them.

'Right, any of you lot got anything to report?'

'No, Sarge,' they choroused.

'Right. Piss off home then.'

Outside, May headed for the car park, then changed tack.

She needed a drink. Returning to the shithole pub of Scott Galbraith's alibi and shaking a confession out of the landlord had a certain appeal but unfortunately wasn't an option. There were a few nice bars in the area, but Scotland's zero-tolerance policy meant even a glass of wine could put her over the limit and land her with a minimum twelve-month driving ban. Dismissal or demotion and desk duties would follow. If they stuck her in an office next to Markie the Meerkat she'd be inside for murder within a year.

The earlier sleet had reverted to a regular drizzle. She shivered as she zipped up her black fleece, wishing she'd brought her hi-vis waterproof. Despite the winter dark and the atrocious weather, the traffic was moving freely. On the corner of the main road the off-licence, and a bottle of good wine to share with Tam, glowed like a beacon. There was no queue for once and she came out five minutes later with an Australian Shiraz she knew he liked, conceding it would likely prompt another conversation about a fresh start in the sunshine.

May picked up the pace back to her car. Sooner she was home the better. She dipped her head against a gust of wind, the rush of raindrops plastering her hair into her eyes as she stepped between two parked cars.

She heard it before she saw it. Instinct made her leap back as the car neatly sliced the empty air where her kneecaps had once been. The granite sett of the kerb caught her heels. The wet pavement seemed to rise, cracking her elbows, tailbone and, finally, the back of her head. The bottle of wine with all its sunshine promise slipped from her hand and exploded next to her on the pavement. For a second, she flapped like a landed fish among the puddles, then rolled onto her side to catch a glimpse between the parked vehicles of the car that had nearly flattened her. It sped up, ignored the traffic, and took a fast left turn. A dark fourbie. No headlights.

'Fucksake!' She slammed her hand into the mix of rainwater and wine. She hadn't even caught the model or part of the number plate. Just when you think the day can't get any worse, there's always someone who'll piss on your chips, she thought, getting shakily to her feet.

CHAPTER 21

When May got home, she peeled off her dirty kit and threw the whole lot in the washing machine along with Tam's running gear. He was in the kitchen cooking a risotto, hair still wet from the shower. A CD of an American bluegrass band was playing in the background.

The bump to the back of her head was no more than a graze. When she told him about the car and her fall on the pavement, Tam frowned and came over from the hob to where she was sitting at the table to make his assessment.

'You've a track record of downplaying this stuff,' he said, shaking his head. 'Sure nobody whacked you?'

She bared her elbows as further evidence of her tumble. 'And I've a bruise on my backside the size of Mull. Play your cards right and I'll show you it later.'

'There's an offer no man in his right mind could refuse,' he conceded, and smiled at her. 'Thank God the wine got the worst of it. Though I plan to visit its family and offer my condolences.' He lifted his chin to the Australian wines in the countertop rack. 'Bad weather. Black uniform. Forgetful driver. Headlights off. I'm just thankful you're in one piece.'

'I was a bit distracted,' May admitted as she thought back

to the incident, and sketched brief details of her encounter with Michael McNally and his henchmen to Tam.

'Might seem a daft question,' Tam said, lifting down two glasses, 'but how come no one's caught these guys yet?'

'They're right clever bastards. It's one thing knowing they're involved in assault, extortion, protection, trafficking, drugs, the lot, but it's another thing having enough evidence to arrest them.' She drew her chair closer, wincing as she rested her elbows on the tabletop. 'They've plenty of legitimate business as slum landlords in the tenements but also the higher-end rental market. Gives them locations to manufacture drugs, house girls, run high-end brothels.'

'The cheek-by-jowl existence of rich and poor facilitates those who are in a position to cross borders,' Tam replied. As well as his work at the youth centre, he was doing an Open University degree in psychology with counselling. She often found some of his musings more theoretical than practical, but on this occasion he was spot on. The rich who preyed on their neighbours were just as dangerous as the poor – more so, since they had greater resources.

Tam put two plates of risotto on the table next to the bottle of wine he'd opened.

'So, this McNally clan,' he began. 'McNally . . . Why do I know that name? The Aspen Trust's major backer is a McNally Enterprises. That's no' them, is it?'

May raised her eyebrows in confirmation as she took another mouthful of risotto. She could feel the first shoots of wellbeing spread through her – home, good food, Tam – a return of equilibrium, despite the topic of conversation.

'Michael McNally is the godfather,' she said. 'He's in his fifties, a businessman and entrepreneur. It's his name you see on the donations to a charity. Ironic, isn't it? He causes the problems, but he tells folk he's the one to fix them. That's either a very guilty conscience, or he gets a kick out of the joke.'

'Way things are going, we've got to take funding where we can get it. But I admit there's a moral ambiguity in trying to help addicts kick the stuff with donations from a drug gang.'

'I suppose you could call that a circular economy. But he's just as likely sending dealers to hang around your centre. Best place to pick up new business is with old customers.'

Tam threw his fork down in disgust. 'How does he keep his hands clean?'

'He's got Liam McNally for that. Nephew, not son. Michael McNally had a brother, Christopher. He died in prison. We think it's his boy, Liam, who's pushing all the shady business. We pick off the small dealers but they just seem to sprout more overnight.'

Now she stopped to think about it, she wondered if the death in prison of both Liam McNally's and Scott Galbraith's fathers had bonded the two men. Liam was ten years older than Galbraith, but that only strengthened her view that it had been a factor – a big brother figure taking a lost boy under his wing.

Tam shook his head. 'If the McNallys ever get caught, the bad press will finish us, and all other small charities like us.'

May got up and Tam pushed his chair back from the table

so she could sit on his knee. She wrapped her arms around his shoulders and kissed the top of his head.

'You're doing good work. You're the good guys,' May reassured him. 'Folk will see that.'

He gave her a squeeze. 'Aye, mibbaes you're right. But if we run out of money, there'll be nothing left for folk to see.'

He looked at her, a tentative question forming behind his eyes and she prepared herself for another quote from an essay in progress.

Instead he said, 'This isn't all because of Isla, is it? You think those who sold her drugs were ultimately responsible for her killing herself.'

'No, no. Isla wasn't an addict. She just dabbled a bit recreationally. All teenagers do.'

'I mean, her counsellor thought drug use was a factor in her depression,' he went on.

'We'd have known. I'd have known. Isla wasn't an addict, so this is not about her.'

'The kids that come to the centre, they talk to us in confidence. Tell us what they've taken. To me it sounds like enough to knock out a horse, but these kids are still standing.'

'That wasn't Isla,' May repeated firmly. 'This' – she stabbed a finger on the table – 'this is about catching a guy who thinks he's got away with murder.'

'Aye, aye, I'm sure you're right,' he said soothingly, taking her hands in his.

'D'you know what I want, Tam? Just once, I'd like to bring them down before they reach peak harm.' She felt it was already too late. Holly was dead, snuffed out, at the hands of Galbraith and his friends. 'Because if I don't, Holly won't be the last. There'll be others, kids like the lads and lassies you see at the centre. Anything – anything we can do to stop it has to be worth doing.'

'I'm not arguing with that, May,' he said, resting his head on her shoulder as he gave her a squeeze. 'Give yourself some time to think things through, that's all I'm saying. Maybe it'll help you put everything into perspective.'

Her phone buzzed on the tabletop and she saw without unlocking it that there was a message from Dimple. Contact details for Holly's friend Mhairi, whom she'd met up with on the night of her death.

She caught a glimpse of her reflection in the kitchen window. In Tam's arms and surrounded by warmth. He was just as determined as she was. It was good advice. She knew this and loved him for it.

CHAPTER 22

The weekend blurred in a run of night shifts for May. Late on Monday evening, she went with a team to arrest a man who'd made more than sixty 999 nuisance calls the week before, claiming everything from that he'd broken all his toes and couldn't walk to that his dog had died. At 2 a.m., a man was found hurling slates off a roof after he'd been chased up there by friends of a woman he'd attacked. Another man fell out of a tenement window drunk, his injuries surprisingly minor. There'd been the usual fights in pubs, drunk drivers, domestic violence calls, drug possessions. Early on Tuesday morning, a woman had mocked a cafe owner's bacon rolls and tipped his cake trays onto the floor. While being escorted out by the owner, she'd punched him, knocking out his front teeth.

By the time May got home she was ready for a soak in the shower and breakfast with Tam before crashing into bed. She woke with a start that afternoon as the light was beginning to fade, convinced she'd forgotten to do something important. Throughout the past few days, she'd kept in regular touch with Dimple and the progress of her enquiries.

She checked the time on her phone. No, it was fine. She fell back on the pillow and went over her plans for that evening.

Tonight, it would be exactly one week since Holly's death.

Dimple had succeeded in persuading her boss to run an appeal on the station message board, but all it had harvested were the kind of crank calls that Ian McDonald had raised as an objection to Jackie's Facebook appeal. Dimple had dutifully ploughed through them, while singlehandedly tackling the CCTV mountain and the increasing backlog of work her inspector was sending her way, perhaps in a calculated bid to get her to drop Holly's case. The media and Jackie's MSP had been wary of touching a story that looked cut and dried. Suicide. Tragic but not unexpected.

It was only when Holly's friend Mhairi McCormack had finally got in touch the previous night, prodded by May's repeated calls, that she'd seen the way forward. If the BTP wouldn't authorise it, she'd need to stage her own reconstruction. There'd be no actor dressed as Holly, but she'd attempt to replicate the route, starting with meeting Mhairi at the bar, the Old Barbers, and taking it from there.

She knew the venue. Tam had played it a few years back. Isla had been there, proud of her dad. Tonight's meeting with Mhairi would remind her that her daughter should be partying with friends, applauding her talented father, and having fun. But May had long accepted the feeling for what it was – a grief so deep in her bones that there was no way of freeing herself from it. It had become a part of her now, and everywhere in this sprawling, vibrant city would go on reminding her of Isla and all she'd lost.

Just after 7 p.m., May stood beneath the clock in Glasgow Central. The station concourse was busy with daily commuters and other travellers. May brought a photo of Holly Campbell up on her phone screen and scanned the folk around her. A lack of potential witnesses wasn't the problem. Holly would've been lost in this crowd. Many were burdened with cases and looked like tourists. They stood squinting at the information boards for destinations to the west on the Clyde coast, Ayrshire, east to Cumbernauld and Edinburgh and south to Lanark, Motherwell, Carlisle, and towns and cities all the way to London Euston, looking as overwhelmed as May felt. She put her phone back in her pocket.

The hands on the clock above her crept to quarter past. Had Mhairi changed her mind? May checked her messages. Nothing. Ten minutes later she was about to give up when a figure approached her.

'Sergeant Mackay? Sorry. My train was delayed.' The young woman who stood before her was taller and broader than May had been expecting. The only photograph on her limited social media had been a headshot that had shown a rather fine-boned, heart-shaped face surrounded by a mass of dark curls. In her long dark coat, she was almost May's height. She'd be an asset on the beat if she ever considered joining Police Scotland.

'Call me May, please. And thank you for agreeing to meet me. I understand this must be difficult.' Perhaps the lassie had had second thoughts; but she was here now and that was what mattered.

Mhairi looked around expectantly at the crowd as if Holly might appear, the last week simply a misunderstanding. *What are you like, Mhairi! I said I was going away to my auntie's!*

May touched her arm. 'Come on, Mhairi. Let's get away out of the cold.'

The Old Barbers was in a cobbled lane around the block from the station's main entrance. The cavernous street-level bar still retained some of the building's original features in its cornicing and brickwork. Upstairs was a multipur-pose venue for bands and exhibitions. It was a no-food, no-frills place that had been in business for twenty years and attracted a younger arty crowd as well as its regulars. This early on a Tuesday, the place was only half full. She showed Holly's picture to the bar staff when she ordered their drinks – tonic water for May, a pint of lager for Mhairi – but the two men and a young woman with impressive tattoos on her bare arms all shook their heads. While she waited, May held her phone screen up for a few customers but without any success.

'It's dead weird without her,' Mhairi said, when May asked her how she'd been since Holly's death.

'And how did she seem to you that evening?'

Mhairi took a long pull of her beer. 'Fine. Well, no' fine, exactly. She couldnae have been, could she?' She gave an embarrassed half-smile and a shrug.

This was common with witnesses who found their own experiences redefined by tragedy. A projection of guilt that they could've somehow changed the course of events and prompted a different outcome. Drinking with a friend who'd apparently then walked out of the pub and thrown themself under a train had to be up there with the worst. No wonder Mhairi hadn't returned her calls.

'So, was anything different about Holly that evening?' May prompted.

'No' different. It was just that she seemed distracted. Always looking over her shoulder or at her phone. When Holly said she was going home, I didn't really believe her.'

'What time was that?'

'About quarter past ten.'

May had imagined that Holly had left Mhairi and gone straight to the station. So what had Holly been doing for the hour before her death?

'Where did you think she was going?'

'Maybe meeting a guy? She hadn't had much to drink.'

'How much?'

'Two or three vodkas – she wasnae drunk.' Mhairi wriggled in her seat. 'I was a bit pissed off at her, cos we were supposed to be going clubbing, and it felt like she was dumping me for a better offer. If she'd been drunk I'd have gone after her, but one of our other mates from college texted and . . . that was it. I went with them.'

'Did she seem worried? Frightened?'

Mhairi screwed up her face. 'I thought she was more . . . annoyed. That maybe she was annoyed at me for something, and that's why she bailed.' She gave May an appraising look. 'Are you thinking it wasn't suicide?'

May considered her next words carefully. Revealing the train driver's uncorroborated account of a second person on the platform might shift Mhairi's recollection. If Scott Galbraith ever stood trial for Holly's murder – and that was still a big if – then Mhairi might be called as a witness. She didn't want to put ideas into her head, or phrases in her mouth, that the defence could later claim had been intentionally planted by a police officer with an axe to grind. Doubt was all the jury needed to return a not guilty verdict.

'Her mother is concerned that when Holly left home that evening her state of mind didn't indicate she was thinking about ending her life,' May said. 'So it's important to understand if anyone was threatening her.'

'You don't think I made her do it, do you?' Mhairi said, suddenly defensive. 'I loved Holly. She was my pal. I wouldnae have hurt her!'

'I'm not suggesting you would,' May said gently, laying a hand on Mhairi's arm. 'I just want to know if you saw anyone following Holly or arguing with her.'

But the girl threw May's hand off. 'I would've said if I had.' She slipped off her stool, gathering up her coat like a shield in front of her. 'I don't think I should be talking to you. I mean, it's no' official or anything. I don't have to.'

'No, you don't. But if you know anything that might explain what happened to Holly, you should tell me.'

Mhairi took a step back, her mouth a firm line. 'I don't know why she did it. Holly was messed up. She had this mad ex-boyfriend.'

Her heart rate jumped. 'You met Scott Galbraith? Was he here last Tuesday?'

But when Mhairi shook her head, May felt a stone drop inside her.

'He came to college a few times. If he was around last

Tuesday I didnae see him.' Mhairi glanced at the door as if she was about to bolt.

'And you don't know where Holly went after she left here?'

Mhairi shook her head again and edged a step backwards. 'I need to go.'

There was no point in trying to detain her. 'Okay,' May said. 'Thanks for your help. I'm very sorry about your friend. If you remember anything, please call me.'

Now she was free to leave, Mhairi seemed to relax a little. Relief flooded her face and she swept her coat around her shoulders. 'You know, Holly said weird things at times. That she knew some big-time dealers and gangsters, and that people were following her. But I don't know if it was true.'

I do, thought May as Mhairi left. I know it's true. I know the dealer who was following her. Mhairi had confirmed that Holly had been agitated, that she'd changed her plans and had left the pub just after she'd received the text – *Meet me, Holls. I only want to talk*. Had she wanted to talk? Or had she just wanted to run and hide? How and when had Galbraith caught up with her? That was what May needed to find out.

CHAPTER 23

There were two options leaving the Old Barbers – left or right? May turned left, back down the lane with its greasy neon-lit cobbles and the sound of revellers gearing up for the night. The logical and most direct route for Holly would have been to retrace her steps and re-enter Glasgow Central by the main entrance. That journey wouldn't have occupied an hour, and despite the BTP's inefficiencies, May thought if Holly had been hanging around the station for all that time she would have been approached by their officers, if only to establish she wasn't a sex worker, a pickpocket, or a desperate addict planning to mug a tourist.

She checked her watch. It was only 8.30 p.m. She was a couple of hours ahead of Holly's schedule. At the end of the lane, she stopped and shivered. The run of night shifts had taken its toll. Her mind raced but her body told her it was dark, time to sleep. She thought of the rest of her officers struggling with the same need to adapt. PC Lauren Paterson had a toddler and a baby she was probably trying to get to sleep right now. Her mother helped out but disapproved of Lauren working, and had no idea of the front-line nature of her job. *She thinks I wear a skirt, carry a handbag and sit behind Cathcart reception desk,* Lauren had once laughed. Her husband was a freelance personal trainer, and they needed Lauren's steady wage to get by, so she didn't have a choice.

Right now, May had a choice. Keep trying to pick up Holly's trail or go home. She knew which one would make Tam happy, but it wouldn't bring her the resolution she craved. Instead, she reframed her choice – the Chicken Shack or Bella Notte? Both options glowed temptingly from across the street. The fast-food place was garishly bright, with a view of the street and a fast turnover of young clientele to whom she could show Holly's picture. The Italian cafe spoke of comfort and restoration, a family business who knew the workings of the street. She decided that as a beat cop she'd served this city long enough to be considered part of its furniture and restoration was what she needed.

An hour later she was back on Holly's trail, refreshed and refuelled, and with a thorough grounding from the restaurant owner as to how the city council could better support small businesses, why fast food wasn't food at all, and the trouble with young people today. She'd flashed Holly's picture around, but wherever Holly had gone, it hadn't been Bella Notte.

May worked along the line of taxi drivers at the main station rank in Gordon Street. Most were polite and sympathetic, and she realised they assumed she was a mother searching for a runaway daughter. That might provide more leverage than a suicide, so she didn't correct them. All she needed to know was whether they'd seen Holly and if there'd been anyone with her. They were apologetic. They hadn't.

She went into the station and approached groups of young

people on the concourse, asking if they'd been there last week and if they recognised Holly from the picture. Most shook their heads and barely glanced at the photo. There were late rail staff, city workers, nurses, care staff heading home, but none recalled the petite young woman with the long dark hair and heavy eyeliner, wearing the distinctive black-and-white skulls top, black jeans, platform boots and a puffer jacket.

The train staff for the Caledonian Sleeper had arrived. Remembering the cleaner's tip, May stopped two young women in tartan-and-tweed uniforms pulling small wheeled suitcases. They were also sympathetic, but staff worked a rolling ten-day rota, and it was unlikely there'd be anyone on the train tonight who had been there a week ago.

Everywhere she went, May noted the position of the CCTV cameras relative to the entrances and the platform where Holly had died. She stopped counting when she got to fifty. There were probably three or four times that many in the station as a whole. Even if the power to the barriers and the lighting had been out, there was no way Holly would have made it that far without being picked up on camera. May's anger bubbled up once more. All it would take for Jackie's daughter to get justice was for the BTP to pull their finger out and review the footage. Instead, here she was, hoofing it around their station at night doing their job for them.

Maybe it was the lack of sleep, her growing frustration, or her active awareness of the CCTV, but she couldn't help feeling there were eyes on her. She looked back over her shoulder but only saw groups of youngsters and a few weary travellers, none of whom appeared to be interested in her.

Perhaps it was just the regular spider-sense every woman developed in crowded public places at night, heightened by the beat-cop requirement to have eyes in the back of your head, or even paranoid guilt. She wasn't in uniform, but if her repeated circling of the concourse had alerted the control room and it got back to Marky the Meerkat, he'd take a dim view. *If that bothers you, go home*, she told herself, knowing it didn't and she wouldn't. But even as she shook herself awake and buttoned up the collar of her coat, she couldn't dispel the chilling sense she was being watched.

May tried the bar and reception staff in the station hotel next, but by the time she was stopping the kitchen workers heading home she'd begun to wonder how Holly could have ended up on the track and not a single person appeared to have seen that journey.

Leaning back against a low ledge outside the station's main entrance, May wrapped her coat more tightly around her and considered her next move. As she did so, she scanned the groups of revellers once more for anyone who might be watching her. The murderer returning to the scene of the crime. It wasn't just in the movies. Plenty of killers revisited the sites of what they considered their greatest achievements, sometimes even offering up helpful witness evidence to the cops. But what did she expect? Scott Galbraith in an *IT WAS ME* T-shirt?

If Galbraith had persuaded Holly to go with him willingly, frightened though she was, they could have gone into any of the dozens of bars, restaurants, fast-food stops or clubs within a ten-minute walk of the station. Without more information to narrow it down, she'd be here all night, and probably every night for the next week.

May was checking through her phone for any likely venues when she became aware of the shadow lingering in the doorway ten metres to her right. Tall. Dark clothing. She felt her muscles tense. Without turning her head fully, she cast her eyes towards the shape. There was something familiar about it. At that moment, a bus pulled up and light spilled from its windows into all the dim corners of the street. When the figure didn't move, she risked a glance.

Was that Holly's friend, Mhairi McCormack?

But when the bus passengers dispersed, and the vehicle moved away, May checked again. The doorway was empty, the figure was gone.

May uncurled her hands, forcing the sudden tension that had gripped her to disperse.

Coincidence. It was getting late. Folk were heading home and she was in one of the busier spots. One more loop to check for possible witnesses and she'd call it a night.

May went south on Hope Street, then steeled herself to turn left under the Hielanman's Umbrella where the low-level station entrance was. At night the stretch of covered road was even more nightmarish than in the daytime. The roar of cars and buses echoed among the shouts, screams and laughter of revellers. This would only intensify over the next hour as pubs and bars emptied and people made their way into the station via chip shops, kebab houses or Thai takeouts. Dark and crowded, it would be a good place to hide, but also a trap.

A street-smart lassie like Holly would have realised this

too. If Galbraith had caught up with her here, she could have expected no help from anyone. May stepped into the road to avoid a pushing match between two guys. It'd just be a drunken argument between a couple, and she could see a few of them brewing.

She'd just passed the spot where she'd found the homeless man, Kit, when a big purple-faced guy in a polo shirt shoved his screaming girlfriend, catching May on the shoulder, spinning her round. She put out an instinctive hand, stopping the lassie from hitting the pavement, at the same time calculating the ways, all of them bad, that this might go. Heads had turned her way, including one she instantly recognised, then the couples' pals streamed in, closing the gap in the crowd.

When they'd parted the combatants, May looked back at the same spot, but Mhairi had vanished into the crowd – although this time there could be no mistake.

She pulled out her phone and called the young woman's number. It rang out then went to voicemail. It'd been hours since they'd met. Had she been following May all this time? And if so, why? She could think of only two possibilities. Mhairi had left the pub in a near panic at May's questions and had been screwing up her courage to tell her something. Or there was a more sinister reason: Mhairi McCormack had been following her because she desperately needed to know exactly what May was uncovering about her friend Holly's death.

CHAPTER 24

May was making her way up Union Street towards the main entrance in the hope of catching Mhairi, when on the opposite side of the street, in front of a brightly lit kebab shop, she saw a familiar figure, sleeping bag draped across his shoulders. He was jabbing a finger into the chest of a shorter man who looked desperate to get away.

May crossed the road and picked up her pace. The wee guy had stumbled back against the shop window and looked about to go down. When she got within a couple of metres she called out.

'Kit? Kit, pal. What's going on?'

James Alexander MacDonald Fraser, ex-Navy and Falklands veteran, turned and stared at her with vacant eyes. His face was red and blotchy beneath his straggly beard and a strong smell of alcohol hung around him. May thought it likely he was using spice to stave off the cold and the nightmares as so many of the homeless did, but as he looked at her, recognition came into his eyes.

'You're the polis woman from the other morning, aren't you? We had a Maccies breakfast.'

'We did, Kit, aye. Can you step back for me? I think this gentleman's a wee bit unhappy you're so close.'

'Aye, well, he should be,' Kit said, indignant. 'He took ma picture. Cannae do that.'

There was something striking about Kit with his height and wild mop of grey hair and deeply lined face. He'd make a distinctive black-and-white in some posh gallery. Poverty porn, Tam called it. She saw too much of the real thing and knew the chaos behind the images too well to appreciate their beauty or ever want any on her walls or bookshelf.

May put out a hand, ordering Kit to stay back while she fished her police ID from her pocket and showed it to the photographer.

He had a wide face and dark receding hair. Around his neck hung one of the small trendy cameras that May sometimes caught Tam looking at on the internet. *Two grand!* she'd exclaimed. *If you want a wee metal box to carry around, I'll buy you a can of sardines and you'll have something to eat for your dinner as well.*

'You okay?' May couldn't see any visible injuries, but she wasn't sure what'd happened before she'd arrived. The camera he clutched to his chest also looked undamaged. 'Are you hurt? D'you need to go to hospital and get checked out?'

He shook his head.

May took a step closer. 'Look, if you want, I can take him in for assault and threatening behaviour.' She indicated over her shoulder at Kit who was still glowering at the man. 'But I have to warn you, you might be at the station for a while waiting to give your statement. So unless you want to press charges, I'm happy for you to go on and enjoy the rest of your evening.'

The man didn't stop to consider the matter. He pushed his way through the small crowd that had congealed around them and scuttled off down the busy street. The onlookers dispersed at a few words from May. She turned back to Kit who scowled as if he were the injured party here.

'It's no' against the law to be taking photos in a public place,' May said, pre-empting any further protests. She wasn't sure how drunk he was, but he should have been capable of understanding that much. 'And I'm not arresting you for laying hands on the guy, but in the future, if anyone tries to take your picture and you're not happy for that to happen, just walk away. Cos then they'll no' be able to take your picture. You get what I'm saying to you?'

He didn't answer and gave her another rebellious look, but she could tell from his slowed breathing, and the relaxation in his shoulders, that the message was getting through.

'No more needless confrontations,' she went on. 'It's a public place. I can't arrest folk for being street photographers or whatever daft explanation they have for what they're doing. You need to be the bigger guy here, Kit. So just chill. Don't you be biting any tourists.'

'I wouldnae be biting them. I don't know where they've been.'

'That's the spirit.'

'What you doing down here again anyway?' he said, his weathered face relaxing into a grin. 'Is it the ambience? Can you no' keep away?'

'Mind that girl I told you about? The one that went under the train?' She was pretty sure he didn't. 'Well, it was a week ago tonight. I thought folk might remember seeing her. Maybe help explain to her parents what happened.'

Kit gathered his sleeping bag around his shoulders. 'Lovely wee doll, wasn't she.'

May had shown him the picture when they'd met previously, but she was oddly touched that he remembered Holly. She realised too that he wasn't as drunk as she'd initially thought.

'She was upset,' he said.

'You saying that you saw her?' May felt as though a cold hand had brushed the back of her neck. She took out her phone and pulled up the picture, turning it for Kit to see.

'Aye, that's her.' He motioned across his chest. 'The wee skulls. She came in that way.' He nodded to the entrance across the road.

'You're sure it's her?' May said, aware that the rolling conformity of Kit's days, as well as alcohol and drugs, might have affected his memory.

'It was her. Tuesday night is kebab night. Freezing, it was. I'd gone into the entrance to sit for a bit out of the wind. She nearly tripped over me. I said I was sorry, and she said it was alright. Gave me a wee smile, but I could see she was in a bit of a state. Been crying. I thought mibbaes she'd had a fight wi' her man. No' long after that the station cops kicked me out intae the cold.'

'You tell the BTP about seeing her?'

'What, that shower? No way. Saving it up for you. Get you a promotion. A nice inside job, off the beat.'

Been there, done that, May thought. 'How did you know you'd see me again?'

Kit shrugged. 'I just knew.'

'What else can you remember from that night? You said *a fight with her man*. Was anyone with her?'

'I remember better with a glass in my hand,' he said, giving her a sideways glance.

'No can do, pal. You know that.'

In the kebab shop behind them, a young guy whose name badge said *Aram* had been eyeing the interaction, probably deciding whether or not Kit was about to put a tourist through his window. May gave him a reassuring smile and he gave her a nod of thanks for her intervention.

'Listen, Kit. Have you eaten today?'

'Don't know.'

'Right, well, I'm gonna get Aram in there to do you a kebab. I want you to eat it now, and while you do, think about what else you saw. Tell him what you want and I'll pay for it.'

'I could pay him myself. Keep my life skills up to scratch.'

'I'm not giving you the cash, Kit. In case you spend it on booze. There, you've made me say it.'

'How no?'

'It'd be bad karma.'

'Aye. Okay.' He leaned back into the open doorway. 'Aram, pal. I'll have my usual.'

A parcel of warm bread and meat with all the trimmings

was handed out the door by Aram. Kit wolfed it down, the light from the shop window illuminating the steam that curled up and around his face, making him look like a creature from mythology. An ancient traveller or seer who May hoped was about to deliver the solution to her quest.

She checked her watch. It was nearing eleven o'clock. If there were such things as ghosts, Holly's would be making her desperate way along Union Street about now.

'Thanks for this,' he said eventually, licking the sauce off the paper. 'I mean, you're doing a good thing for the family, and you've got a lot to put up with.'

'What? Cos I'm a cop?'

'Cos you're a bird. I mean, a woman.'

'You gonna start talking about hormones then?'

'No, no, I don't mean that. I mean you're a *woman*, and a cop. But the biggest bit of you—'

'This better not be about my arse.' May narrowed her eyes at him, only half in warning.

'No, the biggest bit of you as a woman is you're a woman before you're a cop. And that makes you a decent person. You're no' a cop first like a lot o' these station guys. They're just uniforms. Tin men. Hollow men wi' nae souls. But you, you're a woman, you see? And you understand the way things are.'

'Aye, well, I'm glad we cleared that up,' May said, with a sinking feeling. She'd lost him. He had no more to tell. Perhaps his encounter with Holly was no more than a recycled memory of some other distressed young woman, merged with the picture she'd shown him.

He looked at her keenly, then said, 'The kebab place has CCTV.' He turned his head to show the direct line of sight from the shop to the station entrance.

'You know, Kit, for someone who spends half their time talking a load of bollocks, that was really useful.'

'Aye, well,' he said, scrunching up the empty kebab paper and dropping it in the wire bin provided. 'It's a yin-yang thing.'

The place was filling up with groups of mostly drunk young men. May pushed her way in, with Kit at her heels doing more to open a route than her elbows. When she asked Aram about the camera pointing at the window he showed no curiosity or surprise.

'If we have trouble, it's usually a fight outside. The other camera is above the till. The staff know I check it if the cash balance is out. I wipe both cards after seven days.'

'Have you still got CCTV from this time last week?' May's heart thumped. 'From Tuesday evening about eleven p.m.?' She looked at Kit to confirm the time, but he just shrugged.

She should have done this earlier, then reminded herself that without Kit, finding CCTV other than the BTP's would've been a needle in a haystack, and she should just be thankful for this opportunity.

Aram beckoned her to the end of the counter and lifted the hinged section. 'Not you. Just the lady polis,' he said as Kit tried to follow May through. 'Can you go outside, please.'

Kit seemed unfazed and did as he was asked.

In a tiny office, two screens were stacked on top of each other and showed live feeds from the CCTV. Aram pulled up a list of files on a laptop.

'You want this time last week?'

'How long is each file?' May asked.

'Ten minutes.'

'Can we start around ten-thirty?' She didn't know precisely how long Holly had spent in the station before her death, and Kit's timekeeping was vague.

Aram glanced meaningfully at the packed and noisy shop, then opened the first file.

The window was partly fogged, but the station entrance was visible. Figures and vehicles moved in the street. Neither Holly nor Kit could be seen.

'Can I?' May indicated the keyboard and when he nodded, she set the image running at double speed as Aram returned to the shop.

The next two files were also empty. Frustratingly, in the third, a night bus was parked, obscuring the view. May checked the time stamp: 10.55 p.m. Her earlier elation had fizzled out, but it was the first solid sighting she'd had, and she wasn't leaving the shop until she'd examined every image from that evening if necessary.

In the next file, Kit was there, bundled up in the station entrance, his sleeping bag across his knees. May held her breath.

At 11.04 p.m., there she was.

Holly.

A blink-and-you'd-miss-it trip and recovery before she

hurried up the steps onto the station concourse, and out of view.

Twenty seconds later, the station cops arrived and hauled Kit to his feet.

Then, just as the file was about to end, she saw him. The image was so clear she thought she must have imagined it. She replayed the section.

The station cops were chivvying Kit as he bundled up his belongings. The man glanced at them as he passed, a spider tattoo creeping above his collar. Then, as if checking the street behind him, he turned and looked straight into the camera.

Scott Galbraith.

CHAPTER 25

In the end, the combined pressure of the CCTV that May had found of Scott entering the station a minute after Holly, Jackie and Ian piling on pressure, and the family's MSP who had, after all, suddenly smelled a media opportunity, was enough to make the BTP inspector shift his position on Holly's death. By 8 a.m. the next morning, he'd agreed to further enquiries and dispatched Dimple to the kebab shop with a warrant to recover Aram's full CCTV files. Since May was the only officer who knew the background on both Holly Campbell and Scott Galbraith, the DI requested to have her onboard, and Marky the Meerkat had to agree. The pathologist had released Holly's body to the family, citing major trauma as cause of death. The toxicology report also indicated alcohol but no drugs. Since no further forensic recovery was possible, the funeral was to go ahead next week.

May stood in her pyjamas in the front room of her flat with her phone jammed to her ear as she and Dimple discussed the options. They could wait until the Central station CCTV was reviewed, but that might take a few days. May argued that they needed to bring Scott Galbraith in now, pointing out his history of violence and previous intimidation of the victim and her mother.

'If you can give me a couple of your guys, I can put together a team to lift him this morning,' May said, as Tam padded through in his boxers and T-shirt to set a coffee down for her. He gave her a look just short of an eyeroll. Today was supposed to be her day off.

She sent her husband a smile of thanks for the coffee, which also conveyed her insistence. She'd be there for Galbraith's arrest and questioning, day off or not.

'I've already got a team on standby,' Dimple replied.

'Okay. We'll see you at Cathcart at ten a.m.,' May replied, taking her coffee and heading for the shower.

In the cramped briefing room at Cathcart Police Office, May set out her plan for detaining Scott Galbraith, including vehicles, the access and layout at the flat, the likelihood of Big Malky, his large and aggressive friend, being on the premises, and the possibility of weapons, though none had been seen on the previous visit. The air was thick with the smell of coffee and a building buzz of adrenaline.

Dimple had brought a team of six with her, all in riot gear, dwarfing the diminutive detective. They wore an almost identical black uniform to the Police Scotland officers, with only the wording on their hi-vis vests to differentiate them.

PC Ross Reid raised his hand. 'Who's taking the lead on this?'

'Cathcart will be facilitating entry,' May said. 'We'll be interviewing Galbraith here. The unexplained death of Holly Campbell at Glasgow Central is the BTP's case, so DC Sharma will be the arresting officer. That's fine by you, isn't it?'

Dimple looked a little startled that May, the senior rank present, wasn't doing it herself, but she nodded her agreement. After her previous encounter with Galbraith at the flat and the debt collector's office, May didn't want his lawyer framing this in any way as a personal vendetta.

'Right,' May said. 'Let's get going. And just watch yourselves. Don't take your eyes off these guys for a second.'

They'd been ready for trouble, but in the end, Scott Galbraith was detained without incident, Big Malky being absent. Dimple made the arrest, but as he was cautioned, Galbraith never took his eyes off May, who stood in the doorway ready to supervise the search of his flat. His look was a snarl of pure malevolence; a wordless promise that he'd make her pay.

CHAPTER 26

Galbraith had been processed by the custody sergeant and was safely in a cell when May returned to the station. She was standing drinking bad machine coffee and looking out at the rain-blackened trees and the low grey flats beyond, turning over the morning's events in her mind, when there was a tap on her office door.

'How'd it go?' Dimple said, dumping the laptop and the bundle of files she was carrying on the edge of May's desk.

May shook her head. 'Place was clean. No drugs. Only one laptop and one phone. We can ask Galbraith to give us the PIN codes, but you can bet we won't find anything on them. Big Malky will've been off on his toes with the rest of the gear.'

All the way back she'd had a growing misgiving that her encounter with Galbraith at the debt collector's had somehow tipped him off that they were coming. Or more likely Michael McNally, who'd then ordered his lieutenant to take the necessary extra precautions.

'Galbraith isn't daft,' Dimple said. 'Must have known we'd be back after you and I turned up at the flat.'

'True,' May conceded.

151

'Should probably take it as a compliment.' Dimple grinned. 'Knew he wasnae gonna shake you off that easily.'

It was a vote of confidence that Dimple had absorbed a valuable lesson in persistence in the short time they'd spent together. May felt a tiny flicker of warmth, as if someone had lit a candle in a dark place. But that light also illuminated how far they had to go.

Conscious of Dimple's efforts, she gave the young detective an encouraging smile. 'Aye, well, we're not there yet.'

'Listen, Sarge. I've drawn up an interview strategy.' Dimple bit her lip.

'Want me to run through it with you?' May said, remembering it was the lassie's first big case and sensing her nervousness.

'Would you? Great.' She pulled up a chair. 'We've got the text messages from Galbraith on Holly's phone, and Jackie's statement about the assault. And that return ticket you found,' Dimple said. 'I checked. The regular late train to Neilston, which stops at Queens Park, leaves from platform nine.'

'So if the power hadn't been out . . .' May let the implication hang in the air. This was Holly's regular route. 'She chose this platform because she was trying to get home.'

'I think so.'

May shook her head. 'Why couldn't the daft lassie have run up a lit platform?' she muttered.

'Maybe because Holly thought she could hide from whoever was after her. It's something I might do,' Dimple admitted. 'Especially if the area was familiar to me.'

Me too, thought May. Small chance of winning a fight so better to run and hide.

'How'd you get on with the diary?' Dimple said.

May sighed. Each time she'd scanned through, her expectations took another blow.

'It's clear Holly was terrified that Galbraith was following her and he was aggressive anytime they did meet. However, the details – times, places, witnesses present – are flimsy enough for a defence lawyer to drive a double-decker bus through, despite the texts.'

'Right.' Dimple made a note but it was clear from her face she shared May's frustration. 'Holly's laptop didn't give us anything either.'

'Where are your guys with the CCTV?' May said.

'We've got Holly.'

'Is Galbraith with her?' May said, sitting up straighter.

'No, but there's more to go through.'

The breakthrough would come soon, she was sure of it. 'And the train had CCTV, didn't it?'

Dimple nodded.

'Can you show me?'

Dimple hesitated. 'The footage isn't pleasant.' Then, mindful of May's years of experience, and the unfiltered nature of her current job, she added, 'Just so you know.'

Opening her laptop, she turned the screen so May could view it too.

'I called the driver, Billy Mackenzie, this morning. Told him further enquiries were being made. He's agreed to amend his statement.'

'Well done,' said May, genuinely impressed.

Dimple shrugged but the slight upturn of her lips showed she was pleased. 'I told him we'd already put a public appeal up on the destination board, and further enquiries were ongoing. I think it gave him the confidence. He said the guilt he felt was less about Holly's death than the sense he hadn't told all he knew, and it'd just eat him up if he didn't.'

'I think that's true,' May agreed. 'He's made the right decision for himself, as well as for Holly.'

Dimple tapped a few keys and a list of files appeared.

'Right, so, all driver's cabs have a front-facing camera linked to the train's black box video recorders. The camera systems are activated when the cab is enabled by the driver and can't be overridden manually. They also run for ten minutes after the train is powered down, about the time it takes for the driver to get his stuff and leave the cab.'

'Will it cover the platform too?' May said, aware that any progress in the case would rest on the driver's assertion of a second person being present.

'The field of vision is as close to the driver's viewpoint as possible, so it shows things like signals, but yes, some of the platform is visible. It's an important factor for through trains in case a passenger unfortunately gets too close to the edge.'

Dimple opened a file and May steeled herself.

'This is the train approaching the platform. The white text shows the train ID, date, time, camera ID, speed, GPS co-ordinates, driver ID and the event trigger – in this case it was Billy Mackenzie hitting the emergency brake.'

'If he had time to do that then he must have had a good view of the platform.'

Dimple made a *maybe* face. 'These guys have fast reactions. And a jury still might not believe him,' she cautioned. 'The driver isn't on trial, but in past cases we've had the defence bring up the idea that memory has a habit of tricking itself so that they could've merged previous incidents. Not just fatalities; near-misses too.'

'I thought that about Kit,' May reflected, 'right up to the point when he pointed out the CCTV from the kebab shop. He was right, and I'm inclined to believe the driver was too.'

'See for yourself,' Dimple said.

In the dark of a winter's night, the dizzying view from the driver's cab was different from what May had been expecting. The track and overhead lines appeared to radiate out from the centre, the altered perspective giving the impression you were being pulled forward into a dark pit. Banks of red, green and amber lights appeared at intervals. The train's speed dropped below 20mph as it approached the snaking tracks that heralded the fifteen high-level platforms of Glasgow Central. The great glass curve of the station's roof glowed like an upturned hull against the regimented lines of buildings that marched away from it on all sides, their lights dim in the low cloud of the city skyline.

'The cameras operate from ten thousand lux – that's bright daylight,' Dimple said, 'to less than one lux – night, storms and tunnels. But the environmental light affects the quality of the image. There's multiple cameras on the train to monitor track debris and passenger safety, set at increasing levels of picture quality depending on whether you want to detect, observe, recognise or identify. The station concourse cameras are all set to *identify* levels, because that's the evidential requirement.'

'What about this forward-facing camera?'

'Set to a high image level to allow differentiation between on-track personnel and trespassers, so we can identify individuals in near-misses.'

As the train drew level with the end of the long platform, May was struck by how impenetrable the dark edges seemed against the brightly lit concourse nearly 300 metres away. Pillars were barely discernible in the by-wash of the train's lights.

Suddenly a dark shape was caught in their beam and May saw just a flash of white as Holly's profile and flailing hands blinked on the screen and were gone as material from the impact hit the camera.

'This is what the driver would've seen,' Dimple said, as May sat silent, overwhelmed by the speed of it. Holly had been no more than pinpricks of light snuffed out. 'Now,' Dimple continued, 'here's the enhanced version. It runs slower.'

May steeled herself.

Propelled, Billy Mackenzie had said, and May agreed.

Holly's fall didn't seem natural. If you jumped backwards, you'd raise your arms to boost yourself, but Holly's hands stayed low, as if she'd been shoved in the chest. May ran the file again, concentrating on the left side of the frame. She wondered, as the driver must have, if her mind was playing tricks on her. On the platform, a fraction of a second after the impact, what looked like an outline of a human form was revealed among the reflections from the giant metal studs on a pillar.

They'd seized and bagged the clothes Galbraith had worn in the CCTV image from the Union Street entrance. A black hoodie, dark jeans. Dressed as he was, he'd be almost invisible here.

May sat back, brow furrowed, and folded her arms. 'Can we get this further enhanced?'

Dimple shook her head. 'We're on the limit, before the pixels break up.' She moved forward to open another file. 'But there is this.'

It was an enhanced still frame from further down the platform. The head and shoulders of a dark figure.

May sat up. 'You sure this is a person?' Watching the camera footage, she'd seen silhouettes of figures against the station lights that had turned out to be just electrical cabinets and platform furniture.

'The Machine Vision programme in image analytics thinks so.' When Dimple saw her blank expression, she added, 'Computer says yes.'

CHAPTER 27

Cathcart's interview room was over-lit and shabby. Previous efforts with carpet cleaner and disinfectant had failed to erase the odour of vomit and stale sweat, along with the mysterious stains on the walls that could be any number of other body fluids. May sometimes wondered if the grimness was intentional, a sensory assault that would encourage suspects to co-operate, even if only to escape the place. Mind you, anyone who'd been in prison before would find it a home-from-home.

May and Dimple sat across the scuffed desk from Scott Galbraith and his lawyer, Peter Mazzarelli, a sharp suited, sharp-tongued silver fox, whom May immediately recognised as one of McNally's men.

Given the paucity of evidence, May and Dimple's agreed strategy was a simple one. Present the abusive texts, Jackie's statement, Holly's diary entries – all circumstantial but pointing to the escalating pattern of violence – and when he relaxed, thinking that was all they'd got, hit him with the CCTV from the kebab shop and the train. Scare the living shit out of him, then offer a lifeline. Confess and he might do ten years and a domestic violence rehab course. Or he could take his chances with Holly's uncle, Michael McNally, on the street. The fact that the lawyer was from the businessman's stable meant he was sure to report back on everything that was said, client confidentiality being no barrier to a man like McNally. And the more May had thought about it, the more convinced she'd become that whatever his relationship with his niece, the longer this case went on, the more likely it was that McNally would see Galbraith as a liability. It was only the slimmest of chances, but Galbraith might jump ship and confess, even if it was just to save his own skin. Divide and conquer was her tactic now.

Galbraith's frown had deepened when she'd come in, and May had wondered if he'd go *no comment*. Dimple took him through the early evidence with precision, making the lawyer shift uncomfortably, but to which Galbraith just shrugged. It painted him in an unfavourable light as a life partner, but with Holly dead nothing legal could come of it.

When Dimple opened the laptop and said they'd be showing him some CCTV, he had the sense to look wary.

The computer had identified the enhanced image as the rear view of an individual about six feet tall, but wouldn't commit beyond these basics, leaving gender, hair colour and type of clothing up to its human counterparts.

'Mr Galbraith, do you recognise this individual?' Dimple said.

Both the lawyer and his client made a show of peering at the screen, their faces registering exaggerated mystification.

'Could be a bystander who heard the commotion,' the lawyer said.

'Could be half of Glasgow,' Galbraith sneered.

'Oh, a much smaller percentage than that,' May shot back.

'But not a definitive identification of my client,' the lawyer said.

'So, just to be clear, you're saying this is definitely not your client?' May said.

Before the lawyer could answer, Dimple said, 'I'd like you to look at this,' and played the CCTV taken from the kebab shop featuring a blown-up image complete with the distinctive spider tattoo visible on his neck.

The men exchanged a glance, but before the lawyer could ask for a pause for consultation, Galbraith sat forward and tapped the table.

'I didn't see Holly or speak to her. It's a coincidence.'

May leaned forward, mirroring his posture. 'When I asked you where you were that night you told me the Nelly Dean pub.'

'My client was not under caution at that time,' Mazzarelli said.

But in the face of the CCTV, Galbraith seemed intent on brazening it out. 'Got my days mixed up. I was in town for a drink. Can't remember the pub. Malky will confirm he was with me in town.'

'We'll be asking your pal about that,' May replied – when they found him. Malcolm McGregor, aka Big Malky, who had a stream of convictions for assault and drugs, seemed to have dropped off the face of the earth. 'Doesn't look like he was with you here though?' May said tapping the laptop screen.

'He'd got lucky wi' a lassie. I was looking for a cab home.'

'Not a train?'

'No' my scene.'

Dimple laid a printed A4 map of Central station on the table. With her pen she indicated the entrances. 'The cab rank is here on Gordon Street. And you came from the north end of Union Street. You'd already have passed the turnoff.'

'I'd had a bit to drink. Wasn't thinking.'

'So why did you enter the station from Union Street?' May said.

'To use the cashpoint, then remembered I had money on me.'

'Taxi drivers take cards or use apps.'

'Not all.'

'Most licenced cabs do.'

'Do they? That's good to know for next time.'

'So you took a cab home?'

He nodded.

'What time?'

A shrug. 'Late. Can't remember.'

May made a note. With that tattoo, the drivers might recall him. The timing was important, and his demeanour. Had he been agitated? Or could he have pushed Holly in front of the train and then calmly hopped in a cab? May thought it entirely possible.

'Why were you stalking Holly? Sending her threatening messages?' Dimple said.

When he didn't answer, May said, 'Had she upset you? Did she threaten you in some way?' She arranged her face like a mother confessor to whom he could admit difficulties in the relationship. The texts clearly showed he was the one doing the threatening, but here was Galbraith's option to defend, even claim a necessity to what he'd done. *It was an accident. She made me do it.* But seeking absolution through self-justification was a trap Galbraith wasn't going to be lured into, and all he gave her was a blank, cold stare.

Another possibility struck May. Was his pursuit of her about more than just the end of their relationship? An ex-girlfriend who knew your business but could no longer be kept in a perpetual state of submissive fear was a liability. There was no evidence to support it, but given the length of time they'd known each other – since school Gemma Thorne had said – it was worth asking the question.

'Did Holly have information about your activities that you were scared she'd reveal to a third party?'

The elephant in the room was large, white and had *cocaine* written on its side.

'I'm an apprentice electrician. Why would I be worried? You think I was bothered about her reporting me for no' wiring a plug properly or something?' He gave her a snort of contempt.

'Will you give us the PIN codes to your laptop and phone?'

'The laptop's for my college work and is none of your business.'

'What about your other laptop, the one I saw at your flat?'

He pushed back from the table and folded his arms with an air of nonchalance, but the cogs were turning behind his eyes.

'And your other phones?'

'Hearsay,' Mazzarelli said. 'Unless you can produce them.'

'But you did try to meet her that night, didn't you?'

May slid a sheet across the desk at the lawyer, her eyes locked on Galbraith's. *Meet me, Holls. I only want to talk.*

Galbraith took an excessive time to read it. To May, this said he was stalling and already knew the contents. He just needed to consider how best to spin them.

Eventually, he pressed his lips together and shook his head. 'Isnae from me.'

There was a flash of something like glee in his expression.

'Holly's family are very upset,' May said, irritation at his cockiness blossoming into a white-hot anger. 'A young woman with her life ahead of her. Tell me, what does your employer think about you pushing his niece in front of a train?'

Dimple shifted uncomfortably in the seat. May felt the disapproval radiate from her.

The colour drained from Galbraith's face.

Galbraith opened his mouth to respond but his lawyer was quicker.

'I don't see how that's relevant, Sergeant Mackay. For the record, Mr McNally is regretfully not in touch with his sister or his niece. He understands both suffered from long-standing issues with drug addiction and alcohol and had a chaotic lifestyle. The support he offered was repeatedly rejected. Mr Galbraith's association with Mr McNally is solely via his charitable trust set up to aid disadvantaged young men in Glasgow into gainful employment through training. Now, if you don't mind, I need a moment alone with my client, Sergeant.'

'Fine.' May gathered up her papers and nodded to Dimple to pause the interview recording. She stood up, conscious

Galbraith was still watching her. Their eyes met and she finally saw the flicker of fear she'd been hoping for. At the debt collector's, she'd felt some pity for him, his life wrecked by his circumstances as much as his choices. That sympathy had vanished in the face of what he'd chosen to do to Holly. Now he had another choice to make. Who to fear most, the law or Michael McNally.

She'd done all she could. Now it was up to him which way he jumped.

CHAPTER 28

May paced the corridor outside the interview room. The narrow space had no windows with which to judge the passage of daylight. Checking her watch, she was surprised to find it was only mid-afternoon. The quick change from night shifts back to days, without a break in between, was playing havoc with her body clock. Although she hadn't eaten any lunch, she found she wasn't hungry. May realised the same probably wasn't true for Dimple. She was about to suggest she grab a bite when the interview-room door opened.

'My client won't be answering any more questions,' Peter Mazzarelli informed them smoothly. 'But he will provide a statement.'

When it came, May felt a plunge of disappointment, echoed in Dimple's slumped shoulders. The statement was nothing more than a reiteration of what had already been said. Galbraith denied speaking to or contacting Holly. They'd no longer been in a relationship, and it was a coincidence that they'd been in a public place at the same time. He expressed regret for her death but couldn't help the police in any way.

Ten minutes later Galbraith was back in the cells. May and Dimple returned to the briefing room and, after the file had been sent to the Procurator Fiscal's office, began the jittery wait for their charging decision. Dimple eyed the dubious coffee. May couldn't sit still and got up from her chair to stare out at the bleak wasteland beyond the car park's perimeter. The shadowy movement of a fox caught her eye as it slipped neatly under a loose panel of the fence.

The streetlights had come on before the call came.

She heard Dimple thank the fiscal and when she turned to look at her she knew instantly what the news was.

'Doesn't meet the evidence threshold to charge him.'

'Fucksake,' May exploded. 'We're letting him go?'

'Police bail. Not allowed anywhere near Jackie McNally's place.'

'Oh, aye,' May scoffed. 'Like that'll stop him.'

'We'll stop him,' Dimple said calmly. 'That station is wired up to foil terrorists, biological attacks and mass shootings. We've still got CCTV to go through and a witness who saw the appeal might still come forward. If the evidence is out there, we'll find it. Don't you worry.'

But May did worry, for Jackie and Holly, for whom the idea of justice seemed to be slipping further away.

Galbraith was bailed. May and Dimple spent the next hour or so reviewing the file to check no potential lines of enquiry were being missed, then the BTP detective set off for her office at Glasgow Central, promising an update on the remaining CCTV as soon as she had it.

There were a couple of urgent messages on May's desk from the fiscal about other cases due before the sheriff tomorrow, but even as she cursed one of her officer's sloppy paperwork she knew she had an even more unenviable task ahead of her. Someone needed to break the news to Jackie and Ian that Galbraith was out and warn them to be careful.

Ten minutes later, as she made her way to the car park, Andrea from the front desk hailed her from the other end of the corridor.

'May!'

'Andrea, hen, there's such a thing as radios these days. Mobile phones too.'

'I used to be a barmaid, can you tell?' Andrea said, walking quickly towards her. 'Listen.' She dropped her voice to a conspiratorial whisper. 'Jackie McNally's out front.'

'Good. I was just on my way to see her.'

'Not good,' Andrea said. 'Can't tell if she's drunk or manic, or just very upset.'

May checked her phone and saw a stream of missed messages from Jackie asking for an update. She followed Andrea back along the corridor. When she laid eyes on Jackie, she saw the woman had already heard the news on the Govanhill grapevine.

'It's no' right. It cannae be right,' Jackie said as she clung to the front desk. 'What about him battering her in the street. What more do you need?'

'Jackie, love, it's gonna be alright,' May said, pushing through the security door and grabbing hold of the woman whose legs threatened to buckle under her.

On the bench a homeless woman May knew as Flarey Mary, due to her preference for 1970s-style flares and tie-dyed tops (which, to her credit, seemed to be making a comeback), looked up from her doze.

'D'you want a drink, hen?' She fished in the pocket of her greasy sheepskin coat and pulled out a flat half-bottle of cheap whisky. 'Look at her, she's all upset. She needs a drink.'

May signalled Andrea with a tilt of her head to unlock the door back into the corridor.

'Thanks, Mary,' May said. 'But not just now. Put the bottle away for me.'

'Mibbaes later,' Mary said. 'I'm waiting for ma man.'

Mary was most often seen in the company of a fellow homeless guy known locally as Johnny Nae Cash, due to his love of country and western, and lack of ready money. There was a craggy resemblance to the singer. Someone had given him a black cowboy hat, and this had enhanced his local celebrity status. In exchange for a drink, he'd give you a rendition of 'Ring of Fire' or 'Folsom Prison Blues'. This ceased to be amusing after seven or eight goes, and landlords, supermarkets or neighbours usually called the police. May sometimes heard him in the cells from the floor above and had frowned at PC Mo Pannu's suggestion that he might like to compose a special 'Cathcart Cell Blues' since he was here so often. *Don't give him any ideas,* she'd said.

Jackie was crying now, her full weight leaning on May who was trying to keep her upright.

Flarey Mary began to sing Tammy Wynette's 'Stand by Your Man'.

'Anytime you're ready, Andrea,' May called, as she

felt Jackie slipping from her grasp, and the door finally buzzed open.

When May had got her into an interview room it became clear that Jackie had been drinking heavily in the hour or so since she'd learned of Galbraith's release.

'Why'd you let him go, May?' she said tearfully. 'I cannae sleep and when I do, as soon as anyone puts their foot on that bottom step of the close, I wake. I hear them even though I know I cannae possibly have heard them. Every time, I think it's her. Any minute she'll be through that door, rolling in maybe a bit drunk, and then she'll be clattering around in the kitchen making something to eat and playing my Dolly Parton records.'

Jackie was in no fit state to understand the finer points of legal decision-making, May decided, so she gave her the short version.

'The fiscal are idiots, but we'll get him. Listen, Jackie. I think you should go home.'

'Ian says I mustn't get a taxi. Said not to waste my cash.'

'I'm going to get you a coffee. Okay?' May sat her down behind the table.

'I had a drink. I'm sorry. I'm really sorry.'

'Look, Jackie, it'll be fine. You've had the worst thing possible happen to you. Everyone understands that.'

But Jackie had started to cry again. Dry, quiet sobs as if she'd no more tears left.

'Ian won't understand. I'm a disappointment to everyone.'

May thought of Flarey Mary out in the waiting room nursing her bottle like a lost child and wondered if it was just such a crisis that had broken her and Johnny Nae Cash so completely. The steep descent from employed to unemployed, from homeowner to homeless was all too easy, as May had seen countless times before. She wasn't going to let it happen if she could prevent it. As Dimple had said that first morning when May had asked her why she was investigating Holly's death, a moment's kindness had the power to change lives.

'Sit there,' May said. 'You're not on your own, Jackie. We're all here to help you.'

If anyone would understand what a blow this was to Jackie it would be her partner, Holly's stepfather, an ex-cop and a fellow recovering alcoholic.

When Ian McDonald arrived, he fussed over Jackie as though she were a lost kitten, hugging her and smoothing her hair back. When she was calm, he took May aside.

'What did Galbraith say?' He kept his voice low but he was watching May intensely, hands on hips.

Technically, she couldn't discuss the interview with him, but there was very little he wouldn't guess from Galbraith's release.

'Denied it, didn't he,' she said, under her breath in case they were overheard.

'But it is him? He was there?'

May nodded. 'New evidence from the CCTV backs up the driver's story of a second person on the platform.'

Ian looked stunned. 'Fuck. Really? Then how can you not get him for this? What are the BTP playing at, May? They need to pull their finger out and get this guy nailed.' He pointed to his partner crumpled in the corner. 'Jackie is at the end of her tether. I don't know what she'll do.'

'We didn't lock him up today, but we will.'

'It needs to happen now,' Ian said, his eyes wild. 'Maybe if someone killed your daughter you might think differently.'

It stung, but May didn't think he was aware of the significance of what he'd said. She hadn't told either Jackie or Ian about Isla. And anyway, Isla had died by her own hand, there had never been any doubt about that. But was he right? If someone had killed her, how would May have felt about them walking the face of the earth when her daughter was gone? Perhaps you couldn't incarcerate anyone for long enough to balance that. The mere fact that they were still breathing would be a twisting knife in the gut.

'The McNallys sent one of their own lawyers,' she said, trying to banish the image of a murdered Isla from her mind.

'Who?' Ian said.

'Peter Mazzarelli. Fifties. Fit. Bit of a snappy dresser.'

'Recognise the name, but I never dealt with him in court.' Ian looked thoughtful. 'The McNallys will want to know if there's truth in it, won't they? Even if they don't care about Holly, they'll be wondering what sort of scrutiny this will bring. I think young Galbraith is a marked man.' He shook his head at her. 'Don't feel guilty, May. He killed Holly and this might be the only way to get him to admit it.'

She'd already thought about this, but it helped to have it confirmed by someone of Ian's experience. It was easy to doubt sometimes, especially after the fiscal hadn't supported an immediate charge. It was good to be reminded that some-times you had to hold your nerve.

Jackie stirred. 'I need to go to the loo.'

May helped her to her feet and down the corridor to the ladies', then returned to the interview room, standing in the open doorway to keep an eye out for Jackie.

'I'm worried that she'll just go downhill without any hope to cling to,' Ian said quietly. 'Her memory's already bad with the alcohol. She talks about stuff that happened with her husband Darren as if it was yesterday. Things he did to her. It's like she believes he's back. And I don't like her being alone at the flat. I worry it makes her think about Holly more, and that if I'm no' there she'll take a knife out of the kitchen and . . . well . . . you've seen her arms.' He looked up at her, pleading. 'Can you no' tell her she has to come to Shawlands to be safe?'

'Galbraith is barred from entering Jackie's street,' May replied. The woman was making her way unsteadily back along the corridor to where they stood. 'But you're right, I think she'd be better off somewhere out of his reach, and not on her own as much.'

She broached the subject and Jackie stared at her as if she didn't understand what was being proposed.

'Jackie, love.' May took her hand. 'Do you not think you'd be better off at Ian's in Shawlands?'

'I want to stay at my flat.'

'Just for a bit,' May persisted. 'A couple of days. Maybe till after the funeral next week and take it from there?'

At the mention of the funeral Jackie crumbled. May hugged her and told her she was doing the right thing.

'We'll go by your place and you can pack a bag,' Ian said.

May couldn't help but remember those terrible days after Isla's death when she'd been almost mad with grief. She recalled only snatches, out-of-order images like scattered postcards. The funeral. The faces of Isla's friends pale with shock. Identifying their daughter's body which Tam had offered to do, but which May had insisted they should do together.

Ian and Jackie stood quietly, holding hands, united in loss. May knew that no matter what she told them, she was leaving them with a world full of doubt and only the faintest glimmer of potential justice for their lost child.

CHAPTER 29

The next day, Inspector Mark Ward sat behind his desk in his over-heated office and May, not wishing to be detained, took up her habitual stance in his doorway. The rest of the team were already out on calls. She'd had a fitful night's sleep and was fighting down a craving to visit the Turkish bakery and ask for the biggest coffee they could possibly make her. They had a bucket they could rinse out? That'd be grand.

'This BTP case,' the inspector began, his tone distasteful, like she'd brought an unpleasant odour into the station. 'No drugs were found in the lassie's system, beyond traces of pre-scribed medication and alcohol. That's right?'

'That's right,' May replied. 'It confirms what Holly's friend and sometime dealer reported: that Holly was clean.'

'So you won't be pursuing Scott Galbraith's dealing, or any connections to Michael McNally? Our interest is purely in whether he pushed his ex-girlfriend in front of a train.'

May looked at him, uncomprehending. She reran what he'd just said, in case she'd misinterpreted it.

'Why are you so interested in defending Michael McNally?'

He bristled at her tone. 'My interest is in preventing this

division being brought into disrepute. And I'm interested in saving you from yourself.'

'I don't need saving, and I'm not ever likely to, sir.' *Certainly not by the likes of you,* she refrained from adding. 'It's the BTP's investigation, as you were kind enough to remind me, but if they uncover wrongdoing on our patch, I can't see how we can refuse to investigate.'

May pushed off the doorframe. It was on the tip of her tongue to tell him what Danny Stephenson had said about DI Andy Wilson's death, but he'd only see it as gossip and question her judgement and fitness for duty in believing it. Suddenly, May realised this must be a tiny amount of the pressure train driver Billy Mackenzie must have faced. He hadn't backed down, and neither would she.

'If that's all, sir?'

'Oh, before you go, May, I've a special job for you,' he said, ignoring the sarcasm in her tone.

'Aye, what's that then?' She took out her Pronto, checking for any tasking. Nothing outstanding.

'Get down to the Dalmarnock Bridge, where that munitions factory used to be. Our old friend Davey Donnelly, the magnet fisherman, is up to his old tricks. He's hauled another World War Two grenade out of the Clyde. We're waiting for the bomb squad. Officers have already closed the road.'

'So why d'you need me? He's not doing anything illegal.' The two cops dispatched would be sufficient to redirect traffic and shoo away bystanders.

'Because he's eating into our budget and resources. Last month we had to shut the M8 motorway at rush hour to deal with a World War Two mortar shell. I mean, this guy and his mates are hauling up stuff that no one even remembers going into the Clyde in the first place.'

Plus, May thought, all the stuff folk do remember and rather everyone forget – guns, knives, machetes, cars, wedding rings.

'I need you to persuade him he's putting the public at risk by his actions. A charge of culpable or reckless conduct could be applied if he persists.'

May saw from her Pronto screen that the officers on site were Ross Reid and Toni McAleer. If anyone could persuade Davey Donnelly the error of his ways it was those two. Now, if the attending officer had been Rab the Kebab then backup would definitely have been required. He'd have been having a go with the magnet lines himself by now and would probably have hauled up a Luftwaffe aircraft complete with full complement of live ordinance on board. Closing the road for a few hours would be the least of their problems. They'd need to evacuate half the city.

She sighed and tucked her Pronto into her utility vest. 'Righto.'

Inspector Mark Ward was flexing his command. Making sure she knew who was boss, and she wouldn't give him the satisfaction of arguing.

It wasn't this bridge her daughter had jumped from but one further up, around the bend of the river. But every time she'd been called out to the magnet fisherman an involuntary and ridiculous hope had risen and she'd wondered, just for a fraction of a second, if this time she'd see Isla dangling on the end of his magnet like a mermaid – *surprise, Mum!* She knew hope like this was just another kind of self-punishment, the spark of anticipated joy quickly extinguished by a heavy blanket of grief.

Jackie Campbell came once more into her thoughts. Her call to the woman this morning had gone to voicemail. When she'd rung Ian, he'd told her Jackie was asleep when he'd gone to work. He'd left her sandwiches and would pop back at lunchtime to make sure she was eating them.

May checked her phone for any messages from Dimple but there was nothing.

The squat figure of Davey Donnelly in his road sweeper's jacket and flat cap, accompanied by half a dozen of his fishing mates, shuffled on the pavement by the cordoned-off bridge, excitement radiating off him. On the far side of the bridge, she saw the hi-vis vests of Toni and Ross. They raised a hand to acknowledge their sergeant's arrival.

'Sergeant Mackay. Didn't expect to see your good self down here the day,' Davey said as she approached.

'You and me both, Davey. How's it going?'

'Aye, no' bad. Yourself?'

'I'm grand, Davey. What have you got this time?'

'Couple of aircraft rounds, mibbaes a mortar, and a grenade.'

'Where are they?'

He nodded towards the council road-grit bin in the middle of the bridge which stood with its plastic lid open. 'In there.'

'Gonna take your word for it,' she replied.

On the ground by Davey's Dookers, as the group was informally known, were a dozen coiled ropes with magnets attached like bathplugs, along with carrier bags containing Thermos flasks and bottles of Irn-Bru. It seemed to have been quite the outing.

'It was me that found the grenade,' a tall lad in jeans and a hoodie piped up.

'Aye, Sergeant,' Davey cut in. 'D'you want to hear a belter? Paul didnae know he had a grenade. Just dropped it on the ground. I admit I said a wee sweary word at him.'

The others laughed and Paul joined them, happy to be the centre of the joke.

'Aye, I thought it was a rock,' he proclaimed to renewed laughter and May reckoned this was the highlight of his year, destined to be repeated at every Christmas and birthday party for the rest of his life. *Paul, d'you mind that time . . .*

'This is Scotland's history we're pulling up out of the Clyde,' Davey declared, and there were calls of agreement. 'But see my wee Connor here.' Davey proudly hauled forward a nine-year-old version of himself in flat cap and waterproof jacket. 'He's a dab hand with the magnet.'

The others all nodded to a chorus of 'Oh aye,' and 'So he is.'

'First go, I found a samurai sword.' The lad's pale round face and light blue eyes shone.

'It was bigger than he was.' Davey delivered the punch-line to what May realised must be a well-worn story, and his audience erupted in appreciation. Connor beamed at his dad.

'That right?' May said to the boy. 'Where's this sword now?'

'In my bedroom.'

Mindful of her inspector's demand that she deter Davey and his mates from their lawful but highly inconvenient hobby on their patch, she weighed up whether a nine-year-old with his own samurai sword required her intervention. Was he potentially a vulnerable individual or just a bloody menace?

'It's no' sharp,' Davey assured her. 'So it isnae an offensive weapon.'

It seemed Davey Donnelly's previous encounters with Police Scotland had taught him enough about the law regarding bladed items for his son to keep his souvenir.

'My husband works with a guy who's a sword expert. Even had a part in *Outlander*.' He was an outreach worker named Sean whose wife, Morag, sometimes sang with Tam's folk band.

Wee Connor looked suitably impressed. 'Has he got loads of swords?'

'He has. Shall I get him to come and have a chat with you? That sound good?'

Connor nodded and gave her a big smile. May hoped the lad was young enough that his enthusiasm for weapons might be channelled into traditional Scottish martial arts rather than gangs. It would save the polis a lot of bother later.

A paramedic and a white lorry with *Royal Navy Bomb Disposal* stencilled on the side had joined the fire crew. Two personnel jumped out of the lorry and began a conversation with Ross and Toni. Further back beyond the blue-and-white police tape, stationary traffic snaked away along the road towards the city centre. There was less of a tailback on May's side of the river, but impatient drivers were getting out of their cars demanding to know what was going on. May got on the radio and asked the control room to divert any resources not currently tasked to help redirect traffic and clear the backlog. Two more units were on their way. Nearly half of Cathcart's officers were now tied up with this. May reluctantly began to see Inspector Mark Ward's point of view.

Davey's Dookers were craning their necks at the bomb disposal operation which seemed to be proceeding at a snail's pace. The temperature had dropped and a drizzle had set in which would turn the road surfaces to ice and lead to the sort of minor shunts that would cause further delays.

'Davey, pal,' May began, 'I have to tell you, my inspector is pretty fed up with the road closures. He's talking a reckless conduct charge. You've worn out your welcome with Cathcart Police Office. Might be an idea to leave Scotland's history where it is for a while. You get what I'm saying?'

'D'you know what I'd really like?' Davey gave her a sideways look. 'I'd like one of my finds to solve a murder. I mean, a guy up in Dundee pulled up a Viking sword. It's in a museum. I did once find a Ford Focus in the Maryhill Canal, but solving an actual murder, a cold case? That'd be grand. Get me on the telly and on one of them true crime podcasts. Smashing.' He rubbed his hands together in anticipation. 'I've met hundreds of folk since I started this. This is a great hobby. Gets you out in the fresh air. Good for your mental health.'

'Not much good for your mental or physical health if one of your hauls goes off with a bang.' May raised a sceptical eyebrow at him, but he shrugged it off with a smile.

'You know what I mean. Awful lot of boys stuck in on their own. They lose hope and turn to the booze and the drugs. We get them out of the house, give them pals and an interest. Ten quid and you'll get all you need to start magnet fishing off Amazon. So you could argue I'm actually *saving* the polis money on the mental health call-outs.' He grinned at her.

May sighed but couldn't help smiling back. 'You've some cheek, Davey, I'll give you that.'

'See, I've been thinking of trying pastures new. Taking the train up to Kirkintilloch. Got a good canal there. Nice day trip for the boys. Might even go to Edinburgh,' he teased.

Both spots were well out of Cathcart Police Office's patch.

May scrutinised him. 'And you just want a wee update with all the knives, axes and guns you've brought in to us, and if any is linked to an actual crime?'

Davey nodded.

May took off her glove and held out her hand. 'Alright, Davey, you've got yourself a deal.'

It was a job she could delegate. Get some specials and probationers phone bashing. Shift Davey and his merry band off her patch for a while. Keep Marky the Meerkat on side.

Paul, the architect of the current stramash playing out on the bridge watched his grenade being loaded into a safe box by the bomb disposal team for detonation elsewhere.

'It's surreal, man,' he said to May. 'Sad to see it go.'

'I'm sure there'll be others,' May said, happy they'd be someone else's problem. 'What are you hoping for next time?'

'A tank, mibbaes?' He gave her a gleeful smile.

May made a mental note to give Kirkintilloch polis a call. Cancel all leave. Davey's Dookers were on their way.

CHAPTER 30

The morning of Holly's funeral, the sun shone a harsh blue between the banks of dark clouds piled up on the horizon. On the stone porch of the crematorium, May stood with Dimple, both of them sombrely dressed in dark trousers and coats. The hearse carrying Holly's coffin arrived, draped with flowers. Jackie and Ian were in the car behind. Jackie got out unsteadily and clung to Ian for support. They were greeted by the independent celebrant they'd chosen to conduct the funeral. The woman was young, with jet-black hair, piercings and purple lipstick, and May thought Holly would've approved.

The group of mourners wasn't large and May spotted some familiar faces. Jackie's downstairs neighbour was there with another couple of women about the same age. Gemma Thorne stood with a group of lads and lassies who May reckoned had all been at school together. Disappointingly, there was no sign of Holly's college pal, Mhairi. May had made repeated attempts to contact her and had hoped this would be an opportunity to quiz her on her odd behaviour the previous week at Central station. She made do with taking a mental note of the faces present in case they should turn up as potential witnesses in the existing or future lines of enquiry.

Scott Galbraith was nowhere to be seen, though May had her Airwave radio in her handbag and had stationed officers discreetly at the main entrance to the crematorium site with orders to keep a look out for his bright blue BMW.

There were a couple of figures – an older man in a dark raincoat and a young woman in flat boots and a long puffer jacket – who May thought were journalists, but given the raised profile of the BTP case, that wasn't unexpected.

The service was short and featured Holly's favourite music: the Jesus and Mary Chain, Joy Division, and a local band, Danse Macabre. Ian gave an emotional eulogy describing the special and talented girl who'd come late into his life. Gemma read a poem she said Holly had liked at school, 'Nothing Gold Can Stay' by Robert Frost.

May thought how her own daughter, Isla, would have known and recognised these touchstones of Holly's. She felt the familiar *perhaps* creep up on her. Perhaps, if an earlier fateful day had brought May and Jackie together, then their daughters, so close in age, would have become friends, and maybe, just maybe, spared both mothers such grief.

May was sitting with Dimple behind the main group of mourners, but she was conscious that a few late arrivals had joined the funeral director's team in the rearmost pews.

When the service had finished and Jackie and Ian made their way out along the central aisle, May saw Jackie start, and her face change from a look of grief to one of horror.

May glanced carefully back over her shoulder. 'The fuck is he doing here?' she muttered under her breath, just loud enough for Dimple to hear.

But the figure who had so terrified Jackie wasn't Galbraith, but her brother, Michael. He opened his arms to Jackie, who stood frozen. May's first thought was that Jackie would have a panic attack or start screaming. But when she didn't move, Michael McNally came up the aisle and embraced his sister. Ian stared, wrong-footed. Mourners who'd got up to follow Jackie and Ian stood awkwardly, half out of their pews, creating a log jam that blocked May's and Dimple's exit.

Keeping one arm around his stunned sister, Michael McNally reached out the other and gripped Ian's hand in a condoling handshake. Then he turned swiftly and escorted Jackie onwards to the door. She stared straight ahead and moved like a wooden puppet entirely under his control. Ian was left trailing in their wake. It was only then that May saw McNally wasn't alone. The blonde head of Liam McNally was visible in the crowd, along with two other faces May knew from previous arrests.

With a jut of her chin, she indicated the young men. 'Keep an eye on those three for me, will you?' she said to Dimple, who nodded.

When May got to the door she found McNally had positioned himself next to Jackie and Ian and was shaking the hands of the mourners, thanking them for their attendance. Most looked sheepishly pleased to be greeted by such a celebrity, a famous benefactor of the community. A few would know the stories about him but, for their own comfort and safety, chose to see him as he wished to be seen today: a fond uncle, a busy man, who'd taken time out of his hectic schedule to support his sister, who, let's face it, had her problems, poor soul.

When Liam's turn came to offer his condolences, he leaned in. 'So sorry, Aunty Jackie,' he said, and kissed her cheek. As he moved on, her eyes followed him, both wary and wistful, and May thought Jackie was having a *perhaps* moment of her own. Perhaps if her family had been different Holly and her cousin would have formed a lifelong friendship, a support-ive bond that would've seen them comforting each other at Jackie's own funeral.

May hung back until she was last in the line. When she drew level with Michael McNally she held out her hand.

'Sergeant Mackay,' he said smoothly. 'Thank you for coming.'

'My condolences, sir,' she replied, just as evenly, but her expression sent a different message. *Not here, not now, but I will get you.* Michael McNally might have a gang, but he was just a ned in cashmere, and her gang was bigger and better. That was the message she wanted him to read in her eyes.

'Jackie, love.' May put her hand under the woman's elbow and attempted to draw her outside, but McNally was faster, manoeuvring himself between them and swiftly taking his sister's arm.

'If you'll excuse us, Sergeant.'

The two journalists were waiting outside, their expectant eyes on Michael McNally.

Ian stepped forward and took hold of Jackie's free arm so she was suspended like a fairground prize between two equally adamant competitors.

'You don't have to speak to them,' Ian said, pleading.

But in a blood-fuelled tug-of-war there was only going to be one winner.

Michael McNally faced down his opponent, and when Jackie didn't object he swept his sister out through the doorway into the harsh winter sun.

May turned to Ian and raised her eyebrows. 'That's a bit of a turn-up,' she said, keeping her tone neutral, giving him a moment to salvage his pride. She was pretty sure neither he nor Jackie had expected her estranged brother and his lieutenants to turn up.

Ian's knuckles were white as he clasped his shaking hands together.

'Yes,' he said, with artificial brightness.

May saw anger, mixed with fear. As a cop he'd have learned to hide his emotions in the face of the unexpected, but they were bursting through now.

'Don't worry,' May said. 'As soon as he's got his headlines, he'll be gone.'

The flush in Ian's cheeks said that couldn't be quick enough.

Ten minutes later, it turned out May was almost right.

Michael McNally whispered something into his sister's ear, then before getting into his car, he made a show of pressing the flesh of the locals once more. Jackie stood, her face a mask.

Dimple had taken up a position reminiscent of a guard dog. Everywhere Liam and his two pals went, they found the BTP detective had them under tight surveillance. Liam, handsome and tall, curled his lip at Dimple. But all three men were continually shooting looks at Michael McNally as he moved through the small crowd, aware any displeasure would be brutal and painful.

May put her hand under Jackie's elbow and felt her shaking. Ian was there but May told him to thank the guests, a move he recognised as the first step to re-establishing his position as Jackie's official escort.

May took a tissue from her handbag. Jackie rubbed her eyes so hard that May was forced to grab her hand to stop her injuring herself. 'Just take a deep breath,' she said quietly.

'Folk are looking, aren't they?'

'They'll expect you to be upset. No one is judging you, Jackie,' May said.

Most of the mourners would have no idea of the bone-deep terror that Michael McNally inspired in his little sister.

'It's good that all Holly's friends are here,' she went on, in an attempt to distract her.

'Aye,' Jackie said. 'It's a pity it's not her wedding. She'd have loved to see everyone.'

The thought struck deep at May's own pain, and she found she couldn't speak, so she squeezed Jackie's hand as the rain began to fall.

CHAPTER 31

Ever since May had left the crematorium, she'd been replaying Michael McNally turning up a dozen different ways. Had
he been pre-empting any bad publicity that might spring from
his association with Scott Galbraith by portraying himself as
a bereaved uncle and brother, rather than a champion of the
culprit? The presence of the journalists seemed to indicate
that. May had heard he was thinking of politics, maybe
standing for the Scottish Parliament. Plenty of other crooks
at Holyrood: why not? But it was the way he'd reasserted his
control of Jackie that she'd found most unsettling. And just
what had he whispered in her ear as he'd said goodbye?

May threw down her pen and stretched her arms up
above her head as she eased out the tension in her shoulders.
Between the vertical blinds, pewter slices of sky and scrub-
land were once more dimming, even though it was barely
2 p.m. The control log was open on her computer desktop, a
steady stream of callouts being added to her team's caseload,
which only ever seemed to get bigger. At moments like this,
Australia looked like a very good idea.

May's call sign crackled on her Airwave and she picked it
up from the desk and told the control room to go ahead.

'Gentleman called us earlier about a possible body in a

warehouse by the Clyde,' the dispatcher said. 'Responders have confirmed it's human. Looks like a suicide. Forensics and CID are on their way.'

'Okey-doke. Give me the address.' May took out her Pronto.

A company name, just off the Glasgow Road in Rutherglen, appeared on the screen.

'Thanks, control. Let me know if there's updates.'

When May arrived, PCs Lauren Paterson and Toni McAleer had secured the scene. They'd taken contact details and a first account from the dog walker, then sent the old man home. He'd let his spaniel off the lead, and when it'd run inside the building he'd followed, worried it'd get injured. Toni and Lauren had checked and found a white male, noose around his neck, hanging from the central beam.

'Okay' May replied. 'Show me.'

The long single-storey building stood alone on the former industrial estate and looked like it had been abandoned for years. The pebbledash render had come away in chunks. Lauren held open a side door which had been forced some time ago, the wood warped and peeling, and they all squeezed through. Those sections of roof that did remain were filthy, and the thin and dusty light filtering through barely troubled the cavernous interiors. Glass crunched beneath their boots like gravel on a beach, edging the greasy pools of rainwater on the pitted concrete floor. The place smelled of damp earth with a strong ammonia overtone of bird shit, probably from pigeons, or possibly gulls due to the proximity of the Clyde.

Toni switched on her torch and small shadows flitted away across the uneven floor and disappeared into the walls. Rats. May tried not to think about them.

The body hung like a grotesque fruit from the steel rafter. May took in the height, hair colour and clothing. Dark jeans, expensive trainers and sweatshirt. She couldn't tell from his distorted face what his age might be, but she thought at the younger end of the scale.

There was the sound of vehicles pulling up outside.

May and the two female officers went back through the door in time to see the CSI stepping into her white suit. In a parked car, two CID guys were taking an interest in their phones. May recognised them both. The tall, skinny one with the thinning hair was DC Alex Watson, the shorter, round-faced individual was DC Kenny Harvey. Despite the fact they'd worked out of the same office for two years, before May's transfer to Cathcart, they both gave her no more than a perfunctory nod.

'Got an ID for the body?' Watson said through the car's open window, barely glancing up from his phone.

'Got a proper hello for your old sergeant, Alex? Or are all uniforms the same to you?'

He looked up with a start. 'Sorry, Sarge. Didn't recognise you in the dark,' he said weakly.

DC Kenny Harvey gave her a quick once-over, followed by a grudging acknowledgement. 'Sarge.'

'The scene is secured.' She clapped her gloved hands together. 'No obvious ID. He's all yours.'

She walked past them and introduced herself to the CSI,

a young woman called Catriona, who had an educated Edinburgh accent and the lean physique of someone who spent
their weekends up mountains.

'You're going to need lights,' May told Catriona. 'And a
ladder. Door's at the side. Watch out for the fox shit.'

Both male officers appeared reluctant to view the scene,
remaining in their vehicle until the four women stared at
them pointedly. Eventually, the men picked their way across
the broken concrete, levered open the door, and disappeared
inside. Moments later May heard them swearing. She hoped
whatever substance or creature they'd encountered was truly
unpleasant.

May turned back to the forensic officer.

Catriona raised an eyebrow. 'Shall we give the lads a few
minutes in there?'

'Oh, aye. I think so,' May agreed.

An hour later, the scene had been photographed and prelim-
inary recording had been completed, but no further forensic
vehicles had turned up. The two CID officers had retreated
to their car.

When Catriona finished her phone call, her face was grim.
'Short of staff. Could be a while.'

It was already getting dark and May wasn't keen on
leaving the body in situ overnight or tying up officers to
guard the scene until the morning.

'I mean, we could wait,' Catriona continued. 'But if you
lot are up for it . . .'

May looked at Lauren and Toni, both of whom she knew

were forensically trained. They seemed to grasp her meaning, and while neither appeared enthusiastic, they didn't outright refuse.

'Better get suited up,' Lauren said, unzipping her utility vest.

It was a uniform constable's lot to deal with anything from catching sheep to detaining serial killers, all with professional detachment. In her younger days, May had once been detailed to recover body parts in the aftermath of a gas explosion. The trick had been not to think too hard about what you were seeing and to get the job done as quickly as possible.

'Right, c'mon then, ladies,' she said.

May knew there was no point in asking the CID officers for help. They'd be telling her why it was outside their job description until the sun came up.

Catriona checked the pockets for ID and shook her head. The body was loosely bagged while it was still attached to the beam to preserve evidence. Then the rope was cut and the corpse was brought carefully down by Catriona with help from May, Toni and Lauren, and was laid on a flexible stretcher.

'I just want to have another wee look,' Catriona said. 'Can you help me turn him on his side?' The head moved unnaturally above the still-intact noose. Toni held the torch as Catriona felt the scalp with gloved fingers. 'Thanks. You can roll him back.'

There was no way to get a trolley across the floor, so each of the women gripped the hand loops at the corners of the stretcher and carried the body out to the waiting fiscal's van, which had just pulled up to collect it and take it to the mortuary for the postmortem.

The two CID officers were still sitting in their vehicle.

Toni and Lauren pulled off their forensic suits and went back to their squad car to update control. The rain started again. Catriona sat beneath the raised tailgate of the forensics wagon and beckoned May to join her as they took off their overshoes.

'It's not suicide, just made to look that way,' she said.

May stared at her, curious. 'How d'you know?'

'He's got a compressed fracture to the back of his skull that probably rendered him unconscious, before someone strung him up,' Catriona said. 'They did a convincing job. The pathologist will tell you more.'

May couldn't help but feel a grim satisfaction that the CID officers were about to get their just deserts, since this was now a potential murder inquiry and they'd be here for hours. But since this was still her patch, there'd be requests for uniform resources to not just guard the scene but do house-to-house. Marky the Meerkat would have the final say, but the bulk of the admin would come her way.

'Time of death?' May said, unzipping her suit.

'Last night sometime. Can't be more accurate. The cold would've delayed the onset of rigor.'

'But whoever did this was forensically aware, right?'

'Yeah,' Catriona replied with a wry smile. 'But everybody is forensically aware now. It's an arms race against these guys. We work out another way of catching them; they work out another way of avoiding being caught.'

'How long will an ID take?' May could already feel herself slipping back into her old investigative ways, but this time her job would mostly be the grunt work. The thought sickened her. Once more she heard the siren call of a return to CID, loud and persuasive, drowning out the faint trill of Australian sun, and with it, Tam's hopes of a fresh start.

Catriona stood up to begin wriggling out of her forensic suit. 'There's minimal decomposition and soft tissue damage to the hands. Should get fingerprints and DNA no problem. Of course we'll get a clearer snap when the rope comes off, but the tattoo on his neck might make an ID quicker.'

'What tattoo?' May said, aware she'd jumped to her feet, startling her colleague. A high-speed jigsaw of detail was assembling in her mind. Height, build, hair colour, clothing. 'Wait!' she called out to the driver of the mortuary van who was closing the back door. 'Catriona, can you show me?' Her heart was thumping, a nerve-shredding mixture of anticipation and dread flooding her system. She could wait for the forensic photographs, but she had a sudden conviction it wouldn't be necessary to establish their victim's identity.

Catriona shrugged, pulling her suit back up over her shoulders and taking a fresh pair of gloves from a box.

They crossed to the open van door and slipped on their hoods and masks. Catriona signalled to the attendants to slide the metal casket out on its rollers and open its top. Then she moved forward, handed May her torch, and unzipped the body bag.

'Have a look,' she said.

May shone the torch as Catriona repositioned the head and

pulled the noose away from where it had bitten into the puffy flesh. Try not to think too much about what you're seeing and get the job over as quickly as possible, May recited, as proximity undermined her mask, and the smell crept into her mouth and nose. She forced her eyes away from the grotesquely swollen and unrevealing face, lower to the neck, for as long as she needed to be sure.

'Thanks, Catriona,' she said, stepping back, pulling down her mask and taking a deep gulp of the damp evening air.

'You know who he is?'

May leaned forward for a moment, her hands on her knees, then stared up at Catriona crouched on the edge of the van, looking equally at home there as she would on a mountain ledge. A dizzying sensation gripped May as if she too had just scaled a mountain, one consisting of all the implications of what she'd just seen.

She nodded. 'Our victim is called Scott Galbraith.'

CHAPTER 32

Curtains of rain swept across the empty warehouse yard. May walked towards the CID car which sat in a corner of darkness, engine running and windows misted up.

It was only natural she should feel a surge of relief that Scott Galbraith was gone. Violence had been doled out to him, the way he'd used it on others. He wouldn't be around now to threaten Jackie and Ian, to peddle drugs and misery to schoolkids, to move on to abusing and perhaps killing other Hollys. But as the elation at identifying their victim evaporated, guilt seeped in. In her desire to pressure Galbraith into plea-bargaining over his involvement in Holly's death, had she goaded Michael McNally into dispensing his own justice? As soon as the thought formed she batted it away. She'd offered Galbraith a lifeline. He'd made his own choices. And there was no way in heaven or on earth that she should feel responsible for his death.

'Not suicide?' Watson said out of the rolled-down driver's window as May turned up her collar against the rain. She gave them a rundown of Galbraith's criminal record and current suspected interest in the narcotics business. She was about to share her conviction that Michael McNally was behind the killing, but the memory of her former colleagues' reactions to her previous accusations over Andy Wilson's death stopped her.

'Okay. So, Galbraith crossed someone in the gang world. A hitman job.'

'We'd all like to lock up a hitman,' Harvey said, leaning over from the passenger seat. 'Wouldn't we?'

May thought of Davey the Dooker, a caped crusader slinging a magnet into rivers and canals, hauling up potential murder weapons and hoping for fame. Yeah, everyone wanted to lock up a hitman, and Davey probably had more chance than either of these muppets.

'It's probably a gang turf war,' Watson said.

'Tit-for-tat,' Harvey agreed. 'Had it coming.'

'Had it coming,' Watson echoed, then turned to regard May, who stood with the rain trickling down her collar and a look of undisguised contempt on her face. 'Surprised you're bothered about this guy. Heard you had him arrested over some lassie's case with the train cops. Hey, have you got an alibi?' he joked, and they both snorted with laughter.

May turned on her heel and headed back to where Toni and Lauren were checking the crime scene tape was secure and were preparing to stay until they were relieved by another crew later. Officers would need to remain all night, guarding the scene until a second forensic team arrived in the morning to do a sweep for anything left by the killer or killers.

May gave them the news that it was Scott Galbraith they'd found hanging, and the CID's immediate pigeonholing of it as a gangland killing.

'Jeezo, what a couple of jokers,' Toni said, mirroring the

look of disgust on her sergeant's face. 'Those two bandits would last five minutes in response.'

'Aye.' Lauren nodded, chewing on an energy bar. 'If we weren't here, any southside posse worth their salt would've jacked their car and had the wheels away while they were sitting in it.' Then her face turned serious. 'D'you think things are warming up to a turf war, Sarge?'

'It's possible,' May admitted. 'But I'd have expected an uptick in dealer-level aggro – stabbings, guys getting jumped for their stash, burning cars – before a hit like this, if it is a hit.'

'Whoever it was they were fit,' Toni said. 'Took four of us to get him down and we're all handy lassies. And I can't see a player like Scott Galbraith walking in there alone if he was outnumbered.'

'Be daft to walk in there at all if it was with someone he didn't know,' Lauren countered.

'Okay, so he came in here with someone he did know, for gear or a cash handover, *and* it was someone who he thought he could take, even if they pulled out a chib and went on the radge,' Toni said.

'Someone he thought he could turn his back on,' May agreed, thinking of the skull fracture. 'One person could do it, with planning. Whack him unconscious. Get the noose on. Throw the rope over the beam and pull him up.'

'So who?' Lauren said, watching her sergeant carefully.

'What about that mate of his, Big Malky?' Toni said.

'Possible,' May said. He certainly fit the bill, but he hadn't been seen in the area since May had visited Galbraith's flat. Officers in Inverness, where Big Malky had family connections, thought he was around the town, but no one had succeeded in catching him.

She told them about Michael McNally turning up at the funeral. Their eyes widened.

'You think it was one of his crew?' Toni said. 'Avenging Holly Campbell's murder?'

Was this what Michael McNally had whispered into Jackie's ear at the funeral? That he'd sorted it? The polis were useless. He'd taken care of it as he'd always take care of her, if she'd let him. Her daughter's killer had been dealt with. McNally himself had been heartbroken to learn what Scott Galbraith had done – a lad he'd taken under his wing. Known him since he was wee, and this is how he'd paid him back. Jackie had natural justice for Holly's death, which was always preferable to the watered-down legal kind. Galbraith would've got a cushy cell and been out in ten years while he was still a young man. And this was McNally sending a warning to those who disrespected him. He'd pay them back in kind. Galbraith had made his niece's death look like suicide so that's what McNally had done to him.

'Michael McNally would be top of my list,' May said. But proving it, she thought, was another matter.

CHAPTER 33

Before she'd left the warehouse crime scene May had phoned Dimple, who'd taken the news of her chief suspect's death with a quiet thoughtfulness and agreed to talk again the following day when the scene had been fully processed.

'You don't think we did this?' Dimple had said quietly, echoing May's own first reaction.

'Absolutely not,' May had replied, and had left it there.

May had also called Jackie so she wouldn't get the news of Galbraith's death online or from the TV. She'd seemed stunned, and May wondered how far-fetched her own idea that Michael McNally had informed his sister at the funeral was. Surely Jackie would have said something? But the surprise arrival of her brother had already put her in survival mode: do and say nothing to provoke the aggressor, even when you thought he'd gone, cos he'd always get you.

When Ian took the phone, May reassured him that the BTP investigation would continue. She'd make sure there'd be a full inquiry with reviews of all the CCTV and any further witnesses who came forward. She wanted to make sure that every question they might have about Holly's death would be answered.

'It's okay for you to stop, May,' Ian said. 'It's enough for

Jackie that he's gone, and she can be sure she'll no' walk into him in the street.'

He might think that now, in the flood of relief that natural justice, if not legal justice, had caught up with their daughter's killer. But May knew from her own experience that the grieving process was a long and twisting path with many hidden hazards. An apparently trivial question could blossom into a doubt that spawned further uncertainty, until all you thought you knew was no more than ashes at your feet and you were caught in a circle of inescapable grief.

May heard a sound at the other end of the phone and realised Ian was sobbing.

'I'll pop round tomorrow,' she said gently. 'We can talk about anything you need to then.'

The next day, May had a late shift but was up early. Tam had booked a corresponding evening shift with the charity, which they were always grateful to accommodate. He'd made breakfast and they sat in the sunny kitchen chatting and reading the papers until she caught Tam smiling at her.

'What?' she said.

'Can I no' smile at my bonnie lassie?' he said.

May narrowed her eyes playfully. 'You want to go back to bed . . . again?'

It was already close to eleven o'clock and neither of them had been in a hurry to get dressed that morning.

He took a moment to chew his croissant, rocking his head from side to side mischievously as if weighing up her offer. 'Well, I wouldn't say no, but . . .'

'Got a better offer this morning, have you?' She folded the newspaper she was reading and batted him with it across the table, before getting up to make more coffee.

He caught her around the waist as she passed, pulling her onto his lap.

'Come 'ere, you,' he said, then kissed her. 'It's just I've got a rehearsal at lunchtime. Maybe you could pop in for a bit. Everyone in the band would love to see you.'

May felt a pang of guilt. 'I was thinking of going over to see Jackie McNally, before I start at two.'

A two-to-midnight shift wasn't always an easy option and she knew she wouldn't have time later. They had a mid-week match at Ibrox, and depending on the score there'd be either jubilant or belligerent football fans to deal with afterwards. Guys rolling in the gutter, stripped off, fighting their best mates. May and her team would be the big broom expected to sweep the streets clean and call them all *sir* in the process.

She knew Tam was disappointed, though he was doing his best to hide it.

'I miss you, May,' he said, his warm eyes serious. 'Your prime suspect is dead. It's CID's business. Can you not let it go now?'

She didn't trust CID to bring in the true culprit in Galbraith's death but was realistic about her power to alter their course. However, sooner or later, Michael McNally would stumble, and she'd be there to make sure he went down.

'You're the second person to tell me to let it go in twenty-four hours,' she said, stroking his hair back from his forehead. 'Holly's stepfather said the same thing.'

'Aye, well, maybe you should listen.' He hadn't stopped caressing her back, but there was an edge to his voice. 'You need a break.' Sensing her posture stiffen, he added, 'And this isnae about Australia. It's about you not driving yourself into the ground. We need to be there for each other now. D'you see what I'm saying, darlin'?'

Guilt of a different shade to that which she'd briefly experienced in the warehouse last night crooked a finger at her. Tam was right, she knew that she was neglecting him, neglecting her own mental health in pursuit of a case which was, to all intents and purposes, resolved.

'Every day, when you go out the door,' he said quietly, 'I think that it could be the last time I'll ever see you. Every time I get a phone call from a strange number I think that you've been hurt or worse.'

'I know,' May said, trying to show she fully appreciated the stress that her job put upon Tam. 'But giving house-room to every risk I might face is counterproductive to my ability to do my job. Keep a cool head, trust your training, and trust that your fellow officers will have your back. That's how you stay safe.'

It's enough for me; it should be enough for you, she wanted to say, because every other way lies madness.

'And have they? Got your back?' Tam challenged.

CID didn't. Marky the Meerkat would throw her to the wolves without a second thought, if it came to it.

'Well, you can't give in to those wankers,' she said quietly, getting up from his lap.

'It's not giving in,' Tam replied. 'It's picking your battles.'

May sighed. 'I know. You're right. I'm sorry I can't be there today. I like your friend Sean the swordsman.' She'd appreciated him all the more for agreeing to take Davey the Dooker's son under his wing. 'And I could listen to his wife, Morag, sing all day. I just need to tie up these loose ends.' She thought of Dimple and her simple take on why she'd pursued Holly's case despite her superior's opposition. 'A moment's kindness can save someone's life,' May said, aware it sounded somehow less wholesome coming from her. 'That's all I'm doing for Jackie.'

But Tam blew out a long breath and nodded. 'Just as long as that kindness extends to yourself, and me.'

'It does,' May said, hugging him. 'I promise.'

CHAPTER 34

Ian's flat in Shawlands was the upper conversion of a two-storey sandstone villa with a square of neat grass at the front. As he let May in she noticed the locks were good, reinforced with metal plates. It confirmed for her that Jackie had been much safer here than in her Govanhill tenement, had Galbraith threatened her in spite of his bail conditions, though she had the sickly sense that they wouldn't stop Michael McNally if he decided to make his way once more into her home and her head.

In the immaculate front room, Jackie sat on a green velvet sofa staring out of the bay window, which filled the room with light. She was composed, smartly dressed, with her hair and make-up done, but her eyes were dull and unfocused, and May thought there was something hollow about her – a Jackie-sized mannequin of the real woman.

'Jackie, love?'

She looked at May a beat too long before she smiled in recognition.

'The doctor's been and given her something,' Ian muttered into May's ear as he passed and took a seat next to Jackie.

'How are you doing?' May said, sitting down opposite.

'It's so much to take in,' Ian answered. 'Isn't it, darlin'?'

Jackie nodded.

'But a relief to know it's over and we can focus on healing,' he continued, with nervous glances at Jackie, as if willing it to be true. 'Isn't that right?'

Jackie looked from Ian to May and smiled. 'Yes,' she said brightly. 'Holly wouldn't want us to be sad. We need to remember her at her best. The special girl she was.'

'We'll be choosing a beautiful memorial stone for her,' Ian said. 'It's important her memory isn't overshadowed by her end.'

May nodded. 'D'you mind if I ask you something, Jackie?'

Jackie blinked at her. 'No, it's fine.'

'How did your brother, Michael, feel about Holly's death? What did he whisper to you at the funeral yesterday?'

Jackie shook her head. 'I cannae talk about it . . .'

'Did Holly and Liam McNally see much of each other as children?' May persisted.

Liam might never have played with his wee cousin. Michael didn't need to have been fond of his niece. Gangs required gladiatorial levels of loyalty. This was about blood; this was about honour. It was about respect, and the particular kind of justice organised crime groups delivered if you failed to maintain that respect.

But Jackie was rocking backwards and forwards, hands clamped to her face. The composed woman of a few minutes ago had vanished. May realised too late that she'd pushed her over the edge.

Ian gathered Jackie in a tight embrace and she burrowed into his chest like a frightened animal.

'I'm so sorry, Ian,' May said, shocked by the speed of Jackie's decline and kicking herself for not predicting it. If the doctor had prescribed her medication then she was more fragile than her outer appearance indicated.

Ian helped Jackie from the room and May heard him hushing her and encouraging her to rest.

As protective as he was, she thought he'd ask her to leave. But when he returned moments later, to his credit and probably due to his long years as a cop himself, he gave May a reassuring nod and held out his hand for her to sit.

'Ian . . .' May began.

'Look, it's fine. I know you're just doing your job. But this is why we're happy to have the case closed. It's making things worse for Jackie and there doesn't seem any point in prolonging it now.' He lowered his voice. 'We're worried, if I'm honest. Jackie thinks the world of you. After Holly, she'd be distraught if anything happened. She knows what her brother's like. And I heard about your colleague, Andy Wilson, and how the investigation didn't take your concerns about McNally seriously. He'll get his comeuppance one day. His sort always do.'

'They only get their comeuppance because someone like me or you makes sure it happens,' May retorted.

'Aye, but you can't do this alone, May.' He spread his hands, palms upwards. 'Look, we're so grateful for all you've done for us, and for Holly. What I'm saying is, it's enough.' He paused. 'I know what happened to your daughter, Isla.'

May swallowed the hard lump in her throat. It was as if her skin had been peeled back.

'None of this can be easy for you.' Ian sat forward, his face earnest. 'But I think I understand why you helped us, and I'm so grateful you did. I think you saved Jackie's life.'

May nodded, not trusting herself to speak.

'For Jackie's sake and your own, let Holly go.'

May forced herself to smile. 'I hope you and Jackie find the strength in each other that my husband, Tam, and I did.'

'She's so special. I'd never dream of letting her go.'

He smiled and May was reassured Jackie was in the best hands.

'I won't tell you it's easy.' She returned his smile. 'Every day is new a battle in some way, big or small. I'm glad you feel I've helped you both.' She got to her feet. 'I'll leave you in peace.'

Ian got to his feet too and, after a moment, stepped forward and gave her a brief hug.

'Thank you,' he said, his eyes wet with suppressed tears.

'I won't call on Jackie for a while, if you think that's best,' she said.

His initial shrug became a reluctant nod. 'Aye, I think that's best.'

'And I won't send you updates, unless you ask.'

'Updates?' He frowned.

'On the BTP investigation. I'll obviously continue to assist them. I'd like to see it through. After the press scrutiny and your MSP's involvement they'll need to do a thorough job. But I doubt anyone will talk to you and Jackie again, if that's what you want.'

'Of course.' He smiled, reassured. 'Look after yourself, May. And thank you again.'

May went down the steps from the flat and out into the cooling afternoon. The earlier rain had gone, the clouds had thinned. The street with its rows of posh cars and well-tended gardens looked somehow different to how it'd been when she'd arrived. It was probably nothing more than a trick of the light. Although she felt a measure of relief that there'd been some resolution for Jackie, and that she'd done her best, it'd fallen short of what she'd hoped. Contrary by nature, she had to accept that everyone, even her beloved Tam, was telling her the same thing. *Let it go.* They were probably right. But it didn't mean she had to walk away completely.

CHAPTER 35

Thirty minutes into her shift, May was on her way out with Rab the Kebab in tow, when Inspector Mark Ward passed them in the corridor.

'Got your own way in the end then, May,' he said with a wink. 'Another ned off the streets.'

His expression said he'd meant it as a joke, perhaps even a congratulatory one, like the gods were on her side, but with the criminal investigation into Galbraith's death under way it was ill-judged and landed with a thud.

She willed herself not to say something she'd regret. Well, not regret exactly, but pay for later.

'While you're here, sir,' she began, 'any news on filling that vacancy on my team? We're all running ourselves ragged, even without assisting CID on a murder inquiry. My lads and lassies are coming in on days off. I appreciate your overtime budget is capped, but time off in lieu is no good to them if they can't actually take it. This is all shaping up to be a Scottish Police Federation matter. So if you could see your way to actioning that replacement as quick as possible, sir, we'd all appreciate it.'

She turned and strode down the corridor with Rab at her heels.

At the squad car she stopped. 'Can I just point out, PC Kennedy, that that is no way to speak to a senior officer, and I'd advise against it in all but the most extreme circumstances.'

'Except when they're asking for it, Sarge?' Rab said with convincing innocence.

'Aye. Just so,' May replied. Rab was shaping up to be a first-rate constable.

Later that afternoon it was already dark when May followed Rab out of the tenement door in Kingarth Street into a stinging wind. Scaffolding erected for roofing repairs had facilitated an enterprising house-breaker to access the two upper flats via open windows one unseasonally mild afternoon the week before. He'd pocketed cash, bank cards and jewellery before, in a moment of madness, attempting to scale down the scaffolding with a moderately-sized flatscreen TV under his arm, and had lost his grip on the item. The resulting crash had alerted the downstairs neighbours.

May had just reached the driver's side of the squad car when she saw a lad in a baseball cap and dark hoodie at the other end of the block walk up behind an old man, shove him to the ground, and rifle through his pockets.

May pulled her cap on more firmly and began to run.

'Rab, check the victim,' she yelled as his assailant took off and disappeared into Victoria Road.

May rounded the corner after him. It was busy with shoppers.

'Oi. You!' she yelled into the street, hoping that not all of the young males in dark clothing she could see were wanted by the police.

Plenty of heads turned, but only one lad took off on his heels.

Got you, you little bastard.

She remembered the diatribe from the owner of Bella Notte on the youth of today and felt glad this particular lad had spent time online gaming and not in the gym or running around a football field.

He tripped and hit the ground with May half on top of him. He was light-boned and skinny beneath the hoodie and the scarf wrapped around his face. May had a flash of memory, of catching her own son, Rory, in a game before he put on the bulky muscle of adulthood. It was a memory that wouldn't be replicated by similar games with her three grandchildren. But this wasn't a game – not for the victim or for the perpetrator.

When he swore at her she got to her knees and hauled his arms back, keeping her weight on him. 'Listen to me, pal. We'll have none of that.'

She'd just got him cuffed when she felt her phone vibrate inside her utility vest. The control centre and all of her team would be on the Airwave. Tam would call only if it was an emergency. Maybe it's Jackie, she thought suddenly.

'Stop struggling!' she yelled at the lad, leaning one elbow on his back between his shoulder blades and pulling out her phone. It was Tam.

'Hang on a minute, love,' she said, still panting hard.

At that moment, Rab arrived.

May tipped her chin up at Rab. 'Is the gentleman okay?'

'He's fine,' Rab said. 'There was a nurse just coming out of Lidl. I've called an ambo just to check him out.' Then, with one hand he grabbed the struggling captive by the scruff of his hoodie and with the other gripped the handcuffs. 'Calm yourself doon,' he ordered the still-wriggling lad.

'Sorry, darlin'. What is it? What's wrong?'

'The police are here, at the Aspen Trust,' Tam said.

'Are you alright?' She got quickly to her feet, alerted by his tone.

'I'm fine, it's you they're worried about.'

'Me? I'm grand. What's going on?'

May covered the microphone with her hand. Rab was checking the assailant over, asking if he'd any weapons on him. When he said he hadn't, Rab put a gloved hand into his pocket and pulled out an old-fashioned purse, which May thought had probably belonged to the old man's wife. Inside was a roll of notes. May shook her head at the lad, who she reckoned wasn't yet sixteen. They both knew it'd be a slap on the wrist from the sheriff, unless the victim's injuries were serious.

'What's your name?' May asked the boy.

'Fuck off,' came the reply.

'I'll get the car,' Rab said.

Another voice had replaced Tam's on the phone. 'Is that May Mackay?'

'Yes. Who is this, and what's going on?'

'I'm a constable with Hillhead Police Office, Mrs Mackay.'

Something had obviously happened to Tam. She could hear him in the background, incoherent and rambling.

Had he come off his bike? Or had a stroke? Panic set in as May calculated how fast she could blue-light across to the West End.

'Is my husband alright? And it's Sergeant Mackay from Cathcart here.'

There was a pause, then the constable said, 'He's fine. We got a call from a woman who received a Facebook message saying your husband had killed you, that he was contacting her as he couldn't bring himself to call us.'

May took the phone from her ear and stared at the screen. Definitely Tam's number.

'I'm not dead. I'm in the middle of a bloody arrest. Is this a joke?'

She could hear voices, including Tam's, in the background, then the constable came back on.

'I'm sorry, Sergeant Mackay, I think it's a hoax.'

'Who by?'

'Impossible to say. I doubt we'll trace them. We've had a few nuisance messages over the last months. I'm sorry to trouble you and your husband, but you understand we have a duty of care to check it out.'

May's panic had subsided, but not to the point she could see the funny side. She doubted she ever would.

'Might be someone you've previously arrested, so worth double-checking your security arrangements.'

'Right, Constable, thank you. Can I talk to my husband, please?'

They put the lad, who was still refusing to give his name, into the back of the car.

The old man who'd hit the ground had gone off in the ambulance.

'So who did it?' Tam said. There was no doubt it was malicious, and personal.

'I don't know, love. Best forget it. I'll see you later.'

That question preoccupied her all the way home. Someone she'd previously arrested the constable had said, someone who had it in for her. Top of the list was Scott Galbraith. The timeline was tight but he could've posted it before his death. His little joke from beyond the grave. Who else wanted to play cruel tricks?

As she made her way up the tree-lined street to her home, she realised it was more folk than she'd admit to Tam. Someone who'd just got out of prison? Or was still inside, given the rate that phones were smuggled in.

To be on the safe side, she checked the road in case any other jokers were waiting. The lightness she'd felt leaving Jackie and Ian's had been thoroughly banished by someone with a dire sense of humour. As she was getting out, her phone buzzed. Probably Tam checking where she was. But it was Dimple's name that flashed on the screen, and May remembered they'd promised to talk. It was after midnight. What couldn't wait?

'Knew you were on lates,' Dimple said. 'I've got some news. I thought you'd want to know straight away.'

May got back in the car and locked the doors. 'Tell me.'

CHAPTER 36

Earlier in the evening, they'd finished compiling CCTV of Scott Galbraith on the station concourse. He'd been following Holly at a distance, entering the area a minute or so after her.

'I thought I'd check out his story that he didn't have any contact with her,' Dimple said.

'And?' May said impatiently. The temperature in the car was dropping fast, but the ignition remained off to avoid disturbing the neighbours, who might either call the cops at her loitering or give her a lecture in environmental vandalism next time they met on the stairs.

'No evidence Holly and Galbraith met,' Dimple said. 'There's something else.'

May's gut told her she wasn't going to like this.

'I went out this evening and talked to the taxi drivers. Someone remembers him. Wasn't keen dropping off at the Govanhill address in case he got jacked. But the fare paid him in cash. Upfront.'

'There's no doubt?' The cold that was creeping up May's legs had nothing to do with the winter night.

'The spider tattoo,' Dimple confirmed.

'Why didn't the driver come forward before?'

217

'Fortnight in Tenerife,' Dimple replied. 'And this cabbie is one of the good guys. Didn't just pocket the cash, but logged it on his app.'

'Timestamped?'

'Aye. Just as Holly was hit by the train.'

'Fuck.'

'Exactly. You know, if Galbraith had just told us all this he'd have walked free. Can't understand it.'

But May could. 'He'd never have co-operated with us, even if his life depended on it. Turns out it did.'

'You still believe his death was revenge for Holly's?' Dimple's voice quivered. It was clear she still felt some guilt, more now that Galbraith's alibi had come good. 'CID seem to think they'll find a gang connection.'

'Couldn't find their arses with both hands,' May said sourly. 'What hitman is gonna bother stringing him up like a suicide. Bang, bang, thank you and goodnight.' Remembering the two bullet holes in her old colleague DI Andy Wilson's skull, she winced. 'So what's the BTP's line now on Holly Campbell?'

She thought Dimple might say that her inspector was planning a case review in a month, or that a new detective was being assigned, but the young detective sounded surprisingly upbeat.

'Start again in the morning. Talk to Holly's college friends. I'm not sure Mhairi McCormack can tell us any more than what she said in her statement, but there were others in her class.' Dimple hesitated. 'If my inspector squares it with your inspector, can you come with me to her college?'

Mhairi's tall presence shadowing May then disappearing into the crowd came back to her. Mhairi hadn't returned her calls or messages. This could be a chance to resolve the matter.

'Consider it squared,' May said. 'Text me a time. I'll meet you there.'

CHAPTER 37

May saw Dimple waiting on the narrow strip of parking places next to the new City of Glasgow College. The glass-and-white-stone building, with its broad facades and central tower, rose up the hill from Cathedral Street like a cathedral itself, a monument to learning and aspiration, shining against the vivid blue of the winter sky. A steady stream of young people were climbing the broad front steps. Isla should be among them; May felt the thought coming and did nothing to stop it. Her daughter had scorned university, but this might have worked. She should be in there now learning to sew, draw, navigate ships, cut hair, design machines or whatever else she wanted. The world where this was reality passed May in a blink, like the flashed reflection in the windows of the buses on the main street below. You could feel nostalgic for a life you'd never witnessed, May knew, and it wasn't any less painful.

A text came from Ian McDonald. In the light of Dimple uncovering Galbraith's alibi, she'd rethought her promise not to contact the family about the BTP's case. A further press appeal might be required, so it was necessary to keep at least Ian, if not Jackie, in the loop. She'd sent a brief message, apologising but stating that there'd been further developments, stopping short of revealing what exactly. His reply said he hoped he hadn't offended her, repeated their gratitude for her work, and said he'd be happy to meet for a chat whenever she was free. May was grateful. His cop's experience would hopefully prevent misunderstandings and make what was bound to be a torturous experience for Jackie smoother.

'Thanks for coming,' Dimple said as May approached. She was wearing jeans and an open-neck blue shirt under a dark jacket. May was in her black Police Scotland fleece and trousers but had left her utility vest in the back of her car, aware a less Robocop approach was required.

'I think we should interview them as a group,' Dimple said. 'Then maybe while I talk to the tutor, you could see if any approach you individually. They might feel they can say things to you they wouldn't want to say in front of their mates.'

May agreed. It was a good strategy and she was glad to have an opportunity to take Mhairi McCormack aside. Her bolting from the pub only to hang around for hours shadowing May was suspect, and she was convinced the young woman had more to say about Holly's life than she'd let on. Whether she was ready to share that with May was another matter.

'You done a background check on the tutor?' May said. College tutors were not beyond conducting affairs with vulnerable students. For all they knew it could be him on the platform attempting to save his reputation or his job, or both. His headshot on the college website showed a round-faced, bearded and bespectacled man with a cow's lick of dark hair above his forehead that gave him a startled appearance.

'His record was clean,' Dimple confirmed.

'Doesn't mean he's squeaky,' May replied.

But as they entered a spacious and bright conference room, May was immediately disappointed. Mhairi wasn't among the young people gathered there. She recognised Holly's tutor, James Gunn, standing nervously to one side of the group. They introduced themselves. He was shorter than his photograph implied, the cow's lick of dark hair more pronounced.

'I've gathered the tutor group Holly spent her time with,' Gunn said.

They were split evenly – three lads and three lassies – their appearances ranging from the staid to the startling.

'No Mhairi?' May said.

'You've already spoken to her, I believe,' Gunn said with a prim look of censure. May could imagine him in meetings tutting under his breath while making an elaborate show of deference to whomever he thought could best advance his career.

'Oh. I was hoping for another chat,' May replied, unwilling to let it go.

'To be honest, we've not seen much of her lately.'

'Why's that then?' May fixed him with a laser-like stare. If the lassie had done a vanishing act then that really was something they needed to follow up.

'I believe she'd been signed off sick by her doctor. I can't discuss that without her permission,' he said, eyeing May. 'But I believe she took what happened to Holly very hard.'

But not so hard that she'd aid the investigation into her friend's death by returning May's calls. 'Thank you,' she said to a relieved-looking Gunn.

The room was warm and Dimple looped her jacket over the back of a chair and motioned the half-dozen students to gather round in a circle. May sat a little way to one side, observing their body language and reactions. Eyes widened when Dimple began by explaining that the British Transport Police, which was separate from Police Scotland but with much the same powers, was treating Holly Campbell's death as suspicious.

'This is Sergeant Mackay,' Dimple added. 'She's liaising with us and Holly's family to understand what happened. We're not ruling anything out at this stage, but if any of you feel you have something to add you can talk to either of us at any time.'

May smiled at them, recognising a few faces from the photographs on the wall in Holly's bedroom.

Dimple leaned forward, drawing the students into her confidence. Smiles and nods for the lads, active listening and head tilts of approval for the lassies. May watched approvingly as she deployed her earnest charm to get them to open up to someone who wasn't much older than they were.

All the students agreed that Holly was smart. A clever lassie going places. May thought they genuinely meant it, that it wasn't just the eulogising of a departed classmate. Some looked as if they were considering the impact their own death would have on their own families, the extinction of their collective dreams.

Holly was popular but quiet. She went out clubbing occasionally, often with Mhairi and the two were close.

On the night of Holly's death, Mhairi had joined the group in Kitty O'Shea's pub after Holly had left, and they'd all gone on to the Culture Club in Renfield Street afterwards. None of them had been contacted by Holly that evening, and none had messaged her because Mhairi had told them Holly had gone home.

'And did any of you ever meet her ex-partner, Scott Galbraith?' May said evenly. Even though Galbraith had been alibied, he was part of Holly's story, and she needed to know how wide his influence extended.

Most gave wary nods.

'Flash car, nice gear,' a lad with close-cropped hair said.

'But a pure bampot,' cut in a young woman with a purple quiff and multiple piercings. It seemed she'd witnessed an incident at a party between Galbraith and Holly where he'd grabbed her by the throat.

'When was this?'

'Six months back. Just after we all started. It was in the hallway of a pal's place. Heavy raging, so he was. Had his face right in her grill, shouting, *Get the fuck in the car*. Don't think anyone else saw. She went wi' him in the end. I told Holly the next day she should ditch him. He was pure shady.'

'Shady how?' May said, careful to glance down at her notebook and not put the girl under pressure. 'Did he offer you drugs?'

May saw the uneasy looks exchanged by some of the group.

'Did he threaten you if you reported him for dealing?'

There was silence until the young woman, whom May had come to see as the group's spokesperson, leaned back in her chair and folded her arms. 'He was just a bam. We said to Holly he wasnae welcome. I mean, he didnae even go to this college. She said she was sorting it.'

'Did she say how she was sorting it?' Dimple said, with a smile of encouragement.

The young woman shrugged. 'Properly dumping the mad fucker would be a start.'

James Gunn frowned at her – *language!* – but she ignored him.

'But she didn't say what she meant specifically by *sorting it*?' Dimple persisted.

The girl shook her head, and a fleeting look of pain mingled with regret crossed her face.

'It's fine,' Dimple assured her. 'None of you are in any way to blame for what happened to Holly.' She dropped into a broader Glasgow accent. 'I'm a polis, I know these things.' She grinned and was rewarded by flickers of responding smiles. Her face became serious again. 'But if any of you remember anything, any threat Holly spoke of, or an incident where you or she felt uncomfortable, get in touch. We'll leave you our numbers, and thank you for agreeing to see us.'

James Gunn was looking pointedly at his watch.

'I'll be here for a while if anyone has any questions,' May said. 'And finally, good luck in your studies. And please stay on the right side of the law, cos I've trouble opening apps and I don't want you lot taking to cybercrime and showing me up.'

The lads had bolted as soon as the interview was over, but the three lassies were hanging on. May couldn't decide if it was because they had something to say, unanswered questions, or if it was purely a chance to gossip and avoid their classes. Dimple sat in the corner of the room talking in a low and reassuring voice with the tutor, James Gunn.

On the way in, May had spotted a coffee machine in the foyer from a high-street franchise that might just be acceptable in the current caffeine emergency.

When she asked the others, Dimple thanked her and said she'd love one, but Gunn just shook his head.

The first drink had been dispensed when May felt a presence at her elbow.

The young woman with the purple hair stood with her hands in the pockets of her bright green faux-fur jacket, apparently studying the coffee menu.

'You know Holly and Mhairi werenae always pals,' she said. 'I heard them arguing and Mhairi call her a jealous cow.'

'What were they fighting over?' May asked casually.

'Don't know.'

'Did Holly have a relationship with anyone here? Could it have been a lad?'

'Or a lassie.'

'You saying they were in a romantic relationship?'

'Nah, don't think so,' the girl admitted. 'But it would've been fine if they were, wouldn't it?'

May looked at her as if to say, *I've done more courses on diversity and inclusivity than you've had birthdays, lady. Don't try me.*

'What's your name, hen?'

'Madison.'

'Well, Madison, was there a bit of rivalry between them? That what you're saying?'

Madison nodded.

'Did Holly ever tell you she thought someone was following her?'

'We've all got stalkers — ex-boyfriends, never-was boyfriends, just lads in general,' the young woman said with unnerving acceptance.

Had this been Isla's view of relationships? May felt a wave of sadness that this had become part of the normal spectrum of young love.

The second coffee was ready but May didn't pick it up, sensing that the student was in no hurry to leave. The other two girls had gone and the college foyer was almost empty.

'Mhairi *was* with us when Holly died,' Madison began. 'But she also wasn't.'

The lassie was obviously comfortable being the centre of attention, but May didn't think she was stringing things out. No charges had been laid against Galbraith, so no announcement of suspected murder had been made in the media. It was more that Madison was revising established facts in the light of Dimple's announcement that Holly's death was *suspicious*, therefore not necessarily suicide.

'We hadn't got to the club yet, and the bar we were in had

just called last orders. Mhairi said she didnae want another drink and was going out for a vape, but she was gone ages. Didn't catch up with us till the Culture Club. Said she got chatting to this guy. She was a bit high. I thought she'd gone up the alley for a shag or mibbaes done a couple of lines, or both.'

May raised her eyebrows. Did Mhairi's edginess in the pub interview stem from a different route? Guilty self-reproach that she'd missed something in her friend's demeanour was beginning to look like a different type of guilt altogether. Was it drug use that had first drawn Mhairi and Holly together, before Holly had got clean? And how did that affect the relationship? If Mhairi had criticised Holly's abstinence then that could've promoted the *jealous cow* comment, or was it something entirely different?

'How long was Mhairi gone?'

'About eleven till mibbaes twenty past.'

'You sure?' May was mind-mapping the pub, Central station and the club. It would've been possible for Mhairi to visit all three in that timeframe. There was no evidence on Holly's phone that she'd been in contact with Mhairi after she'd left, but they'd been on regular nights out and Mhairi could've known which train Holly usually caught. All she had to do was lie in wait near the platform. But why?

'I'm sure about the time,' said Madison. 'You look at me and I see what you're thinking, but I don't drink, I don't do drugs. My ma died a jakey. I fuckin' hate drugs. I know Holly was an addict and she got clean. I admire her for it, but I dinnae believe she was an angel.'

'What d'you mean?' May said, studying Madison's defiant expression.

'I think Holly could manipulate folk when she wanted. If it wasnae suicide or an accident, then mibbaes it was someone she pissed off.'

'Who?' May said, but Madison just pressed her lips together and shook her head.

'Okay, thank you.' She took a card from her pocket. 'Will you call me if you think of anything else?'

Madison nodded, shoved the card in her pocket, and walked away.

May and Dimple paused outside the college, soaking up some vitamin D before the sun disappeared behind the city centre's tall buildings once more.

'What did the tutor say?' May asked.

'Said Holly had been an excellent student, focused on her studies and a career that would get her out of Govanhill. They'd talked about university as a next step, but an IT company up in Dundee had offered to take her on as a trainee, and she planned to start there when the year finished in June.'

A clever lassie, going places had been Jackie's assessment of her daughter and it was proving to have been, quite literally, the truth.

'I think,' May began, 'that Galbraith was using Holly as a kind of Trojan horse to get drugs into this college. Look at the size of this place. There's more than thirty-two thousand students here. It's new and maybe not established territory for another organised crime group. He could go to parties with her, recruit dealers. That lad with the cropped head believed Galbraith was living it large with his nice car and clothes.'

The most dangerous time for a woman was when she left a coercive and abusive relationship. But often what prompted her flight was not concern for herself, but concern for others – her children, her friends.

'I think she didn't want him getting his hooks into her mates,' May said. 'Galbraith had an apprenticeship and attended Clyde College at Langside one day a week. We've been onto the campus with a drugs dog as part of our regular sweeps, and our furry friend was alerting left, right and centre. Can't link it to Galbraith, but in light of him hanging out here I'd say that was his business plan.'

Dimple nodded. 'Might have put Holly in the firing line. She'd be a soft target.'

'Other gangs, you mean? Easy way to get to him?' May considered this. 'Possible. But officially the relationship was over. And before you say it, I still don't think that points to why he ended up dead.'

'There's something else,' May said, and recounted what Madison had told her about Mhairi, and how she was sure Holly's friend had tracked her the night they'd first met. 'She was wearing a long black coat, black jeans and boots, and she's got distinctive dark curly hair.' The more she thought about it, the more it seemed possible. 'It'd be easy enough to hide that under a beanie. She's the right height and build. Because hair aside, that lassie is the perfect fit for our mystery assailant who pushed Holly in front of the train.'

CHAPTER 38

It had only taken a few minutes of consideration by Dimple to agree it was possible the enhanced train CCTV could be a match with Mhairi, but they'd need more than that to pull her in. Dimple would review what they had both from the statements and the station footage and let her know.

May had just returned to Cathcart Police Office when a priority call came in. Report of a shotgun being discharged into a four-in-the-block flat off Allison Street, home to a woman named Shannon Hope and her three-year-old son, Jack. While units were racing to the scene, May double-checked the address and occupant on the system and found no links to any previous callouts.

May arrived to find PCs Ross Reid and Mo Pannu had cordoned off the cul-de-sac and had evacuated the neighbours to a nearby community centre.

'What happened?' May said to Mo from the driver's seat of the squad car when she drew level with the exclusion tape. The main window of the top left flat was shattered, ragged curtains and a blind hanging from the frame.

'Couple of guys pulled up in a van, climbed on top, and let go with both barrels. Balaclavas, the works.'

'She and the wee lad okay?'

'Aye, they're no' injured, just shaken up. They've gone into one of the neighbour's up the street while we crime-scene guys get busy.' Mo pointed to a ground-floor flat where a woman in her sixties stood on the step with her arms folded watching them. 'Toni and Lauren are with her.'

'Thanks, Mo. I'll go over there now. Buzz me when forensics are finished.'

Her neighbour's front room was crowded with too-large furniture and a riot of swagged curtains and oversized cushions in peaches and browns. Shannon Hope was petite and in her early twenties. She ran a mobile hairdressing business, a fact efficiently advertised by a waterfall of silvery-blonde hair that fell almost to her waist. She sat on a plump sofa with her legs curled under her and the boy, Jack, next to her. He had her fair colouring and Lauren was expertly distracting him with a game that involved dinosaurs climbing up a mountainous cushion and sliding them into a ravine beyond. Toni had her Pronto out taking a first account.

May introduced herself and then beckoned Toni into the kitchen where Shannon's neighbour had indicated they could help themselves to a pot of tea already brewed.

'She's saying she can't think why anyone would do this and that it must be mistaken identity,' Toni said.

'What d'you think?'

Toni hooked her thumbs into the top of her tactical vest as she considered. 'Lassie's local but not known to us. Clean record, no drugs. These guys weren't messing about.'

'Could this have a domestic element? Vengeful ex-boyfriend?'

'Have to be pretty vengeful to shoot into a room with a mum and toddler,' Toni replied doubtfully, but her tone stopped just short of saying it was impossible. 'The kid's father is out of the picture. I asked if he needed to be informed, but it was a holiday hook-up in Ibiza, she said. Bonnie wee lad, though. Not the worst souvenir you could bring home.'

Through the half-open kitchen door, May saw the child climb into his mother's lap. Shannon hugged him, swinging the child from side to side until he laughed.

'She got family nearby?'

'Says not. She wants to go back to the flat as soon as she can.'

May raised her eyebrows. Most folk would be offski after an experience like that. But then if it really was mistaken identity, Shannon would be thinking there was little chance of a return visit, and perhaps that flat was the nicest place she'd ever lived.

'It's a rental,' Toni continued. 'We're running a check on previous occupants in case they were a more likely target, but quite a few of these flats have been empty the past year while the refurbishment scheme's been ongoing, and I remember there was an issue with squatters.'

The neighbour had come back into the kitchen with mugs she'd collected from the front room.

'This kind lady is Mrs Kennedy,' Toni said.

'You know who used to live there, Mrs Kennedy?' May asked her.

The woman had close-cropped steel-grey hair and intense brown eyes. 'I can't mind who was there last. It was council;

this is a bought house,' she said, as if to distance herself from the kind of transient folk who'd occupied such a place.

'Been here long?'

'Thirty-five years.'

'You must be one of the street's longest residents,' May said, and saw a touch of pride in the woman's face that her achievement had been recognised. 'Been any trouble in the cul-de-sac recently?' There was nothing in the log, but May thought she was exactly the sort of woman who'd know everything that went on.

'Not that I can recall,' she said formally, drawing together her cardigan and folding her arms in what May recognised as a gesture of self-defence. If she did know anything about the previous occupants it was clear she wasn't keen on revealing it to the police.

May lowered her voice. 'Anything you tell us will remain anonymous.'

Mrs Kennedy gave May a sceptical look. 'I'll not see Shannon and the boy stood out in the cold, but with her sitting in my front room, how anonymous d'you think I'd be?'

May knew further reassurances were pointless. She nodded and Mrs Kennedy refilled the cups and left the kitchen.

'Have the flat's owners been contacted?' May said to Toni. Whoever it was would need to call their insurers.

Toni nodded. 'The agency is Southside Lettings, but the actual owners are the sister company Southside Holdings, part of the McNally Group. The two top flats are theirs.'

The McNallys again. Was there a pie in this city that they didn't have their fingers in?

'Alright, Toni. Get the nearest CCTV and see if you can trace the van. We've guys down the community centre doing the rounds of the neighbours. And let's see what forensics say, though *it was definitely a shotgun and it made a big hole* might be all they can give us.'

CHAPTER 39

May went to say goodbye to Shannon Hope, but the young woman said she wanted to walk up and see what was happening at the flat, and find out when she might get back in.

'I can't let you past the cordon tape,' May warned.

'That's okay. Jack's gonna stay here for a bit. She'll give him his tea.'

Mrs Kennedy and Jack were on their knees in front of the open freezer door choosing the appropriately shaped chicken nuggets – dinosaurs or dippers – and May thought he was probably a regular visitor when his mother was working.

'Okay, that's fine,' May said. She was pretty sure Shannon knew more than she was saying and, given she had no previous, a vengeful ex-partner was May's number-one concern. She'd met plenty of victims who couldn't or wouldn't see themselves as such.

Walking Shannon up to the tape before it was completely dark might also make her change her mind. The windows would be boarded up for a day or two, the broken glass swept up, the units replaced. If there were no substantial repairs required, Shannon and Jack might be back in a week. The damage to their peace of mind might take longer, no matter what the young woman said.

Shannon's head barely reached May's shoulder and she had to shorten her stride to allow the young woman to keep up.

'I saw you on the street outside Jackie McNally's, didn't I?' Shannon said as they crossed the road. 'Her daughter got killed with a train. I was going over to visit her. I was pals at school wi' Holly.'

May slowed further. 'Were you still in touch?'

'No' really.'

No' really – what did that mean? She wanted details. Times and places. But she sensed that Shannon had engineered this chat in much the same way as the student Madison had approached her at the coffee machine, and if May made any sudden moves or demands she'd spook her. Instead, she waited and was rewarded for her patience.

'We had the same birthday,' Shannon continued. 'People used to say we looked alike and could've been twins. This isnae my natural colour, by the way.' She indicated her blonde tresses with an ironic flip of her fingers.

There was some likeness. May knew Holly only through photos, CCTV, and other folk's memories. Shannon was a more robust version of the girl whose life had ended on the tracks, but there was something in the eyes. *It was her birthday just by. She had money to spend*: Jackie's words about Holly came back to her.

'You'll have just had your birthday then? What did you do?'

May was rewarded with a gratifying look from Shannon. If she could gain her trust then maybe she'd have some background on Holly. Neither Holly's friends at college nor her old dealer Gemma had shed much light on what might have been going on in Holly's head. What did a girl from Govanhill want out of life when she grew up? To be rich and famous? Travel the world? Or maybe just to be safe. Holly had a dysfunctional family. Shannon, it appeared, had none at all. Perhaps their playground chat had amounted to more than clothes and boys.

'For ma birthday me and Jack went to Edinburgh Zoo,' Shannon said brightly.

'Cold?'

'Freezing.'

'Favourite animal?'

'Well, Jack was disappointed there was no dinosaurs, obviously, but he loved the chimps.'

'What about you?'

'I liked the tank with all the fancy fish and all of them parrots. Imagine being able to swim in a sea like that.' She gestured to the grey-harled flats, the patchy grass and bare hedges, fourteen hours of darkness already closing in. 'And have all that colour just flying around you. It'd be amazin', wouldn't it?'

'Sounds like it was more a party for Jack, no' for you.' May smiled, remembering similar sacrificial outings herself.

Shannon looked thoughtful. 'No, it was for both of us.'

May smiled at her again, to show she understood. Shannon was reclaiming her own childhood through her son and was laying down good memories for them both.

'Holly was going shopping with her birthday money,' May

said casually, bringing the conversation back to her primary objective.

'Aye, she had good taste,' Shannon said.

'Beautiful hair,' May said as the thought struck her. 'Did you do it for her?'

'Sometimes. No' for a while. She was at college. Different world.'

'You didn't go to City college then?' May was recalling the hairdressing courses she'd seen listed on the website.

'Did go one day a week when I had an apprenticeship, but that was yonks ago. It's how I know it's a different world.' In the half-light, May thought she saw some shadow of regret pass across the young woman's face, but then she brightened. 'But I got ma own business. Look at me now.'

'Aye, you've done well,' May said, because Shannon seemed to expect it and, after all, she had – her own place and she was supporting her son. 'We'll get you somewhere to stay for a week or so.'

'No, it's fine. I've rung the letting place and they say I can stay in the next-door flat. Only part furnished, mind, but it'll be fine. Can I get things out of my own flat?'

'Yes, we'll find someone to take you in,' May replied, admiring Shannon's organisational abilities in the face of the shock she'd just had, and also relieved that a job had been crossed off her team's list. With so many officers tied up on this she wanted the scene processed and the neighbours back in their homes ASAP.

'And all my business stuff is in there so I need to be around when the workmen come,' Shannon added.

May was about to reassure her she could probably trust the window fitter not to nick hair products, but then she remembered what her own hairdresser had said about the cost of hair extensions – a hundred quid a throw, and likely a substantial investment for someone like Shannon.

'Hope they don't faint fae the smell of chemicals,' Shannon joked. 'Lads don't know what we put ourselves through, do they?'

'Don't worry, we'll make sure you're back in your home as quickly as we can.'

Just before they reached the tape, May put her hand on Shannon's arm, drawing her to a stop. Ahead, P C Mo Pannu pointed to the flat and gave his sergeant a thumbs-up to indicate forensics were nearly done.

'Listen,' May began. 'Did Jackie McNally tell you why I was at her flat?'

Shannon looked around her for a moment. The sweeping blue lights from the emergency vehicles had been switched off. The low blocks of grey flats were empty and hushed and their windows were dark, waiting for the residents to return and the daily clock of their lives to begin ticking once more.

'Jackie said that it wasn't suicide,' Shannon said eventually. 'She said Scott Galbraith killed Holly and you were gonna help her get him.'

'You knew Galbraith?'

'Course,' said Shannon. 'Knew him from school same as Holly. Galbraith's dead now.' She shrugged. 'So I guess that's that.'

'The British Transport Police's case is still ongoing,' May said carefully. 'Did Holly tell you anything you think I should know?'

'Would it make a difference?'

May frowned. 'What d'you mean, Shannon?'

But the young woman batted away the comment. 'I just mean there's no justice for lassies that get treated like Holly did, is there?'

'Do you know anything that might relate to her death?' May persisted.

'No,' Shannon replied with such certainty that May didn't believe her.

She raised her eyebrows at Shannon, an invitation to reconsider. 'Sure?'

'Aye, I'm sure.' A hint of impatience had crept into her tone. She'd just had a shotgun fired into her home so May let it go and tried not to read too much into it.

'Fine,' May said. 'But if you need someone to talk to, about anything, you come to me, okay?' She took out a card and pressed it into Shannon's hand.

They'd reached the tape and Mo held it up for them both to enter.

'Ms Hope will need to collect some personal items shortly,' May said to her officer. 'She's going to sit in a patrol car till I get back.'

Mo nodded.

May turned back to Shannon. 'Okay?' The question was more than an agreement to wait for an escort into the building, and they both knew it. Shannon would come to May if she changed her mind.

'Okay,' said Shannon eventually.

May watched her walk away and prayed whatever it was Shannon Hope had to say about Holly she confessed it soon.

CHAPTER 40

May was on her way back to see Lauren and Toni at the neighbour's flat when her phone rang. The number showed *No Caller ID* but she answered it expecting to hear again from Madison or one of the other students she'd spoken to earlier, but when the voice came, it sounded like an older man.

'Is that May?'

'How can I help you?' she said. Further down the road she could see a gang of kids close to her squad car. She waved at them and they bolted.

'Is Friday night still good for our date?'

'How's that?' May frowned.

'It's Gerry. We've been messaging all week.' When May didn't respond he added, 'You know? On BUNK.'

Toni and Lauren had come to meet her, keen to get on with the job so their shift wouldn't run over.

May covered the mouthpiece. 'Lauren, what's BUNK?' She didn't think it was a police acronym but systems changed fast and it sounded half familiar.

The constable's brown eyes widened and she looked half shocked, half impressed.

Beside her, Toni gave a snort and her hand went to her mouth.

'BUNK's a dating app, Sarge. Ross Reid's the guy to speak to if you're having account issues.'

'It's not . . .'May began, when she heard Gerry's voice in her ear.

'You said dates and hook-ups in your profile. Bondage and submission. Is that no' right?'

He sounded like an aggrieved customer who'd been short-changed. May wanted to laugh.

'I'm sorry, pal. I think you've got the wrong number.' She caught Lauren's eye and the young officer suppressed a giggle.

'We were supposed to be meeting up,' he persisted.

'I think you've been catfished. Did you disclose any financial details? Did you send explicit pictures or exchange sexual messages that would leave you open to blackmail?' She knew from an online exploitation course that a third of dating site users had been asked for money to help with a problem or to facilitate a meet-up. 'I'm a police officer – if you'd like to send me your details I'll—' The call went dead.

It was only as she checked the screen that it hit her. How could it be a wrong number when he'd asked for her by name?

'You okay, boss?' Lauren said, sensing her change of mood.

'Aye, fine.' May frowned, still trying to make sense of what had happened. 'You two can get off now, if you want. Mo is taking Shannon Hope in for some essentials, and her accommodation is sorted.'

'Okay, Sarge,' Lauren said, still watching her. 'Sure every-thing's okay?'

'Off you go.' May waved them away.

By the time May reached the car, a text showing a BUNK account had arrived on her phone – sent, she assumed, by her erstwhile date. She walked around to the driver's side, pausing to click the link.

It was her alright. A BUNK profile with all her details on it – a photo *in uniform*, personal details like the areas where she lived and worked. She was looking for men to date and for hook-ups – one-night stands. Whoever had done this had been chatting with men online, leading them on. Suddenly it didn't seem so funny any more.

What had the creep who'd been impersonating her said to this Gerry? How many people had seen that profile? She couldn't help but imagine the vilest of images it conjured up. Try not to think too much about what you're seeing and get the job over as quickly as possible, she recited. But in this case, it was impossible. The creeping panic was beginning to set in, and no matter how hard she tried she couldn't evict it.

There was no way May could tell Tam about this. She couldn't pass it off as a joke – *you'll never guess the call I got today* – he'd be just as horrified as she was. But it also felt wrong to keep anything from him, especially something this personal. It was like she had a dirty secret.

By the time she got back to the station, she'd already called the site. She reported it, told them she was a police officer, which was apparent to anyone who looked at the profile picture, and did they not think that was suspicious? The poor guy at the call centre nearly had a heart attack, couldn't get the profile down quick enough.

May's mind began to whir with possible perpetrators. She faced harassment on the street every day and had learned to distance herself, but this was different.

The profile picture was likely from the internet. She didn't have social media, but a few press releases had gone out over the years with her headshot. Must have been in the last two years if she was in uniform. Anyone could've set up a fake email, but who had her phone number?

That wasn't as small a group as she'd first imagined. She'd given her number out to not only potential witnesses like the student that morning, but also to those she'd thought vulnerable. Women who wouldn't talk openly to the officers attending a treble-nine call but might just speak to her if they were truly scared. And plenty of officers had it.

Was it someone she'd pissed off at work? Surely not one of her own team because she'd bollocked them about a messy squad car? Rab the Kebab took those things in his stride. It was the kind of sleekit wee jab that Marky the Meerkat was capable of, but she couldn't see it. Ross 'Keep the Heid' Reed, was, on paper, the best equipped. Toni had said he had a profile on most dating sites and was often juggling any number of women. No wonder he never had time to actually sit his sergeants' exam.

She steeled herself. Stop. This is what they want, spreading fear and making her question the strength of her relationships. It had the same feel about it as the Facebook message saying Tam had killed her. Cowardly. Online, remote, and the same small chance of catching who'd done it. She had to screenshot it and file it away. Nothing else could be done for now. She certainly wasn't about to report it to CID so they could piss themselves laughing at her all over again.

CHAPTER 41

May spent the next morning tidying the flat and sorting the laundry. Tam looked pleasantly surprised to see her at home. She listened as he talked about his dreams for the community centre and his ambitions for the young people they'd already welcomed in. It was a tonic just to sit with him, and she felt her mood lightening, her faith in good restored after so much darkness. He looked impressed when she told him she'd be taking time off to come with him on the band's proposed tour of the islands in the summer. He was less impressed when she said she was meeting Ian McDonald for a coffee before her shift started.

'It's just a brief update for them,' May insisted.

'Shouldn't your mate Dimple be doing that?'

'Probably. She's good, but she's just a kid. Maybe I have been swayed by Jackie McNally's distress,' she said, seeing his expression. 'Ian McDonald was a detective sergeant like me. This is a chance to work out what resolution might look like for the family.'

She saw Tam's mollified expression, that he'd taken that to mean that this whole case was entering its endgame, and she didn't dissuade him on that point.

When she was ready to go, May gathered up her jacket and

a sandwich Tam had made her. On late shifts it was sometimes
tricky to find places still open when they got a meal break, the
timing dependent on how busy they were. When she reached
the front door she saw he was waiting, helmet on and his road
bike hoisted on one shoulder. For a second she thought he
was planning to come with her, to make sure she really was
putting an end to her involvement in the investigation.

But he smiled at her concerned expression. 'You don't
mind, do you? We're just doing a quick ride. Up to Loch
Lomond. Three hours, fifteen minutes round trip. Wi' a coffee
stop. I'll be back afore it's proper dark.' He knew she worried
about him on the roads in winter.

She came forward and put her arms around him, hugging
him tight. He smelled smoky and sweet and made her think
of music-filled nights by a roaring fire.

'Hey, hey,' he said, almost knocked off balance. 'I'm only
going to Balloch, no' the Russian Front.'

'You just be careful. I know what you boys are like when
you're out to play.'

'Gonna check my lights, officer? Or the rest of my equipment?' He gave her a sly look followed by a quick kiss on
the cheek.

'Want me to take down your particulars?'

'Now you're talking.'

'Get moving.' She gave him a playful shove. 'I've the law
to uphold and you've an espresso to drink on the bonnie,
bonnie banks of Loch Lomond.'

When they reached the street door, he gave her
another kiss.

Even before she got to her car, she could see something was wrong. The cover for the fuel cap cover stood open. She tried to push it shut, but it wouldn't budge.

Then she saw the petrol cap itself had been levered off and a rag stuffed in. Put a flame to that and the whole thing would go up.

'Did you drive home like that?' Tam asked, coming up behind her astride his bike, one foot pushing along the pavement.

She was sure she hadn't.

'Must have.'

She nodded to reassure him, because the alternative was worse and she didn't want him thinking it. A dashboard light would've come on, and it hadn't.

'This is why we're never moving to the southside,' he said. 'It's bandit country over there. You'll need to take a cab to work. I'll make some calls. See if I can get a new petrol cap fitted and the car checked. You're off all day tomorrow, aren't you?'

May nodded.

'Hallelujah to that.'

She knew he was looking forward to her coming along to a gig and an after-party at the weekend. She started on earlies on Sunday. The days when she could roll in at three in the morning, catch a couple of hours' sleep, then be on shift at 6 a.m. were long gone, but she'd make the effort to show her face at least, so as not to disappoint him.

'Well, if you're on lates,' Tam said, 'I can find a garage.

The car should be ready before you go on shift tomorrow night at nine.'

May nodded. Tam with his practical efficiency had offered a solution.

The taxi app said a car would be there to pick her up in ten minutes. She sent a text to Ian McDonald that she was running late, and waved Tam off with a cheerful smile.

Only once he was gone did she allow the reality of what had happened to sink in.

She checked the other cars on the street. There was nothing to indicate they'd suffered the same fate. No vandalism spree by tanked-up teenagers.

This wasn't random. Someone had targeted her car.

And whoever had done this had known which one was hers, knew where she lived.

The BUNK hoax had felt personal; this, even more so.

She remembered the constable who'd called her over the malicious Facebook post. *Worth double-checking your security arrangements,* he'd said, in case it was someone she'd previously locked up.

But were the two incidents even related?

The street door to the flats was secure, and their neighbours were vigilant about letting strangers into the close. They even had a video doorbell as an extra precaution.

Setting her car up as a bomb on wheels was the best way of targeting her without accessing the building. And she'd seen it before. It was an established practice of gangs burning out stolen vehicles in order to erase DNA.

She thought of calling it in, but there'd be no prints. This was a nice area. The nearest traffic camera or CCTV was too far away to be useful. Even if she could persuade CID to investigate and canvass her neighbours for dashcam footage, that'd likely show nothing more than dark figures in hoodies and maybe another vehicle with cloned plates. Or even just an untraceable lad on an untraceable bike.

With shaking fingers, she checked the alert that had just landed on her phone. The taxi was here. But as they drove away, May couldn't help looking over her shoulder.

CHAPTER 42

The Pollokshaws Road cafe was busy with dog walkers and families. A long countertop, laden with cakes, led through the depth of the building to a rear seating area. A toddler had kicked off, the decibels rising. Ian had bagged a table near the window. As May navigated the parked buggies, he got up and held out his hand for her to shake, giving her a guilty grimace at his choice of venue.

'We can go somewhere else, if you like?'

'No, it's fine. I've two probationers and seven lads on my team. I'm used to bawling weans.'

'Sit down,' he said, indicating the chair opposite. 'I'll get you a coffee.'

Everything May had seen so far showed that Ian was clearly fond of Holly. There'd been mentions in the diary of gifts and outings to computer shows and trade exhibitions. He'd taken an interest in her life, so perhaps there was some nugget of information the investigation had overlooked that would give them a new prime suspect. She checked her watch. She didn't have long.

It turned out he didn't intend to waste time with pleasantries either.

'Do you really believe Scott Galbraith killed Holly?' he said as soon as he returned with her Americano.

'What's your view?' she replied, unwilling to show her hand this early in their meeting.

'Jackie thinks so,' he replied. 'She told me about the abusive texts, and the journal. If I'd known what that bastard Galbraith was doing to Holly . . .' He shook his head, his pain clearly visible. 'Didn't like him. Thought Holly could do better.' A tear ran from the corner of his eye and he quickly wiped it away with the back of his hand.

May crossed her arms and rested her elbows on the table and thought hard about what she was about to say.

'Truth is,' she began, her voice low enough so it wouldn't carry above the hubbub to nearby families, 'Galbraith's alibi stands up. It wasn't him on the platform.'

He'd have had to hear this sooner rather than later. Better he thought she wasn't keeping things back from the family.

Ian's hands flew to his head and he rocked back in his chair. The gesture was dramatic enough that other diners stared at him. May could see the curiosity on their faces as they tried to work out what she'd just told him. She was pregnant. She was having an affair. Never in a million years would they guess the truth.

'Right from the start,' he said, jabbing an index finger into the table, 'this whole case has been about proving his guilt. Jackie believes, heart and soul, that he did it. If it wasn't him, then who?'

'We're following a number of leads.' It sounded lame, even to her ears.

'But Galbraith was there that night?'

'Oh yes.'

'Maybe one of his psycho mates was with him. Couldn't do the deed himself. Too much of a coward. Pointed Holly out to some executioner who just did it for money?'

May remembered what Dimple had said the day they'd first met. It seemed too elaborate. Why go to all that bother? Why not just grab her off the street? Men who wanted revenge liked to strangle women so they could see the life leave their eyes.

'Did Holly ever talk about her friend Mhairi McCormack?'

Dimple was trying to find the young woman on the station CCTV, but anything May could harvest on the dynamic of their relationship would be helpful.

'Just a college pal,' Ian replied, brushing the question aside. 'Michael McNally could still be behind this. My Holly was smart. She had something on him. You know yourself how these guys operate. Escalating pattern of intimidation to make you back off. Maybe he even set Galbraith on her, told him to keep her in line, then had to tidy him away too. What?' he said, looking at her curiously. 'Have you remembered something?'

An escalating pattern was certainly a way to describe what was happening to her.

'It's just some stuff that's been going on recently?'

'What?' he said, his face creasing with anxiety.

She told him about the hoax Facebook message, the fake dating profile, the petrol cap, and then it occurred to her that the car that had nearly missed her – headlights out, fast down the side street near (but not too near) Cathcart Police Office with its cameras – might have been the opening salvo in this barrage of intimidation.

It had all started after Galbraith had seen her sitting in full view of his customers outside his flat, and had escalated as the investigation had shifted gear after Galbraith's death and she'd continued to pursue it. It couldn't have been Galbraith alone. This went all the way to the top of the tree.

'McNally knows you're after him. Shit, May. I told you what he was like.'

She felt a curl of annoyance that he, formerly a fellow police officer, should criticise her actions in pursuit of his stepdaughter's killer.

'I put myself in the line of fire every time I go out there in a uniform,' she reminded him. It came out harsher than she'd intended. 'This is no different.'

'Of course, I'm so sorry,' he said quickly, setting down his cup and touching her arm lightly in apology. 'It's just . . . I'm trying to get Jackie to stay at my place in Shawlands, out of harm's way. She doesn't think he's a threat to her, but if he killed her daughter, what else might he do? We've both known guys like this. He thinks he's got away with it. Any impulse control will be out the window – it'll have made him bold. I'm at work, I can't be there all the time to keep Jackie safe.' He looked mystified and panicky.

'She wants to go back to Holly,' May said quietly.

He looked at her, not understanding. 'What d'you mean?'

She wanted to tell him how Jackie heard Holly moving around the flat. That she sometimes felt her own daughter just behind her in the kitchen or heard music coming from Isla's bedroom. She knew it was only the heart reaching for a moment of comfort, the sense that the person was not gone, but just in another room. In the absence of anything more solid it was a powerful anchor to a place and time. Perhaps you had to experience it to understand.

Instead, she said, 'It's the grief. I appreciate your worries.'

She hadn't intended to share the recent incidents with anyone but Tam. After all what did she have? Some practical jokes and a bit of mindless vandalism. If she reported it, her inspector would think she was paranoid or on a witch-hunt for the McNallys. He'd be more concerned about souring relations with the BTP, getting Police Scotland in serious legal bother, or prompting a raft of media stories from McNally about police harassment.

'Fucksake, May. We really need to get this guy before someone else – you or Jackie – gets hurt.' He edged forward in his seat. May recognised the familiar look of a cop picking up the scent, determined to follow it. 'Who else could it be?'

But May shook her head. She wasn't prepared to share any more.

'She was a smart lassie,' he said with obvious pride. Then he sat back in his chair and let out a long breath. 'Jackie and Holly had nothing to do with that family,' he went on. 'It doesn't mean their lives weren't ruined by them. You need to watch yourself, May. It's not just McNally and his thugs. He's got powerful friends everywhere. Still time for you to walk away.'

When she'd come to this meeting with Ian McDonald,

she'd had no notion of recruiting him into pursuing his step-daughter's killer. He was a sounding board, no more. But there was no doubt he was passionate and motivated and that he'd loved Holly like she was his own.

May drained her cup and checked the time. She'd have to make a move soon.

'Can I ask you something?' she said. 'Why did you really leave the job?'

He'd cited his relationship with Jackie and his battle with alcohol, but if she was going to trust him she needed the whole story, and there was a story, she was sure.

He gave her a resigned smile, as if he'd been expecting the question.

'It's simple. Between you and me, I was asked to falsify evidence. I refused and suddenly my face didn't fit any more. Questions were raised over my drinking, which was fair enough, but that wasn't really the problem. I'd stood up to my boss and been ostracised. I decided going quietly was my only option if I wanted to keep my pension.'

May understood this dilemma better than he could have guessed. It was another reason she was uneasy about going back to her old CID team. She suspected something similar had happened on the case of a missing teenager who'd turned up dead. The mum's boyfriend had gone down for it. He was probably guilty, but some of the evidence was made less shaky. She'd felt grubby at the time, and further contaminated now that she didn't have the guts to do anything about it. But they'd got the right result, hadn't they? Maybe. Though you could never be sure. If you did it once and got away with it, falsifying evidence began to feel like a legitimate shortcut when resources were scarce. Locking up the bad guys was the big picture. It sounded like Ian had been a good cop, but sometimes that wasn't enough. *You've got to be willing to wade into the cesspool* was what her DI had claimed, and it seemed neither of them had had the stomach for it.

She nodded to indicate his brief explanation was all that was needed. She recognised the scenario. Best he didn't tell her any of the sordid details.

'Did Jackie ever talk to you about Holly's problems?' she said.

'Yes, sometimes. She and Holly would fight, and then they'd be best friends again. I've no kids myself, felt out of my depth. I didn't know how to parent her, and Jackie and I aren't married so I wasn't really her stepdad, not in law anyway. If I'm honest, I was wary about getting caught in the crossfire and then ending up in the wrong with both of them no matter what I did. Mostly, I just tried to de-escalate the situation, calm everyone down. But I could have done more. I see that now. What can I do to help now?'

May considered. She didn't want him wading into an active investigation and maybe ending up like Scott Galbraith.

'DC Sharma is a good detective. You can trust her to be thorough.'

'If you let me have Holly's phone and laptop I can go through it and see if there's anything significant. You can release them back to me, can't you?'

'We'd better hang on to those.' She didn't want the evidence chain compromised when a suspect was found.

'Okay.' He nodded.

'All I can think of are the questions I asked at the beginning. Go back over the last three months. Talk to Jackie if she's well enough. Anything that Holly said to either of you that seemed odd. Changes to her plans where she might have been avoiding someone. Incidents where there'd be witnesses or CCTV. Maybe Galbraith wasn't the only one she was frightened of.'

'What are you going to do?' Ian said.

'Keep looking.'

CHAPTER 43

May found it hard to do anything on her day off, even the most mundane task. Sorting laundry resulted in mis-paired socks, and even an attempt to make breakfast saw orange juice instead of milk being added to a cup of tea.

Dimple had re-interviewed Mhairi McCormack, who'd categorically denied she'd gone to the station and had a confrontation with Holly the night she'd died. She insisted she'd just been vaping and chatting during the time she was out of touch with her friends. CCTV had failed to find any sign of her. May had felt exasperated, sure that putting Mhairi under pressure would've worked, but she pulled back when she heard Dimple's own tiredness and frustration, though she insisted she was as committed as ever to solving the case.

May considered heading for Glasgow Central and finding Kit, the homeless man, who'd proven such a charm in tracking down Galbraith, but instead she got back into bed and began working through Holly's diary again. The notebook was less a chronological list of events than a journal of thoughts, and had likely been recommended by her psychiatrist as a way to track mood, document symptoms and improve patterns of thinking. May hoped it'd helped

Holly. She dropped the journal onto the duvet cover. Isla had completed a similar exercise but hadn't found it a useful experience. She'd scoffed at the idea she should practise gratitude for small things, peppering her journal with the kind of heavy sarcasm – *I found a nice yellow leaf. Wow* – that May had dealt with on a daily basis whenever she'd tried to elevate her daughter's mood with a suggested activity. *A walk. Wow. Learn to knit. Wow. A trip to the cinema. Fucking brilliant idea, Mum.* It had felt pointless and exhausting, but it had never stopped May from trying. But had she tried hard enough? Could she have stopped her?

She threw back the covers and winced as she stood up. Her muscles felt heavy, but conversely her whole body was an eggshell that might crack apart at any moment. Maybe Tam was right. She lifted her arms, stretching out her back. She was getting too old for this caper. She'd had a hot shower when she'd come home last night, as she usually did after a shift. A chance to sluice off the dirt, stale beer and bodily fluids of strangers that clung to her. But now she felt like she'd need another one to even make it down the stairs to the car.

It seemed as if all May's cases were facing brick walls. The scene of the shooting at Shannon Hope's flat had been processed by forensics and the case handed over to CID. The spray of shotgun pellets embedded in the wall of the flat was unlikely to give them much because the cartridge, on which DNA of whoever had loaded it might be present, had been retained within the shotgun.

Lauren had succeeded in tracking the likely vehicle – a white panel van with roof rack – via traffic cameras to an industrial site where it disappeared into a warren of warehouses, scrapyards and small industrial units. It was a useful lead for CID to chew on but May knew Lauren would get none of the credit should it come to anything.

May went through to the front room and busied herself with the Saturday newspapers, attempting to concentrate on the here and now. It was often this way after a run of shifts, and by the time she adjusted to a slower pace it would be time to go back to work. Tam was moving around gathering what he needed for that evening's gig. May was conscious that just by her mere presence in the flat she was in his good books again, and the thought warmed her.

After the mix-up with the orange juice earlier, however, he declined her offer to iron his shirt for the evening, which was probably a wise move if he wanted it in one piece. The venue would be warm with the BBC's studio lights and the audience at full capacity. She'd picked out her outfit, a pale blue Paisley-patterned chiffon wrap midi-dress, teamed with boots, which would be fine under her long wool coat for the short journey.

'You're wearing that?' Tam said, his eyes widening when he saw it hanging on the wardrobe door.

'Too much?' May said, suddenly questioning whether she'd be overdressed for a folk night, even a televised one, and it was rather low cut.

'No, no, it's lovely,' Tam said, one arm circling her waist.

'Just don't sit in the front row, lassie: you'll be too distracting, and I'm only flesh and blood.'

'Not very professional if you can't keep your mind on your work,' she teased.

'I'm a musician. Chasing bonnie lassies is part of my job description,' he said, nuzzling her neck.

'Is that right?' she replied with mock indignation. 'Just as long as you're only chasing the one lassie.'

'You'll always be my girl,' he said.

'Good', she said, kissing him. 'Cos the ironing can wait to later.'

The gig was scheduled for eight o'clock that night, but Tam needed to be at the venue with the rest of the band for sound checks at least two hours before. His friend Sean would be there with his wife, Morag, who wasn't singing on this occasion. Morag was vivacious and funny and had a ready store of anecdotes from her job teaching in one of the most deprived areas of the city, including the time she'd silenced a room full of stroppy teenagers by hitting a top C.

They were just leaving the flat when May's phone rang. She checked the caller ID.

'It's Jackie McNally,' she said to Tam. He gave her a warning look as her finger went to the accept button. 'She probably just needs a chat. Go on, the cab's waiting. I'll catch you up.'

It suited her to go separately since she was on earlies the next day and planned to be back before Tam anyway. If she took the car, she wouldn't be tempted to drink. She pointed to the screen and threw out her hand in a *what else can I do?* gesture. 'There's loads of time before it starts – go on.'

Eventually Tam conceded defeat and tucked his fiddle under his arm. *Don't be late,* he mouthed as he opened the door, then sent her a goodbye kiss.

CHAPTER 44

As soon as May picked up the phone she knew Jackie had been drinking.

'Are you on your own, Jackie? Where's Ian?'

'Out. He'll be angry. He'll say I'm weak an' he'll be right,' she slurred. 'I wasnae strong enough to save my own wee girl,' she said, and began sobbing.

'Look, Jackie . . .' May checked her watch, there wasn't time to get over to Shawlands, calm Jackie down, make sure she was okay, find Ian, and get back for the concert. 'You're not weak. You've had a terrible time.'

'He was here, you know, Galbraith. I thought he was gonna kill Ian. They were fighting in the garden.'

'Scott Galbraith is dead, Jackie. You're safe from him now.'

'I want to be with her, I want to be with her.'

'Jackie? Jackie . . .'

The line had gone dead. May hung up, tried again but got the busy tone.

'Shit, shit, shit,' she muttered, searching for Ian McDonald's number. It rang, then went to voicemail.

She was out the close door and halfway to her car when it struck her.

You're not the only polis in Glasgow, Tam had often said in frustration at her workload, and he was right.

She rang the control-room direct line.

'It's Sergeant Mackay. Can you do me an urgent welfare check on Jackie McNally?' She gave them the address in Shawlands. 'She rang me very distressed. She's a history of substance abuse and self-harm. I can't raise her. Who've you got nearest?'

May heard the tap of a keyboard. 'PCs Toni McAleer and Lauren Paterson are closest,' the operator said.

Perfect, thought May. 'Thank you. Get them to call me when they've seen her.'

'Will do, Sergeant Mackay.'

May rested her back against her car and looked up at the dark sky. No guiding stars for this city, just clouds reflecting the perpetual sulphurous glow of its streets and inhabitants, all seemingly intent on doing harm to themselves and others.

Prompted by Jackie's panicked call and the dark and deserted street, she felt her sense of unease return. She jumped as her phone buzzed in her hand, then the call cut. Tam, wondering if she'd left yet. She got quickly into the car.

Ten minutes later she left Byres Road and cut up a side street looking for a parking spot. She drove parallel to the main road, scanning the street until the tenements opened up again on the left and she could see the pub's front door. Outside it, the flashing blue of the ambulance's lights made her hit the brake. At the same moment, Tam's pal Sean's call lit up her screen.

'May? You better come.'

She dropped the phone and hung a hard left, screeching to a halt behind the ambulance, not caring that she was boxing it in. Her heart rate jumped when she saw the doors open but no one inside. Cursing her stupid heels, stupid outfit, she ran into the foyer, catching sight of Morag's distinctive red hair. She was crouching by a figure sitting with a foil blanket around his shoulders, a paramedic in green next to her.

The world tilted as a wave of nausea and panic crashed over her.

'Tam!' she howled, staggering forward and falling to her knees, patting him down for broken bones or life-threatening injuries, despite the paramedic in plain view beside him. Miraculously, the only damage seemed to be a deep gash on his scalp.

'Everyone's a critic,' he said into her shoulder as she flung her arms around him. 'Somebody doesnae like my music.'

'Are you really okay?' she said, continuing to run her eyes and fingers over him as if she couldn't believe he was still in one piece.

'I'm fine, I'm fine,' he insisted, with the air of someone whose pain was numbed by adrenaline.

'We're gonna have to take you up the hospital now, Mr Kinsella,' the young paramedic said. 'That'll need stitches, I'm afraid.'

'What about the gig?' Tam stared at the lad, who'd probably seen this reaction many times before.

'There'll be other gigs. Your head's more important.' May struggled to keep her voice steady and not scold him.

She turned to his friend Sean, aware she was treating him

like one of her constables but unable to stop herself. 'Where'd this happen?'

'In the alleyway. Right outside the stage door.'

'Robbery?'

'Didnae take anything,' Tam replied. 'Just came up behind me and banjaxed me over the head. The worst thing is . . .' May saw a look of deep distress cross her husband's face and she followed the direction of his gaze to the instrument case at his feet. Morag leaned forward and opened it. Inside, his fiddle lay on the green velvet lining, a deep crack across the spruce top of the soundboard.

It had belonged to his mother.

'Much worse than a bash on the head,' Tam said quietly.

May didn't trust herself to speak. She wanted to yell at him that it was just wood and glue and strings and was replaceable, whereas he was not. She'd lost a daughter, and Tam was selfish to think she could bear losing him too.

'At least you still have it, Tam,' Morag said gently, with a fellow musician's understanding. 'It can be fixed. I know someone.'

'It'll never be the same,' Tam said, and May regretted her harsh thoughts and saw his heart was breaking, even if his head was still in one piece.

'No, it'll probably play differently,' Morag conceded. 'But that will be its history. And maybe, when one of your grandchildren draws a bow across it, all the way on the other side of the world, they'll tell the story of this instrument's survival, of its journey, and that'll make it sound all the sweeter.'

Tam gave her a sad, knowing smile and patted her cheek,

but already his face was less bleak than it had been a moment ago. Morag, it seemed, wasn't only in the business of fixing broken children and violins; she could work her magic on concussed old fiddle players too.

In that moment May was profoundly grateful for Morag's words and for Tam's survival. But as the paramedic ushered Tam into the back of the ambulance, and May said she'd follow in the car, her mind was already turning to who might have done this. Tam would think she was overreacting, but after the conversation she'd had with Ian McDonald about her run of bad luck, it was as if a switch had flicked on inside her. Hypervigilance they called it, the body's response to sustained stress. Putting a name to it didn't make it any easier to bear.

She pulled out, letting the ambulance go first, wishing she had her squad car and could blue-light Tam all the way to the hospital, though he didn't need it. As she waited at the traffic lights, a text flashed up on her phone. It would be Sean or Morag telling her to call them at any hour if she needed them. She opened the message.

May hadn't been sure before. There'd still been a kernel of doubt, a residual belief that fate could be a right bastard when it wanted to be.

She was sure now.

Stop and no one else will get hurt.

May checked the sender and felt a jolt of recognition. It was the number on Holly's phone. The one that had sent the last message before she'd died.

Meet me, Holls. I only want to talk.

CHAPTER 45

The first thing May did on reaching Cathcart Police Office on Sunday morning was phone Dimple. She didn't care that it was early. The Royal Infirmary's A&E department hadn't discharged Tam until 4 a.m. Two hours later, May had welcomed Morag and Sean into the flat. They'd volunteered to keep an eye on him for concussion until she got back. Calling in sick, pleading personal circumstances were options – sensible ones – but she knew she'd just fret and bark at Tam unless she put on her uniform and took active steps to hunt down whoever had attacked him. Officers from their local Hillhead police had arrived to take a statement, but it was clear they hadn't believed this was part of a pattern or that there was much hope of finding the culprit.

Dimple was horrified when May told her about the attack on Tam.

'Oh my God, Sarge – is he okay?'

May reassured her that he was. There seemed to be no reason to hold back from telling Dimple she believed they'd been targeted via a series of escalating incidents, culminating in the violence against her husband and the text she'd received shortly afterwards.

'Step back,' Dimple said immediately. 'We can assign another liaison. Someone from CID. You can brief them.'

'There isn't time. Whoever is doing this killed Holly and the only way to stop this is to catch them.'

'How?'

May bit the soft skin of her thumb as she tried to put some order into the jumble of facts that threatened to overwhelm her.

'Holly and Galbraith's murders, how are they linked?' May began, a curious, calm determination settling on her now she was taking action. 'Are they sequential or parallel? Was Galbraith murdered in revenge for Holly's death, or were they both killed because they knew something about Michael McNally?'

'It's sequential,' Dimple said firmly. 'Why wait? If you didn't want either to reveal anything, it makes more sense to kill them at the same time, or the other one would get spooked. Why not kill them at the same time?'

'I want to talk to Mhairi again,' May said. 'She's the key.'

'You don't think she did this? We excluded her.'

'It's too coincidental that the incidents escalated into physical violence right after you reinterviewed her. She followed me that night at the station, she's not been in college, she'd been obstructive by not returning my calls, *and* she has a background in computers so setting up a fake dating profile or Facebook post would be meat and drink to the lassie.'

In the face of May's reasoning, as well as her resoluteness, Dimple conceded. 'When can you get away?' she said.

'Where does Mhairi live?'

'Just off the Gallowgate.'

May checked the schedule. 'I can get to you in an hour.'

Quickly, she gathered up her papers and made her way to the briefing room.

PC Toni McAleer came in shortly afterwards and set down her coffee. 'Mornin', Sarge. Your husband okay?'

May assured her he was. Toni had called last night, while May had been at the hospital, to report that they'd got to Jackie's but she couldn't or wouldn't let them in. Luckily, Ian McDonald had appeared shortly afterwards and the situation had been quickly resolved. Jackie hadn't harmed herself. May's call to her this morning had gone to voicemail, though Ian had texted to say they were both fine.

Ross Reid was next. After he too had enquired about Tam, he said, 'Your pal Davey the Dooker? Most of the stuff he's hauled up is languishing in boxes in the forensics unit at Gartcosh. I managed to talk to someone at the lab and asked if they knew of any forensics students on work experience who might do an initial assessment in terms of age and the likelihood of recoverable data. She did. Be pretty good for their CVs if they helped solve a cold case, wouldn't it?'

May was tapping the table impatiently with her pen, anxious to get over to Mhairi's. 'That's good thinking, Ross.'

'And they'll give us a budget estimate for the tests themselves, minus regular staff costs. I thought we could maybe do the top three items likely to yield good forensic results.'

'Aye, sure,' May said, distracted.

Straight after the briefing, as May hurried to her car, she called Tam.

'Could it have been a lassie that hit you?'

'Could've been the prime minister and I wouldnae be able to tell you.'

'Think. Anything at all? Smell of perfume. Woman's voice.'

'Sorry,' he replied.

'But you're okay?'

'Morag and Sean are making breakfast. I promise I'll sit on the sofa and watch old episodes of *Celtic Connections* until you get home. Happy?'

'Yes,' May replied. 'But I'll be checking.'

Mhairi shared a flat with three other students on the ground floor of a tenement building that overlooked a sports field. This early on a Sunday morning all the curtains were drawn, and May doubted the others would be up. A text told her Dimple had already arrived, but May remained in the squad car turning over an idea that had occurred to her on the journey from Cathcart. She'd sifted through Mhairi's odd behaviour, forming it into a new alignment. It was the only thing that made sense.

Mhairi was wrapped in a dressing gown at the kitchen table when Dimple led May through from the hall. The young woman eyed her with alarm as if the uniform and squad car outside signified an imminent arrest.

Dimple stood beside Mhairi as May sat down and looked the young woman square in the face.

'I know Scott Galbraith recruited you as a dealer. That's why you were following me at Central station, why you've been targeting me online, vandalising my car, and seriously assaulted my husband.'

Mhairi's eyes widened in horror. She pushed away from the table and half rose, but Dimple's surprisingly forceful hand on her shoulder forced her back into her seat.

'It's no' true. I never did those things.' Mhairi looked between the two officers.

May leaned her elbow on the kitchen table and pointed a finger at her. 'You told DC Sharma you weren't on the platform when Holly died. We have video evidence someone matching your description was. D'you want to rethink what you said?'

Tears sprung to Mhairi's eyes. 'I wasnae there, I swear. I never saw her after the pub.'

'But Galbraith did recruit you?'

Mhairi bit her lip, then nodded.

'And is that why you argued? Why you called Holly a jealous cow?'

After a moment, Mhairi nodded again, her face a picture of regret.

'Holly was trying to stop you getting dragged into her ex's dealing, but you thought it was territorial? That she wanted Galbraith back? I think she just wanted you to be safe.'

Mhairi put her hand to her mouth and sobbed. 'I did follow you at Central station – Scott said I had to, just to see who you were talking to. But I didnae tell him anything, I swear, and I didnae do all those other things you said. I've no' been to college, I switched off my phone, and I went to a mate's house for a bit, but then I heard Scott was dead . . .'

Mhairi had a clean record and her horror seemed so real that May was inclined to believe her.

'Listen, love,' May went on. 'You're no' in trouble, but I do need to ask you some questions and it's really important you're honest with me. Okay?'

'Okay,' Mhairi sobbed, and Dimple sat down beside her and took out her Pronto.

It wasn't until she'd been driving over that she'd realised what had been bothering her about Holly's diary. There was nothing *really* personal in it. The other student, Madison, had said the two young women had argued. Falling out with your best mate would merit pages of indignation. Holly likely knew her mother was reading her diary and had constructed a fantasy that was just real enough for Jackie to believe.

She'd also said her daughter was clever, and her tutor had confirmed she was talented enough with computers to be headhunted out of college by a tech company and would be off to Dundee. And Ian McDonald had had a point when he'd said that Holly would know things about the McNally drug operation – enough to get her killed.

'If Holly wanted to keep information secret – a journal or a diary – how would she do that? There's nothing on her laptop.'

Mhairi scoffed. 'Of course not.'

'Online then?'

'No. Worse. Cloud storage is ultimately hackable,' Mhairi said, with the scorn the young reserved for anyone who hadn't grow up in the internet world. 'Poor cloud infrastructure and stolen credentials will get you in.'

'How then?' May said, her patience growing thin. 'Where would it be, Mhairi?'

The young woman must have heard the edge in May's voice, so her reply was serious, the tone respectful.

'She might have had another laptop and air-gapped it. Not connected it externally to the internet or any kind of network, so it'd be secure.'

'We talked to the tutor in case she'd left any devices at college,' added Dimple. 'Nothing's been found.'

'It could be a Raspberry Pi.'

The name triggered a vague memory with May, some project Isla had done as a teenager when she'd had a brief obsession with science and building her own music computer.

'What would it look like?'

'Anything. Lego. Jewellery. There'd be a USB-type connection but it wouldn't be obvious. She could have used that on her laptop, with an internal air-gap, and you'd never know it had been there.'

'If you saw it, would you recognise it?' May said impatiently.

Mhairi shrugged. 'Aye, mibbaes.'

'Okay.' May got up. 'Listen, Mhairi. I want you to stay in the flat and keep your phone off until DC Sharma comes back for you later today. Understand?'

Mhairi wiped her eyes and nodded.

'I mean it,' May said. 'Don't even go to the corner shop. Send one of your pals. And don't answer the door to anyone you don't know.'

Once they were outside, she turned to Dimple. 'I need to get back. Search Holly's room. Take the lassie with you. I think we missed something when we were there.'

'Alright,' Dimple said. 'I'll get on to it.'

At the end of the shift, the team were in the locker room and May was just stowing her utility vest when Toni came in.

'I meant to say earlier, Sarge,' she began. 'When we went to Jackie McNally's last night, she said something weird.'

'What was that?' May said, pulling on her fleece.

'She said something about Scott Galbraith being in the garden.'

May nodded. 'She said the same to me. I think she's very mixed up. She's on pills, though I'm not sure how that'll help her long term.'

'Thing is,' Toni went on, 'Lauren and I were chatting to a neighbour afterwards. She'd seen the squad car draw up. She told us the same story.'

May stopped, the zip halfway done, and frowned at her constable. 'Galbraith's dead. You helped cut him down.'

'Oh aye, but this didnae happen yesterday,' Toni clarified. 'Seems it was the night before the funeral. Get this: Galbraith was shouting the odds in the front garden, saying Ian owed him. The neighbour said Galbraith meant the family owed him for all the presents and money he'd spent on Holly over the years. Can you believe it? You've been bailed on suspicion of pushing your ex-girlfriend under a train and you want cash off her parents for expenses.'

May shook her head. 'Unfortunately, I can believe it.

Abusers like Galbraith find it all too easy to cast themselves as the victim in any scenario.'

'Anyways, I hope your husband's okay and they catch the guy who did it,' Toni said, swinging her rucksack over her shoulder.

'Thanks, hen. Safe home,' May said, closing her locker door and fishing in her pockets for her car key as the other constables added their good wishes. All she wanted now was to get home and see with her own eyes that Tam was safe, and lock the door, just for a few hours, on the world.

CHAPTER 46

When May arrived home she felt a surge of panic. Looking up from where she'd parked the car she saw all the windows of the flat were in darkness. Where was Tam? Sean and Morag were supposed to stay with him. She checked her phone. No messages. She was about to phone the hospital, convinced he'd been readmitted with a blood clot to his brain, when another vehicle pulled up further down the street. Her heart soared at the sight of him getting out of Morag's car.

The streetlights caught the sheen of raindrops on his dark jacket and his hair. He sparkled as he moved, as if the light were coming from within him.

'Hello, bonnie lass,' he said, drawing her close and kissing her cheek. 'Thought I'd be back afore you.'

He'd been to see Morag's musician friend, who also repaired instruments, and judging by the smile he gave May, and the violin case he was carrying, the trip had been a successful one.

'C'mon, you,' she said, hooking her arm through Tam's. 'Let's get inside and you can tell me interesting fiddle facts. I can see you're bursting to.' He looked tired, and perhaps not as recovered from the attack as he liked to pretend.

As she pushed open the flat door, a stack of flyers that was wedged in the letter box fell to the floor.

Tam scooped it up and carried it into the kitchen, laying his fiddle case on the chair by the window. She gave the pile only a cursory glance. A sales pitch from a conservatory company – in a top-floor tenement, really? – a cruise brochure to Australia, local arts venue leaflets.

'I'm going for a shower,' she said.

'Okey-doke. This'll be the gig pictures,' Tam said, picking up a stiff brown envelope with no name or address on it. It'd likely been dropped off by a bandmate buzzed in by the neighbours.

May put her hand on his shoulder. 'I'm really sorry you missed it.'

'Not your fault,' he said with forced cheerfulness, though she could tell he resented the curbs on his freedom, even while understanding vigilance was necessary for them both. He'd greeted news of the text May had received with defiance, and fear for May rather than for himself. She'd promised it wouldn't be for long, and that Dimple was throwing all she could into finding Holly's killer. Until then, May didn't want him out on his own.

'I've been thinking about Australia. Just a holiday,' she added quickly, seeing his hopes rise. 'It was what Morag said about the grandchildren. I want them to see you play, know what a talented grandpa they have. Can we organise a wee tour for you? Pubs and folk clubs. That'd be possible, wouldn't it?'

He smiled, but his eyes went to the fiddle case. 'Need to get the old girl fixed first.'

She hugged him. 'Right, it's settled. Soon as that's done.' She hadn't wanted him to open the envelope, see his fellow band members exalted on stage, without something of his own to look forward to. 'I'm off to the shower. You can show me in a minute.'

Thirty seconds later she was crossing the hall, fresh towel in hand, when she heard him shout.

'May! You need to come.'

His face was etched with panic, and when she looked at the photographs he'd dropped on the table she saw why.

They showed May with four men. Naked. Hardcore pornography.

For a full second, there was only numbness, then a succession of blows rained down on her – horror, incomprehension, panic – followed by the aftershocks of fear and crushing humiliation.

She snatched up the washing-up gloves, partly from forensic awareness and partly from an instinctive revulsion, and stuffed the prints back into the envelope.

'Don't think about them,' she ordered Tam. 'Wipe them from your mind. It's not real. Photoshopped. Some bastard's idea of a joke.' Her voice didn't sound like her own, even to herself. It was shrill and shaky.

'I know, May. I know it isnae real.'

She knew he meant it, as far as he could, but his face was ashen below the bandage that covered the cut on his head. Suddenly, she worried the shock would tip him into some kind of crisis.

'Sit down.' She hustled him into a seat by the window.

A dozen priorities crowded in, each clamouring for her attention. Prioritise Tam's wellbeing and safety. Secure evidence. Create a timeline.

'Tam, where's your phone?'

'Doorbell camera,' he said, immediately understanding her line of thought and opening the app.

The envelope had been shoved through the letter box just before 3 p.m. by someone in the standard dark jeans, hoodie and with a scarf wrapped high around their face.

'Fuck. Just a delivery boy,' May said, though she'd half expected this. When Tam looked disappointed she added, 'Send me that anyway.'

'Are you going to report this?' Tam said.

'Who to?' May said, exasperated. 'The local cops? CID?' The pictures would end up in WhatsApp groups and online before the day was out. Oh, God, she thought. What if they already were?

'Must be someone you trust?' His face was desperate. More than anything he needed to see confidence that she could contain this, deal with it.

May wracked her brains. She'd have to tell Dimple, but she didn't want the BTP dragged in, and how could they help? She'd been on a course last year, stalking and cybercrime. Just a day, but May recalled there'd been a female Glasgow DI who'd given a talk and seemed efficient and empathetic. They'd chatted afterwards about rolling out training for all constables, and had exchanged numbers.

May scrolled through her phone, unable to remember the woman's name.

Then she saw it. DI Jennie McBride.

Five minutes later, May was back on the phone to Sean and Morag, asking if they could please come back to the flat and keep Tam company as she had to go out.

She held Tam for as long as she could, willing him her strength, knowing he was doing the same for her.

Ten minutes after that, May was putting her uniform fleece back on and heading out the door. Her legs shook and she felt hollow with fear. She'd never experienced anything like this powerlessness. But then she remembered she had. Losing Isla would always be the worst thing that would ever happen to her, no matter what lay ahead.

CHAPTER 47

Detective Inspector Jennie McBride was smartly dressed, and had gravitas, just the way May remembered her. Thank God it wasn't one of her ex-colleagues interviewing her. That would've been unbearable.

They went into a corner office with a view of the ring road.

Jennie took the envelope from May and dropped it into an evidence bag and put it on her desk. May felt the physical relief of not carrying it on her person any more.

'When stuff like this happens, it's common to look at your friends and colleagues and ask, *Could they possibly be behind this? Does this person have another side that I just can't see?*' Jennie told her, as if reading her thoughts. 'Commonly, it's an ex-boyfriend.'

'I know who this is,' May said. 'I just don't know their identity.'

When May explained the case, Jennie frowned and shook her head. 'Whoever it is, it's because they're obsessed with you. Used to be just celebrities,' Jennie said, directing May to a chair by a low table and sitting down opposite. 'Now it's everyone. Who have you been in touch with recently, because it may not be who you're expecting.'

She outlined her belief that it was ultimately a criminal

gang that were behind it. 'But this case I'm liaising with the BTP on, it also involves a group of computing students.'

But Jennie shook her head again. 'You wouldn't need much knowledge to do this. It used to take specialised computer skills and lots of available images, which is why celebrities were the early targets. Now websites and apps will do it for you. It's not on the dark web any more, it's a quick search on Google. YouTube tutorials. One photo where the person is looking straight into the camera is enough. If your Facebook or Instagram accounts are set to private, then it's likely someone that you're friends with.'

'I don't have social media,' May said.

'Probably wise,' Jennie agreed. She leaned forward, hands clasped in front of her, elbows on her knees. 'After you called, I did a quick search. I'm sorry to say I've already found quite a bit online.'

'I want to see it,' May said.

Jennie paused. 'Are you sure? Normally, I'd caution against it. But I'm sure you encounter plenty of unpleasant-ness in your day job, and you might spot a pattern that'll help.'

Jennie went behind her desk and May pulled up a chair next to her.

'Right, let's start with this Reddit post.'

It was headed *Shag, marry or kill?* Different photoshopped pictures of May's head on a nude body had been posted. One hundred and sixty-five people had commented.

'Let's move on,' Jennie said.

There were message boards and threads. *Pervchief. Slut shop. MILF machine. Hornyboss. Real Scots Mammas.*

Conversations between lots of men on what they'd like to do to her. Front or back. Filthy old slut.

'A lot of these are people posting pictures of people they know with sexual questions attached. Usually an ex-partner, someone who doesn't like you. We've thirteen-year-old boys using these chats to blackmail their sisters into giving them their pocket money.'

'Fucksake,' May said. Was this a world that Holly and Isla had faced? She was a grown woman, a polis, a sergeant who dragged hardmen to their knees and even she was shaking with horror and disbelief at the damage this could wreak to her life.

More nude photoshopped images. Photos and videos. Fake, but some of it looked real. Humiliating. Violating. Thousands had seen it. A cesspit of online abuse.

May felt a deep wave of nausea in the pit of her stomach.

'It looks like this started about ten days ago. We'll go after everything we can under the Online Safety Act, get it taken down, and try to find the perpetrator, but you know yourself it's whack-a-mole.' Jennie sat back and regarded May. 'So, any likely culprits spring to mind with your murder case, we'll look at them too.'

'The victim was one of the computer students I mentioned. She was very smart by all accounts, and I think her former partner set himself up as a techno-dealer under the auspices of an organised crime group. He was found dead and is the object of a separate murder inquiry.'

'Multiple aliases make it tricky, but some of this material was uploaded today, so if he was involved, he has accomplices.

Other OCG members are a possibility. We can look at what we've got, if you give me names. Be comprehensive, particularly with anyone who you've come into contact with recently.'

'What about the prints in the envelope?'

'Possible, but these guys — and it is usually guys — are forensically aware.'

May thought about what the SOCO had said when they'd found Galbraith's body. An arms race. *We work out another way of catching them; they work out another way of avoiding being caught.*

'But look at this.' Jennie took one of the online images and drew a box around May's head, disengaging it from the foreign body. 'If you've no socials, then how old would you say this headshot was? Any idea where it would've come from?'

May's hair was a little longer, with fewer highlights. 'Maybe a couple of years ago.' She peered closer. 'The earrings,' she said.

They were the ones Isla had given her. She'd lost one just before Isla's death, and her daughter had been so angry with her that May had been shocked, which was why she remembered them.

'The picture must be from before I left CID.' She swallowed. 'It wasn't a happy farewell.' Was someone in her old team tied up with Michael McNally? Is that why the investigation into her partner Andy Wilson had never gone that way? It felt like a fit.

'If it's someone inside who's targeting you, we'll find

them,' Jennie assured her, and May saw she meant it. 'Look, you've had a shock. Leave this with me. Go home and try to forget about it until tomorrow. I'll call you when I have anything.'

May walked down the steps outside the building, the cold air hitting her like a slap. The exchange with DI Jennie McBride had left her a fraction lighter, less isolated. She wasn't the only one who had faced this. If it was the McNallys she had an ally in the fight now.

Her phone buzzed and May's breath caught in her throat. A text from the same number as before.

Want to keep playing, bitch? Your daughter next.

May felt her legs go from under her. Reflexively, she grabbed the handrail, but it wasn't enough to keep her from hitting the step. She felt a pain rush through her as the phone and the ultimate horror it had delivered fell from her grip and lay still on the ice-cold stone.

CHAPTER 48

May didn't sleep that night. She'd assured Tam that the pictures were a one-off and that DI Jennie McBride had matters in hand, but she knew by his breathing and restlessness that he hadn't slept either. Telling him the full extent of what was out there would be of no benefit, but she emphasised that he shouldn't go looking. He was horrified that she even needed to say it, and she hoped that sentiment would be enough to stop him considering why she had said it in the first place.

By lunchtime, her earlier resolve to concentrate on the job list she had in front of her was slipping. With nothing but paperwork to distract her, her office was beginning to feel like a holding cell.

Dimple called to say she'd pulled together a team to search Holly's room for further evidence, but Jackie and Ian weren't answering their phones, and she was reluctant to break the door down in the flat if keys couldn't be found.

'I'm a bit worried,' Dimple said. There was no need to expand on her concerns. With Holly's killer unidentified they were both on edge.

'I'll send a car round to check on them,' May replied. 'You could try the downstairs neighbour. She might have a key.'

The woman hadn't been willing to make a statement about Galbraith's abuse of Holly, but she might agree to this. 'Is your boss okay about you taking Mhairi with you?'

'I've told him she's a specialist IT consultant and won't be doing any searching herself, just viewing anything we find.'

'Good thinking,' May said. 'Let me know how it goes.'

She put her phone down on the desk, then flinched as it buzzed. Ever since the message threatening Isla had arrived, she'd regarded the device like one of Davey the Dooker's grenades, and was relieved when she saw DI Jennie McBride's name on the screen.

'That threatening text message you received last night pinged off a single mast near Queen's Park,' Jennie said. 'Looks like the phone was switched on just before sending, and then off immediately afterwards. Same with your previous message. The BTP report the same pattern with the message sent to Holly Campbell. Single mast near Glasgow Central. Someone savvy and being ultra careful.'

If Galbraith had been alive, May would've said it fit perfectly. Multiple phones, techno-dealer, tech back-up extracted from Holly by promises of affection or threats of violence, whatever did the job. Now it felt like it could be anyone, the forensic arms race in action once more.

'But don't worry. This all builds a picture,' Jennie said.

May's heart sank. It was a phrase she recognised from her time in CID. It meant *we're currently chasing our tails but hope that will stop soon.*

'There's something else,' Jennie said, her voice dropping.

'Just between you and me, I think you're right about OCG activity with the names you gave me.'

This was hardly new. As Ian McDonald had said, CID had been chasing the McNally operation for years and had got nowhere.

'We had a records request in cybercrime about one of your recent contacts.'

'Who?'

When Jennie hesitated, May said, 'I'm liaising on an active murder inquiry and these bastards are after me. Who was flagged?'

'Shannon Hope.'

May was momentarily wrongfooted as she struggled to fit the young woman whose windows had been put in with a shotgun blast into an already-complex picture. 'The lassie that's the hairdresser?'

'She must be a damn good hairdresser,' Jennie said. 'She's turning over fifty grand a month through various accounts.'

'Why hasn't she been lifted?' There was no record of any arrest on the system and May felt a wrinkle of annoyance that no intel had been passed to her that CID had a person of interest under surveillance on her patch.

'I don't know why she hasn't been questioned,' Jennie said. 'I think they're letting things run in the hope of catching bigger fish.'

So both the OCG and the polis were putting Shannon and her son, literally, in the line of fire – CID by not offering her protective custody, and the McNallys by parking her in a flat next door to one that'd just been hit. It wasn't on.

Was that why Shannon had hinted to May that she knew something about Holly? Scouting out if a deal could be done? If May could persuade her to tell what she knew about Holly's death and the McNallys, then she could get resolution for Jackie and Ian, and proper justice for Holly. She'd also free herself, and Tam, and Isla's precious memory from the threat hanging over them.

'May,' Jennie said, her tone a warning, 'I can pretty much hear those cogs turning from here. Don't step in. Just let CID get on with the job.'

'Aye, of course,' May said. 'Let me know if you hear anything more.'

She ended the call and began replaying what she'd just heard. If Shannon had known Holly from school, then maybe there was someone else within their circle of friends. Money-laundering on the scale Jennie had mentioned could only mean drugs. May dialled Gemma Thorne's number.

'How did Shannon Hope and Holly get along?'

'Fine,' Gemma said, brightly. 'Holly would've loved being an aunty to wee Jack. Watch him get bigger and go to school and that.'

'How d'you mean?' May had grown up with a host of aunties and uncles, people she wasn't related to – but it was a term of respect for your elders across many cultures, Scottish working class included. Shannon hadn't given her the impression that she and Holly had still been close.

'She wasn't really his aunty,' Gemma confirmed. 'Cousins, maybe.'

'Are they related to each other then?' Shannon had pointed out their likeness when they were younger – *could've been twins* – so maybe they were half-sisters via the same dad. Jackie hadn't mentioned it, but perhaps she didn't know Darren Campbell had played away.

'They're no' related to each other as such,' Gemma said. 'But through Jack's dad, Liam.'

'Holly's cousin is the wee boy Jack's dad?'

Shannon had deliberately concealed that fact from May. So much for the holiday romance in Ibiza. Maybe she was estranged from Liam, but you'd hardly live in one of the family flats if you were. And what about the shotgun incident? Liam McNally warning her to stay in line after some argument? No, May couldn't see it, not with his son in there. That left the opposition, whichever gang the McNallys were butting heads with now.

May was torn between excitement at the new connection she'd found and trepidation at what a potential gang war meant for Shannon. The young woman and her wee boy were not safe where they were. May needed to shift them, sooner rather than later, or risk both their lives.

'Thanks for the chat, Gemma,' May said.

Then she got up, picked up her utility vest, and headed out the door.

The windows were still boarded up on Shannon Hope's flat. There were no lights on next door, but her bronze Nissan Qashqai sat a few doors up. May knocked, and a minute later Shannon answered. She had her coat on and May reckoned she'd been expecting someone else. They stared at each other until Shannon looked away.

'Thought I might be seeing you again. I suppose you better come up.'

At the top of the stairs sat two suitcases. Jack also had his coat on and lay on the sofa watching a video on an iPad.

Shannon leaned against a side table and folded her arms. From this position she had a good view of the cul-de-sac outside and anyone approaching.

'It was my only way to keep Jack,' she said to the question May hadn't asked. 'I'm not using, and nobody's using me – as a sex toy or a punchbag.' She shrugged. 'Somebody's going to supply it, you can't stop it. If it gets me out, why not? I've a good bit put away. And the taxi will be here in a minute.'

She gave May a look that was half hope, half challenge.

'You need to let me go, Sergeant Mackay. Because you and I both know how it'll finish for me if I don't. Prison, or maybe rehab, or maybe the morgue.' She nodded towards her son. 'Care system for him. This way it's no cost to the taxpayer. I can't ever pop up in the drugs business again cos McNally will find me.'

'Tell me about the McNallys,' May said.

Shannon smiled like it was a joke. Like May was trying to catch her out. 'Don't need me for that. Holly will have told you.'

'How?' It confirmed what May had always expected. Someone as smart as Holly would have insurance. 'There's nothing on her laptop,' May said.

'Well, it's up to you to find, isn't it, cos this is my way, and that was hers.'

'We know Galbraith didn't kill her, so who did?'

'He was a dangerous bampot, mind,' Shannon said. 'But he was soft on her. Always thought she'd come back to him.' She gave May an ironic smile. 'Aye, even with the things he said to her. But women hear that all the time and don't leave. Holly was smart, but not that different.'

'Did the McNallys know that?'

'Liam did, and he and Scott were like brothers.'

'Is that why they killed him? Because they thought he'd pushed Holly?'

Shannon raised her eyebrows at that. 'Didn't think he had.' She paused. 'I've heard it said you only need one bit of luck to turn your life around.' Her eyes constantly flicked between her son and the street outside. 'Not talking about lottery wins, just a time when a good thing happens to you instead of a bad thing. One bit of good luck is all I need. You can give me back my life, as it should have been. And in return I'll give you something.'

'You know I can't authorise anything straight away.' Shannon handing over the McNallys was the break they needed, but careful protection arrangements would be required. 'But I can talk to CID.'

Shannon snorted. 'That lot are useless. They've been watching this place for weeks and they still havenae worked it out.'

'They've all the online evidence needed to arrest you,' May warned, 'wherever you think you can run to.'

'I'm a hairdresser. By the time I get where I'm going, I won't look like this. I won't even be the same person. And it's not that they havenae worked it out. There's a fuckin' cannabis farm in the roof. That's why the opposition put my windows in.'

The two upstairs flats had a communal loft, it seemed. She remembered Shannon joking about the odour from her hairdressing chemicals. That had been her cover story just in case anyone complained about the smell.

'Here's what I'll give you. It's about Holly. There was someone she really didnae like.'

'Who?'

'That stepdad of hers. Used to talk about it to me sometimes when the two of us were pals.'

'What'd she say?'

'That he creeped her out.'

May studied Shannon. 'You're the only one who's told me this. Ian McDonald has a clean record.'

'Maybe you need to look a bit harder. Guys like him are everywhere, hiding in plain sight. You should know. CID are full of them.'

'What d'you mean?' May frowned.

'You need to let me go,' Shannon said. 'Call it payback. There was this cop. I moved all the way from Bearsden to get away from him, and he turned up round the corner. He lifted me, and it never went to court. He did me a bad turn. You can do me a good one.'

'Why did it never go to court?' Given Shannon's current sideline, she could guess the charges. Possession with intent to supply. Something that'd put her inside.

'Because I did what he asked. Favours for him. Favours for his creepy mates while he watched.'

'What was this guy's name?'

The story wasn't an original one, but it had the ring of truth. She'd heard the rumours too. It could be about any one of a number of officers across the divisions.

'His name is DI Andy Wilson,' Shannon said.

May stared at her. The lassie was definitely making this up.

'You report this to anyone?'

But Shannon just laughed. 'Like that would work.'

May thought of her own reluctance to report the BUNK hoax, the cyberporn. A lassie like Shannon wouldn't have stood a chance.

Outside, a black rain cloud passed in front of the sun, plunging the room into darkness.

May saw a car with *ABC Taxis* emblazoned on the side pull up. Shannon pushed off from the side table, her face pinched and uncertain, the window of possibility for her new life closing fast.

May glanced up at the ceiling trying to calculate how many plants you could've crammed into the space. The attics were high. A fair number. She put her hand on her Airwave. 'I'm going to have to call this in.'

May watched as Shannon stared at her, expression draining away. She'd gambled and lost, like Holly, like countless other young women sucked into crime. You only needed one bit of luck to turn your life around. Dimple's act of kindness. What if Isla had been luckier? What if someone passing had seen her and had stopped her from jumping? Got her to hospital. She might have been here now.

May's hand froze on her radio. A single act of kindness. Shannon was no angel, but she was as much victim as perpetrator. Her hand dropped. 'But before I do, I'm just going to check the back garden.' She turned and moved towards the door.

'May,' Shannon called after her. 'Thank you.'

May looked back, the cloud had moved on, and she saw the young woman kneeling by her son lit by the sun and the glimmer of a different life.

CHAPTER 49

It took some time to process the scene at Shannon's flat. Two
SOCO wagons and three uniform units would be tied up for
the rest of the day. May sat in her squad car at the end of the
cul-de-sac and directed her officers, who interviewed the same
neighbours they had after the shotgun blast and got much the
same replies. No one had seen a thing.

Between flurries of activity, May snatched moments to
make some calls.

She couldn't put her finger on why she believed what
Shannon had told her about Holly's stepfather. It hadn't been
much of a bargaining chip, but it had awakened something
unresolved in her own mind.

May called Dimple. 'D'you still have Mhairi with you?
Put her on.'

There was a pause then she heard the young woman's
voice.

'Mhairi, how did Holly get on with her stepdad?'

'She didn't like him much, but he took her to computer
shows and he got her some cool kit, and they talked all that
cybercrime stuff cos of his job.'

'Why would they talk about that?' There was nothing in
Ian's CID history to say he had dealt with cybercrime.

'You know, the maritime security stuff,' Mhairi said. 'Trawls around the dark web looking for terrorism threats and stuff.'

'That's helpful, Mhairi. Thank you,' May said evenly, a cold uneasiness climbing up her spine.

Had it all been Ian? The fake dating profile, the cyber-porn. He'd have the knowledge to do it. The rag in the petrol tank to make it look like it had a gangland link was something any CID officer could pull off. And worst of all, the attack on Tam.

She couldn't be sure. Not yet. There'd been so many missteps in this case, and Ian McDonald had an alibi for the time of her death. A room full of colleagues and a taxi receipt from Central station. And what was his motive? Had Ian been the abuser the therapists wouldn't name? No, she couldn't see it. Holly would've told someone if he'd abused her. It wasn't that simple. But no one got to be that accomplished a manipulator without leaving a trace.

Her next call was to DI Jennie McBride. An *anonymous source* had suggested Holly's stepfather had knowledge of cybercrime and the dark web. Could Jennie look into it?

'What's his name?'

When May replied, Jennie came straight back.

'I can tell you now. There were always rumours about him.'

'He told me he was forced out because he refused to falsify evidence.'

'He went because he was a drunk and a crook and couldn't keep his hands off young women,' Jennie said. 'It seemed easier to pension him off rather than trying to prove anything, but if your *anonymous source* is pointing his way, I'm happy to check.'

May thanked her. The unease she'd felt earlier was solidifying into anger that Ian had played her.

She called Dimple again and this time she told her what Shannon and DI McBride had revealed.

'You know, when I was going through Holly's diary, I never got the sense she was talking about Galbraith specifically. She knew her mother read it, but occasionally, she was so angry and scared the truth burst through. *I THINK HE'S FOLLOWING ME. I CAN'T TRUST HIM.* It don't think it was Scott Galbraith she meant. I think it was Ian.'

'Oh my God,' Dimple said. 'We're nearly finished here. What d'you want me to do?'

'Can you place Ian at Central station that night? I need to be sure.'

'I'll get my CCTV guys onto it.'

An hour later, May was still outside Shannon's when Dimple called back. Her tone was cautious, but it definitely held a note of suppressed excitement.

'We can't be certain, but someone matching Ian McDonald's description can be seen entering the station just after Holly. A minute after she died, there's a similar figure running into the low-level area of the station and jumping onto a train to Motherwell. There's three other stops on that route. We'll have to access those stations' CCTV, and we'll look at enhancing the images.'

'Okay, thanks, Dimple,' May said, trying to keep the

disappointment out of her voice. 'Well done. It's a start. We really need that ID confirmed.'

May swore silently and smashed her palm against the steering wheel. It wasn't enough. He had work mates who'd likely back up his alibi, and a taxi receipt home from town to his Shawlands flat.

May opened the picture of the receipt on her phone, then googled the price of a taxi from Glasgow Central to Shawlands – £15 to £30. Ian's fare had been at the upper end of the scale, but it was the correct amount.

Outside, the streetlights were coming on. She tapped her phone against her chin, then looked at the image again. It had been an ABC cab that had come for Shannon, but the logo on this receipt was different. She frowned and searched online. The first result showed a company of that name for central Glasgow, but there was another ABC taxi company based in the suburbs, fifteen miles outside the city. Her pulse raced as she saw its logo matched the receipt. She called them and asked how much from the station to Shawlands on a weekday evening. Thirty pounds, came the reply – did she want to book?

She could've punched the air. Instead, she got straight on the phone to Dimple.

'It's Motherwell. I think your guy that matches his description *is* him. I think the bastard pushed Holly in front of that train and escaped on another to Motherwell. Fucksake. I can't believe he had the gall to flash me a cab receipt to confirm his alibi.'

She was almost speechless with anger, at Ian McDonald, but also at herself for falling for his lies.

'But why did he do it?' Dimple said. 'Why now?'

She's so special. I'd never dream of letting her go.

May thought he'd been talking about Jackie.

Meet me, Holls. I only want to talk.

'Who knows with these sick bastards. But Holly was moving out of his grip. She was already at college. Now she was off to Dundee.'

'Right, let's arrest him,' Dimple said. 'We can't wait. He's too big a risk to you and Tam, but if we go to his place there might be a risk to Jackie too.'

'I agree,' said May, remembering the locks on the doors and the flat's position in the upper part of the villa, which sat in the centre of a long, straight road. Even without blue lights, there was a good chance he'd see them coming. 'And he'll smell a rat if I ask him to come into Cathcart.'

'Can you get him to our office at Glasgow Central, d'you think?' Dimple said.

Wired up to foil terrorists, biological attacks and mass shootings, the BTP detective had said.

'I can do that,' May replied.

CHAPTER 50

Half an hour later May was on her way to Glasgow Central, having left Ross Reid in charge of the house-to-house operation at Shannon's cosy neighbourhood cannabis farm.

The lie to snare Ian had been easy enough. His advice was needed on a small item, recently recovered at the station, that might have belonged to Holly. Yes, the BTP were useless, hadn't done a proper search, a shitshow from the start. Five minutes of his time and the case could probably be tied up. She didn't want to upset Jackie by showing her it. The item might be jewellery, might be something else, she said, borrowing Mhairi's line. He'd know what that meant: a possible data-storage device. Did it implicate him? That was what he'd need to know.

'I'm just on my way home,' Ian had said. 'I'll pop in.'

'Great,' May had replied. 'Meet you under the clock.'

Glasgow Central station was busy with teatime commuters. Some folk navigated the crowd hauling bags and children in their wake, others less encumbered sliced through, phones to their ears, eyes on their destination. The signature smells of coffee, deep-fried food and heavy engine oil hung in the air, and train announcements rebounded off the hard surfaces of the glass roof and tiled concourse.

May stood beneath the famous four-faced hanging clock. She turned a slow circle, fixing in her mind the exits and the pairs of BTP officers who stood near them. Arriving by car, Ian would likely look for a parking space on the Hope Street side.

On her way to the station, she'd pieced together a possible timeline for the minutes before Holly's death. If Ian had been following Holly, there was a good chance Galbraith would've been behind them both. Perhaps he hadn't realised what he'd seen until afterwards and had tried to blackmail Ian. It seemed to May a reasonable interpretation of the argument witnessed on the lawn by Ian's neighbour the night before Holly's funeral. Maybe he'd just wanted money, or maybe he'd believed that bringing in an ex-cop to do some dirty work would impress McNally. Shannon thought Galbraith had loved Holly, but May didn't. The texts, the threats, the actual punches pointed in only one direction. He'd used Holly in life, he'd tried to use her in death, it'd gotten him killed, and Ian McDonald was responsible for both deaths.

May's stance was casual, moderately alert. Waiting for a friend, but keen to get on with the job and get home. Ian had the drive to reconfigure May's words into multiple meanings, and his ex-cop instincts might be jangling. She didn't want him spooked.

A familiar shape was coming towards her through the crowd.

'Kit, pal. Not now.'

'Too good for your old friends, eh?'

James Alexander MacDonald Fraser looked the worse for wear. His sleeping bag lay in a roll across his shoulders. The cardboard sign advertising his patriotism and service to his country was tucked beneath his arm, and the paper cup in his hand was half filled with change.

A couple of the BTP cops were moving quickly towards them, eyes fixed on Kit.

'Target has just entered the station via the hotel entrance,' Dimple said into May's earpiece from her vantage point in the CCTV control room.

May turned away from Kit, keen to get a fix on Ian.

'Hey, yous.' Kit's hand brushed her shoulder.

May looked back in time to see two BTP officers take hold of Kit, who was staring at her with bemused hurt.

'It's fine,' she told the officers. 'We're old pals. But I'm a bit busy now,' she said to Kit. 'Can we catch up later?'

Kit glared at her as the officers gripped his arms.

Ian was coming forward through the crowd. His sandy hair was darkened from the rain and he pushed it back from his face as he walked. He wore a navy suit over a sweater, collar and tie, a look shared by a good proportion of the middle-aged males in the station.

When he spotted May, his pace slowed and he frowned at the BTP officers at her shoulder.

She smiled and raised her hand in greeting. For a second they all stood frozen, May smiling and Ian looking from her to Kit, to the BTP guys, and back, as if trying to make sense of the strange tableau before him.

Then he bolted.

CHAPTER 51

The crowd swallowed him whole.

'Fuck!' May ran towards the spot she'd last seen him. 'Where is he?' she shouted into her radio.

'He's not gone back the way he came in,' Dimple confirmed. 'He's still in the station.'

'You two,' she said to the BTP cops. 'Get back to your exit.'

They'd let go of Kit, who stared at her bemused.

She spotted Ian among a group of businessmen heading for the travel centre. He'd skirted behind her, aiming for the stairs down to Union Street. But when he saw the cops, he changed tack, moving at a speed through the crowd that May hadn't thought possible. She began to run, swerving past wheeled suitcases and passengers who were still staring up at the destination boards, unaware of the drama unfolding around them.

The barrier to the platforms on the far side from her had been opened to allow food trolleys through. Ian pushed past the startled steward in West Coast Mainline uniform. Ahead, the London train stood at platform 2, doors open, a mist of condensation streaming from its cooling wheelsets.

'Move!' May barked at the startled steward as she went

through the barrier, four BTP cops on her heels. On the platform, guards and station personnel were ushering everyone to the far wall, away from the train. She checked their frightened faces in case Ian was hiding among them but found no one she recognised. He couldn't have sprinted to the far end of the platform, across which curtains of rain swept, lit only by dim station lights. He had to be in one of the carriages.

She sent two cops to the front of the train, and two to the rear to begin a methodical search. Choosing a middle carriage, she stepped aboard. The space was brightly lit and hushed after the noise of the concourse. Ian wasn't armed, she was fairly sure, but still there was a claustrophobic sense of threat.

Dimple kept up a commentary in her earpiece, accessing the onboard carriage cameras. Officers were sweeping the train. More were on the platform.

May's breath slowed. Ian McDonald had run out of luck. There was nowhere to run.

She went cautiously forward, checking the luggage areas and toilets.

Suddenly, the sound of an alarm blared out.

'May,' Dimple said, 'an emergency door release has been activated in the carriage ahead of you. He's trying to get out on the trackside.'

May ran through the connecting passage. A train was approaching along the parallel track, heading for the neighbouring platform.

Ian stood poised on the threshold of the open carriage door, and in that moment she saw what he intended to do.

'Ian. Stop!' she yelled, but without turning to look at her, he jumped.

The oncoming train sounded a long blast.

May lurched forward. The train driver would have seen him jump and would have hit the emergency brake. She felt a brief flash of malevolence that the driver hadn't been quick enough, that the pendulum had swung, some balance in the universe had been activated, and Ian McDonald's life would end the way Holly's had, on the tracks of Glasgow Central.

But as she made it to the carriage door, she saw Ian heave himself up onto the far platform. He shot her a look of triumph. For the briefest second she thought about following him. They were so close. She could catch him. And then the train with its screaming brakes blocked her path, making the decision for her.

Through the slowing windows, like juddering frames in an old movie, she saw another train on platform 4 had also just pulled in, and to her horror, Ian McDonald was swallowed by a crowd once more.

As May sprinted from the London train, a wall of jarring sound hit her once more. Travellers had witnessed the concourse flooding with police and had begun to look nervously for the source of the trouble. What must be going through their heads? Suicide bomber. Lone gunman. Station announcements said there'd been a security incident and asked people to leave the building in a calm and orderly manner.

The flow of panicked passengers towards the now-open ticket barriers and exits picked up, concentrating the crowd. But

Ian McDonald was there, somewhere, among those nervously streaming from the newly arrived trains on platforms 3 and 4. Officers were at the barrier, but the press of the crowd threatened a different kind of tragedy, forcing them to let people through the bottleneck without checking every single ticket.

'Can you see him?' May radioed Dimple.

'He's in that crowd. We'll get him.'

May reached the barrier. Her height was an advantage, and she concentrated on any sandy-haired males, around six foot tall, in suits, who were keeping their faces lowered.

Other officers had made it to the train, searching the carriages in case Ian had got on and hidden, hoping it would pull out again to another station or marshalling yard from where he could escape on foot. He was in maritime security, was fit and tech-savvy. If they lost him now, May knew he'd have ways to disappear. Fake passports, mates who could get him aboard a ship.

As the minutes ticked by, May's hope diminished in proportion to the thinning crowd. It seemed unthinkable that Ian McDonald could vanish in a place that Dimple had told her had the highest proportion of surveillance technology in the city. But it was also Scotland's busiest rail station, the very definition of the kind of haystack into which a needle might fall.

There was a tap on her arm and Kit stood regarding her with wary eyes.

'No' now, Kit, please,' May said, sure her lack of grace would confirm for him that maybe she was not the cop he'd thought she was. He'd believe that her gratitude for the

CCTV had been short-lived and he was no more than street furniture. The thoughts passed quickly through her mind, but she couldn't spare the mental energy to persuade him otherwise.

'May,' he said, and something in his tone cut through the hubbub of anxious travellers, public information announcements and the radio chatter in her ear. She turned and looked at him.

His face was lined with dirt, and the matted grey hair to one side gave it an uneven slant. She realised he had always been a creature of the night to her – in the sparse shelter under the Hielanman's Umbrella or in the rain-streaked midnight street outside the kebab shop – that she'd never looked at him under such industrial illumination. Everything about him was worn and faded, except his eyes. They were the deep blue of the winter sky above Glasgow. The blue eyes met hers, then he slowly moved them in the direction of a dark-haired woman and a hunched older man standing ten metres away as the crowd washed around them.

May saw with a lurch in her gut that the woman was Jackie McNally. The man grasping her tightly, Ian McDonald – not old, just slouched to disguise his height. He'd ditched the suit jacket and picked up a baseball cap from somewhere; perhaps he'd even had it in his pocket.

His grip on Jackie was so tight that May believed the pursuit of an individual had just become a hostage situation. There'd been no suggestion so far that he was armed, but any sharp metal object he'd picked up could be the weapon digging into Jackie's ribs.

But now May had him in her sights. Technology, it seemed, was no match for an old sailor with a sharp pair of eyes. There was still a way to detain Holly's murderer and save Jackie.

She took a step towards them. Kit looked set to come with her, but she stopped him with a gentle pressure on his arm.

May walked slowly towards the couple, who seemed intent on each other, ignoring the agitated people around them. She didn't dare to even lift her radio to report the target's position, fearing the movement might break whatever spell was holding them immobile.

May was two metres away when she finally spoke.

'Ian. Let Jackie go.'

His exits were blocked. Hostage-taking was a last-ditch attempt to escape capture, and rarely succeeded. Enough of the station cops were armed to make the outcome inevitable.

But May's priority now was Jackie's safety.

'Ian,' she repeated, louder this time. 'Let her go.'

Ian clung to Jackie, then sank to his knees as if pleading for her forgiveness. Surely he didn't think she'd forgive him for what he'd done? That he'd even ask was a mark of how justified he thought his actions had been. *I didn't mean it. She made me do it.*

Ian's grip loosened.

When Jackie stepped back, May saw it. The knife in her hand. The blood spread across the ice-white of the station concourse. The tide of commuters flowed out and away from the man on the ground. Beside May, a woman began to scream.

CHAPTER 52

Six Months Later

May drew up in the car park of the women's prison just north of Stirling. At the murder trial, Jackie's defence had pointed to the coercive nature of her relationship with Ian McDonald. The self-harm marks on Jackie's arms, she'd finally admitted, were anything but. On the night May had thought Jackie might kill herself, and had sent Toni and Lauren round, it hadn't been that Jackie wouldn't open the door. She couldn't. Ian had locked her in. There were countless other examples. May had convinced Jackie to go to Ian's in Shawlands, believing she'd be safe. Thank God he hadn't killed her, too. As she sat for a moment, taking in the new two-storey buildings, the sports field and the gardens behind the high fence, she realised she would carry the burden of that guilt with her. She welcomed it. Perhaps it'd stop her making the same mistake again.

The visitor area was designed to look like a cafe, so it would be less traumatic for family members and any children visiting their mothers. Jackie was waiting, in jeans and a blue sweatshirt, looking better than May had seen her in a while.

They sat opposite each other, as they'd done on the day they'd first met, only this time May wasn't in uniform. They were just two women having a coffee and a chat about their kids.

'I see Holly all the time,' Jackie said, her hands around the paper cup and its tepid contents. 'Yesterday, there was all this rain on a tree and the sun was behind it. She was really wee, inside the drops, and she was laughing. Sometimes she's a massive cloud in the sky. Other times she's just normal-sized. Sitting in the kitchen.'

May nodded, understanding on a level beyond words.

'I know it's the pain,' Jackie said. 'But you cannae get away from it, so sometimes you just have tae let it hurt. I mean, it's love, int it, and that doesnae just vanish. It has to go some-where. Maybe it's like tiny bits of Holly are all around us, like in one of them snow globes, and when we brush up against them, there she is. So she'll never really be gone, will she?'

'No, she won't,' May agreed.

'I'm sorry, May. I know you wanted to put him in the jail, but I couldnae let you. He'd just be breathing, allowed phone calls. It's not just her life he took, it's mine too. I mean, I'll get out, sometime, but I'll serve a whole-life sentence. Not for what I did to Ian, for what he did to me and Holly. Can you imagine how much she could have done if he'd allowed her to live? I'm no' living. I'm just existing, marking time till I can join her.'

May sighed. 'I thought that too, once.'

'Aye, I reckoned mibbaes you'd lost someone, else how would you understand so well?'

'My daughter, Isla. She killed herself two and a half years ago.'

'D'you want to tell me about her?' Jackie said.

So May did, and the hour slipped by. May told her all about Isla, her dreams, her troubles, and she told Jackie she must go on for all the Hollys and Islas. For all the Mays and Jackies, cos they weren't the only ones. That would be Holly and Isla's legacy.

'I'm lucky.' May smiled. 'I have a son in Australia.'

'Grandkids?'

'Three.'

Jackie clasped her hands together in glee, like she'd won a prize at the fair.

'I'm going out to visit them in a couple of weeks,' May said, the thought like a bubble of joy she carried inside her.

Jackie's eyes widened, then her look turned coy. 'Can I ask you a big, big favour?'

'Sure,' said May, not at all sure what was coming.

'Will you send me a postcard from Australia? A proper cardboard one with a picture and a stamp? I can put it up in my room.'

'Course.' May smiled. So much of Jackie's life would be lived vicariously through the experience of others that she thought it would be cruel to refuse.

'Jackie, can I ask you something? You don't have to tell me if you don't want to.' She paused. There was phone evidence that showed Ian had called Jackie when he was on his way to Glasgow Central, but it didn't tell the whole story. 'How did you know Ian had killed Holly?'

'I'll tell you. But I doubt it'll help. Be my word against his.'

And without Jackie saying his name, May knew it was Michael McNally who had revealed to her what Ian McDonald had done, having worked it out, perhaps from a message, a parting gift from Shannon, just before May had.

'He said that I had twenty-four hours to decide what I wanted done with him. The police or the river. But he just did it so I'd go back to him, be in his power. I had to fix Ian myself.'

She wouldn't utter Michael McNally's name if she could avoid it. But it wasn't fear, it was contempt. He was no family to her, nor ever would be now. Perhaps it was killing her abuser, her daughter's murderer, that had freed the small, frightened creature that had been trapped inside her.

Jackie smiled. 'Some of the women in here think I'm a hero for doing what I did. They fix my hair for me and give me sweets. I feel so sorry for them. They've had it worse than I did. But I'm no' a hero. I couldnae save my daughter, and that's all that mattered.'

Maybe Holly's evidence would convict Michael McNally, May thought, and Jackie, when she got out, would have a new life again, a real freedom. The data storage had finally been located with Mhairi's help. A Lego Wednesday Addams figure, containing an SD card, had been sitting on the shelf in Holly's bedroom in full view of the searchers. Mhairi had said when she'd found it that she could hear Holly laughing.

There were spreadsheets of dealers' names, debts and amounts of drugs supplied. There was a crude command structure for the OCG, including some previously unknown names.

Michael McNally himself had proved elusive, but his turn would come, May felt sure of that. His gamble of associating himself publicly with Jackie had backfired – now it was clear who his family was. His sister had killed her partner who'd killed her daughter.

It was also beginning to look like his nephew was in the frame for the murder of DI Andy Wilson. Davey the Dooker had got his wish after one of the guns recovered from the Clyde had shown Liam McNally's DNA inside the barrel, the ballistics a match for the bullets recovered from DI Andy Wilson. Perhaps Liam had done it as an act of love for Shannon, but May found she no longer cared about her former colleague's fate.

Michael McNally's political ambitions were in tatters – *get you own hoose in order afore you tell us what to do* was the dominant sentiment. May had worried about the knock-on effect of this for Tam's charity, but they seemed to be weathering the storm. And it was entirely possible Michael McNally might too, that he'd spin his misfortunes and bounce back stronger, and Holly's murder would fade from the public's consciousness until it was just another death in Glasgow. May hoped not.

Other visitors were gathering up bags and putting coats on struggling children.

They never spoke about Scott Galbraith. On the first visit, Jackie had said she didn't care that Ian killed had him. He was scum anyway after what he'd done to her daughter. And May had never told Jackie what McDonald had done to her, what he'd threatened to do to Isla. She knew from the investigating officers that cyberporn featuring Isla had been found on a hard drive, but most of what had happened was ruled inadmissible at the trial as it didn't directly relate to Jackie's relationship with Ian and her killing of him. May was mostly just relieved that she hadn't had to go through it all again on the witness stand. Other women wouldn't have been so lucky. The law surrounding cyberporn had been tightened, but the arms race still hadn't been won. As soon as a law was passed, criminals would find ways around it. May didn't think DI Jennie McBride would be out of a job anytime soon.

May hugged Jackie, who was trying to put on a brave face at her departure. There was no one left for her now. Perhaps her neighbour downstairs would visit. Or maybe she might even see Shannon Hope, with a different name and a different look, and Jackie's great-nephew Jack, in the visitors' room, or if Shannon's luck ran out, in a neighbouring cell.

'I'll see you in a couple of months, Jackie, love. And I'll have pictures of the grandkids with me.'

Jackie's face brightened. 'Aye, I'd love that.'

May got back to Cathcart Police Office in plenty of time for her shift. Two lates, then two nights before a four-day break. Tam was due to play a gig in Oban, a warm-up for his Australian dates. He'd confessed to nerves. She'd said she'd go with him, and he'd looked pleased. That he didn't in any way blame her for the misfortunes he'd suffered in her pursuit of Holly Campbell's killer was all to his credit, and May hoped that the depth and breadth of their love for each other was such that they'd never reach its edges.

She pulled her tactical vest from her locker. Outside in the corridor, Rab the Kebab was arguing with Lauren about the legal blood alcohol level for drivers.

'It's fifty-five mg,' Rab said.

'It's fifty mg,' Lauren said, incredulous. 'How can you no' know that?'

'Lauren's right,' May said as she swept past. 'I'm gonna ask you key operational questions later, Rab, and none of them will be what time does Maccies open.'

'You'll no' catch me that way, Sarge,' he replied. 'It's twenty-four-hours. Doesnae close.'

She turned and pointed a finger at him. 'I mean it, P C Kennedy. Don't make me send you on a course.'

May had the satisfaction of seeing his face fall before she pushed the door open to the car park.

Outside, the cold and the fiery sky of another dimming day lay before her. Somewhere close she heard the opening bars of a siren as Glasgow, her Glasgow, prepared once more to sing its full repertoire of tragedy, violence, hope, and startling acts of human kindness. Sergeant May Mackay pulled on her cap and stepped out onto the tarmac, ready for whatever might come.

Acknowledgements

Every book is a collaborative process and I was exception-
ally blessed by all my fellow travellers in this project. I am
particularly indebted to highly talented fellow Glaswegian,
Rachel Imrie, from whose original idea the novel grew. We
were both inspired by the strong women upon which the city
was built and all those who continue to keep it flourishing.

I am deeply grateful to the team at Cornerstone – my
editor Annie Peacock, Publishing Director Claire Simmonds,
who contributed so much to the development of the book,
and to Managing Editor Laurie Ip Fung Chun, who made the
later stages run smoothly. My thanks also go to former editor
Charlotte Osment, and also to freelance copy-editor Alice
Brett for sparing my author blushes. I appreciate you all for
your guidance, wisdom and inspiration.

Special thanks to my agent Anne Williams at KHLA for her
unwavering belief and encouragement. Her insightful com-
ments on the manuscript raised the bar wonderfully, as usual.

My heartfelt thanks to Paul Lyons of Central Station Tours
for his knowledge and insight of the issues faced on the rail
network and those employed on it. I'm also indebted to the
response officers of Police Scotland and elsewhere who have
shared the highs and lows of this difficult and rewarding
calling.

ACKNOWLEDGEMENTS

The insights that make up the writing process often arrive at unexpected moments and my thanks go to the staff and my fellow alumni of the University of East Anglia Creative Writing programme, who continue to be such a source of support and inspiration.

Finally, a big thank you to my home team – John, Netta and Eric McEwan, Catherine Oliver, Chloe, Leo, Sam and Mickey – for their steadfast support and my friends who listened to my ideas and provided such invaluable feedback – Charles Simpson, Virginia Cole, Sarah Barnes, Fiona MacDonell. You all made it happen.